OTHER B(
CORALIE H

L'ORO VERDE
IL PANE DELLA   A
WINTER HARVEST
LETY'S GIFT
PASSUP POINT

Chianti Classico

A Sister Angela Mystery

Coralie Hughes Jensen

Copyright © 2015 by Coralie Hughes Jensen

ALL RIGHTS RESERVED

This is a work of fiction. Names, characters, places, and incidents are drawn from the author's imagination or used fictitiously and are not to be construed as real. Any resemblance to actual events, locales, organizations, or persons, living or dead, is entirely coincidental.

No part of this book may be used or reproduced in any manner whatsoever without the written permission of the copyright owner, except in the case of brief quotations embodied in critical articles and reviews.

To my father
John
who inspired me to become a writer

ACKNOWLEDGEMENTS

Cover: Dar Albert of Wicked Smart Designs

Thank you to my editor, Bruce. To our dear friend, Cinzia and Giorgio, owners of La Chiusa dei Monaci Bed and Breakfast in Arrezzo, who helped me find the places we needed to see in the Apennines. To the members of the Rhode Island Romance Group who helped me to go independent and to New England Sisters in Crime who kindle my interest in mysteries.

Chapter One

The darkness murmured, the silent night not so hushed when beds lined each wall of the attic room. Sheets rustled, bed springs squeaked, lips muttered, but the small bodies seemingly dreamed on, still fingering dolls, stuffed animals, and silky blanket edges.

The soft footsteps that ascended the wooden staircase could be heard if one of the pillowed heads strained an ear. But would someone have questioned or even noticed? The centuries-old building was never without noise of some kind, and eyes usually followed the children wherever they went, even in sleep.

The soft warm air in her ear roused her. Pia didn't startle because that was often how the others awakened her for breakfast. The rough hand stroked her face and urged her to sit up.

A whisper floated on the air like a melody. "Come, we must go. Someone's waiting for you."

Too tired to question her, Pia slipped into the jacket the nun held for her, and taking the old woman's hand, the two crept down the stairs and ambled out through a door into the damp night air.

Darkness faded with the chirping of birds and the smell of fresh-baked bread. Sister Carmela bellowed from the bottom of the stairs at the young girls just beginning to rise. Through the small window at the end of the room, sunlight streaked the floorboards.

Allegra pushed the hair from her face. "We're up, Sister," she said.

A head popped up over the top step. "Terza, I don't see you. You must still be under the covers. Sister Edita made fresh rolls with strawberries this morning. The other girls are trying to stuff themselves already. You'll be too late. Where's Pia?"

"She must be in the toilet downstairs," said Allegra. "I haven't seen her."

"I don't think so. Grazia was in there. Pia? Are you here? Check under the bed, Allegra." Sister Carmela's voice rose as she barked instructions. "Did anyone see her leave? How long has she been gone?"

Terza shrugged her shoulders. "Maybe the nun took her."

"What nun?"

"One of the nuns came up here last night. I really didn't notice who. She just checked on us, I guess."

"Did anyone else see a nun?"

Cammeo sat on the edge of her bed, dangling her feet. "I saw a ghostly old woman come up here."

"You dreamt about that hag again, Cammeo," said Allegra. "You always tell us you see ghosts strolling around up here."

"No. They float. This one was dark, and her hands were all shriveled. I figured it was the same ghost in a different outfit."

"Why didn't you scream?" asked Terza.

"Because you get mad when I wake you up. I rolled over and pretended I didn't see her."

"Did she take Pia?" asked Allegra.

"I don't know. Maybe."

Sister Carmela was already halfway down the stairs again and didn't hear the last exchange. She had to get to the phone and call Mother Faustine. Something wasn't right.

Sister Daniela entered the door at the back of the old stone building. She was late and concerned the nuns would be in a tizzy, worried about who was keeping the girls organized while they tried to change shifts. She placed her heavy briefcase on top of her desk in the large classroom and glanced at her watch. It was quiet—too quiet for the beginning of the school. She walked into the hallway and gazed toward the laundry door to her right. The door was still closed, presumably locked. No one had started washing the sheets or towels. She glanced to the left where the outside basement door still stood open. Had she failed to close it or had someone entered behind her? She peeked up the stairs to the main house. Where was everyone?

Sister Daniela was just a few treads up when she

heard the heavy footsteps in the passage above. Her heart began to pump harder. Should she stay downstairs and hide? Was the orphanage being taken over by a marauding army? She took a deep breath and let it out. Then she continued up the stairs and opened the door.

Lined up along the walls of the passageway, at least twenty of the girls of all ages and sizes stood at attention. Sister Edita carried a ruler, daring them to move. When she heard the door close behind Sister Daniela, the cook turned to face her.

"What's happened?" asked Sister Daniella.

"Sister Carmela, and Sister Natalia, who just got here, are conducting a search."

"Who's missing?"

"We can't find Pia." Tears began to fill Sister Edita's eyes.

"Mother Faustine's on her way," said Terza. "Allegra and Evelina are going room by room."

Sister Edita shot Terza a menacing gaze, but Terza ignored her. The tears began to track down the nun's cheeks, making her threat ineffective. Instead, Terza walked forward and slid her small hand into the cook's.

Sister Carmela descended the stairs and noticed the young nun. "The police have been called. Sister Daniela, please take the children downstairs to the classroom. I think that they'll worry less if they're kept busy. Sister Edita, please continue with your duties. In a few hours, lunch needs to be served in the dining room."

Sister Daniela opened the basement door and motioned for everyone to enter. Sixteen-year-old

Evelina was the last to approach the door. Sister Daniela stared into her gray eyes. "You and Allegra didn't find anything upstairs?"

"No. We looked in every hiding place we've all used at one time or another. Nothing. I sleep in one of the rooms on the second floor. I heard nothing, but Allegra said that some of the girls in her room saw a nun come up. She believes they thought it was old Sister Octavia so they didn't stop to consider that Sister Octavia would never be able to climb all those stairs."

"Or stay up that late," said Sister Daniela. "Maybe we can have the girls in that room draw us pictures of what they saw or dreamt about. Could you do that, Allegra? Could you take them aside and have them work on the project? Don't forget to draw what you think you saw too. Everyone else can sketch pictures in the classroom with me. Perhaps they saw something through a window or on a trek to the toilet."

"I think you would prefer being with the police, wouldn't you?" asked Evelina. "Didn't you mention that you and another nun did detective work when you we're at the *scuola media* in Montriano?"

Sister Daniela smiled as she closed the door behind her. "Yes well, right now I can help more by taking care of my students. Hopefully we won't lose anyone else." Stopping at the bottom of the stairs, she shivered. Considering the damage she could do to possible evidence, she walked to the door leading outside and carefully latched it.

Sister Daniela kept her mind on the task at hand, even when the police began to remove her students one at a time to interview with them. She longed to ask questions herself, but didn't dare. Instead, hoping they would draw a picture of the intruder who may have visited while they were supposedly asleep, Sister Daniela waved the most-likely witnesses to the back of the room. Maybe she should have had everyone involved in the lesson together. What if a child was finding her way to the toilet and seen someone in the hall? Perhaps the child didn't remember what she observed, and another's drawing suddenly sparked a memory? The teacher's head spun.

When classes were over, she dismissed the students into Sister Carmela's capable hands. Those assigned to preparing dinner would report to the kitchen while others studied and got extra help with assignments in the dining room upstairs.

Evelina approached Sister Daniela's desk as soon as the students had left the room. "I watched to see if anyone examined the room at the end of the hall. No one even came down to inspect it."

Sister Daniela kept writing. "I assume they checked down here this morning before I arrived."

"But the police didn't. They lined us up as soon as I came downstairs."

"So what do you think we ought to do?"

"You have the keys, don't you?"

"Yes. I assume we're talking about the laundry room. Since the laundry was done yesterday, it's been quiet. I usually pray for quiet while we study, but it did seem a bit eerie down here today." Sister Daniela opened the desk drawer and retrieved her ring of keys. "Stand by the door after I open it. If you hear anyone descending the stairs, please warn me."

Evelina followed the nun into the hallway and stopped in front of the door.

Sister Daniela slid the key into the lock and slowly turned it. The door squeaked when it opened. The nun stuck her fingers through the crack, fumbling with the switch. "The lights won't come on," she said, her voice husky with fear.

Evelina pushed open the door to let a swatch of light from the hallway cross the polished floor.

"Pia?" whispered Sister Daniela.

The two listened but heard no response.

Evelina suddenly disappeared and soon returned with a flashlight. She aimed it at each wall and then followed the contour of the floor.

"I don't see anything amiss," said the nun.

Evelina aimed the light toward a vent along the far wall. "That looks like someone's fiddled with the grate, doesn't it?"

They suddenly froze at the sound of a door slamming shut somewhere in the house. Was someone coming? Evelina fidgeted with the flashlight, trying to shut it off. The two women retreated to the hallway, and Sister Daniela quietly shut the door behind them. Sister Carmela appeared halfway down the stairs.

"There you are, Evelina. I thought you were going to help me. The homework seems to be hard for them."

"Yes, I'll be right there. I had a question about the assignment for Sister Daniela, and she came out here to explain it before I disappeared up the stairs."

"Thank you for that, Sister. I certainly can't explain it to them. I have no idea how to do that with numbers." Sister Carmela started back up the stairs.

"Maybe we can examine the laundry room again later," said Evelina.

"No. I'll make sure the police have searched the area around the vent. You run along to help everyone with homework. I have to get to my sister's house and make her husband something to eat.

Sister Daniela scooped the broccoletti and ricotta mixture into the small paccheri pasta bowls she'd prepared by standing the hollow noodles on end. Then she sprinkled the tops with breadcrumbs and hot pepper flakes. She placed the bowl into a tray of water in the oven to steam.

Michel walked in to wash his hands in the kitchen sink. Sister Daniela said nothing. It wasn't her place to tell her brother-in-law to wash his hands in the washroom when it was his house.

"Did you talk to Susanna today?" she asked. "I went to take her espresso, but she was asleep."

"She was okay this morning. There's an apron in the drawer if you want to keep your habit clean."

The nun looked down at a stain on the front of her black blouse. "Luckily, I have another. I can wash it out and hang it on the line so I have a backup. You're right, of course. I should keep myself tidier. I'm just not used to cooking for everyone."

Michel smiled. "I'm very grateful you came to help out. Susanna doesn't do well after one of her chemo sessions. I found I wasn't spending enough time on the vineyard when I alone had to care for her."

"What can go wrong during the summer before the grapes are picked?"

"A lot, actually. Weather can affect the grapes. We have to make sure we minimize the effects of too much heat or cold. I also have to supervise when the aging wine's checked for irregularities in the process. Anything can happen when you leave others on their own. Classico can have a life of its own. If I want the DOCG label from the control panel so that it's even called Chianti, I have to have my eyes on the whole process. Too many vintners have sent second-class wines to restaurants, giving a bad name to the rest of us."

"You use the oak barrels, don't you?"

"Yes. I went the traditional route. I have to work hard but can achieve a beefier taste while the wine's aging in the barrels. If for some reason the taste is off and I can't adjust it, my investment's lost."

"Sounds complicated. You know, we had a young child go missing from the orphanage today," said Sister Daniela, chopping tomatoes and tossing them into a bowl of lettuce.

"Did you find her?"

"No. I tell you this because the police might come knocking on your door, wanting to inspect the house and outbuildings. At least, I hope they do because I want them to find her."

"You think she might have come here?"

"Or was brought here or any other place within walking distance of the orphanage."

"Maybe I should check everything out right after dinner," he said, taking time to savor his glass of wine."

"That'd be nice. I'd help you, but I want to make sure Susanna's fed before she falls asleep again."

"What am I looking for?"

"She's six years old with black curls that fall to just below her chin. She was last seen wearing pajamas, but the woman who supposedly walked her out of the orphanage might have had another set of clothes for her."

"Woman? What did she look like?"

Sister Daniela grimaced. She hadn't really concentrated on how the woman was described. "She supposedly wore a habit and was old. I had my students draw pictures of her but haven't had time to looked at them yet. I haven't accomplished much to help them, actually."

"There's still a lot of light left. I'll have time to check out the buildings to see if anything might have changed. I think my fellow winemaker, Lucardi, is probably still around. He can help me."

The nun served Michel his dinner and sat down to pick at her own. "Maximo Lucardi, isn't it? I met him yesterday. He asked me about Susanna. He's a very nice man. "

"And he knows what he's doing. I'm lucky he works for me."

After she finished wiping up and washing dishes, Sister Daniel grabbed her folder of pictures the children had drawn and lay over her full bed in the guestroom across the hall from her sister's to examine them. She looked at the first, drawn by Terza. The woman she sketched was clearly a nun, her habit completely enveloping her body, and her head practically a tiny dot under the weight of an oversized, bulging wimple. The equally tiny hands, barely peeking out from her sleeves, were skeleton-like. The next sketch was Allegra's. The more mature artist drew someone hunched over the nearby bed. Below, she drew a profile of the woman's face, perhaps seen after the woman got up to leave with Pia. The hair peeking out from a wimple was stringy, maybe gray— hard to tell because the pictures were in black and white. The nun's face was lined, and her nose was long and crooked. Did she look like Sister Octavia? Sister Daniela couldn't tell. Another picture showed a nun on a broomstick.

This must be Cammeo's, said Sister Daniela to herself. *Is there anything to glean from this?* She stopped and laid out the pictures side by side. All three drawings showed a woman in a long habit and wimple—something worn by sisters in fewer and fewer convents nowadays. The figures in all sketches were tall and thin.

She turned over a few more drawings and wrote down some of the details. Within fifteen minutes, however, she was asleep, dreaming of witches and nuns herself.

An hour later she startled. What time was it? She heard a noise downstairs.

Michel held onto the front doorknob while he slipped out of his muddy boots.

Sister Daniela descended the stairs with some dishes. "She's awake if you want to see her. She looks quite good. Maybe she can get out of bed tomorrow. I'd like that. It's easier to help her wash her hair when she can stand up. Did the police ever come by?"

"Yes, but Lucardi and I had already checked everything. Nothing new except…"

"Except what?"

"You know how it drizzled last night—not a lot, just enough to make it difficult to walk between the rows of vines to check the grapes. It's clumping now, but I still need a stick to clean my boots."

"Yes. It was sunny this morning, though."

"Well, a car turned around in the drive sometime during the night. The police noticed it and asked if we'd been out during the night or early this morning. Lucardi said he left about eight to pick up a date and take her to a bar in town, but it hadn't yet rained. He was the last to leave. They took casts of all the tracks, including the ones for our trucks."

"And you were here. I know because your bedroom door was open, and I could hear you snoring." Sister Daniela felt her face grow hot. "I didn't mean that it kept me up."

"Susanna complains about my snoring too. Don't worry about embarrassing me."

"Susanna must have eaten heartily. Her dishes are empty. That's a good sign. I sat beside the bed and examined those drawings I told you about."

"What did you find?"

"Most were nothing. I really wanted to examine the ones drawn by Pia's roommates. One of them said she dreamed of a nun in the room. It looked the same as one of the others who said she awoke and saw the nun but went back to sleep. They figured it was Sister Octavia, an elderly nun belonging to the same order in Siena. Most of the drawings do look like her, but Sister Octavia doesn't go out much anymore. She's in her nineties and can only get around with a walker. I'm not sure a walker could help her get up to the attic. And nobody heard or saw a walker."

"So they thought it was this Sister Octavia and drew how they remembered Sister Octavia. Perhaps they didn't really see the old woman."

"The main thing is that Sister Octavia's very tall and skinny. That's how they described the woman who took Pia. I tend to believe the girls actually saw a nun or someone who looked like her."

He walked into the kitchen as Sister Daniela took the phone out of her pocked and pecked at the tiny keypad. She waited for the older nun to pick up her red cell phone. When it went to her voicemail, Sister

Daniela left a message, "Sister Angela. I need you here. Please get Mother Margarita's permission to visit us and get here as quickly as possible."

Chapter Two

Sister Angela waited outside Mother Margherita's office. She squirmed. Her chair was far too small for her ample backside. There should be chairs for adults. What happens when the parents have to meet with the mother superior? Is this waiting room designed to make everyone uncomfortable?

She heard Sister Marcella put down the phone with a click and looked up. The headmistress' secretary gazed back at Sister Angela and smiled.

You think I look funny in this chair, don't you? Sister Angela thought. She sat up straight and glanced away. *Well, I'm not going to give you the pleasure of making your day.*

The door to the office suddenly opened, and a man and a woman walked out. Behind them, Sister Margherita paused in the doorway and gestured for Sister Angela to enter. The nun started to stand when her knees resisted. Praying that God spare her the humiliation of asking for help getting out of this devil of a chair, she was finally able to extricate herself and move slowly toward the office. Is that Sister Marcella quietly snickering?

"Sister Angela, I know why you're here," Mother Margherita said before she returned to her seat across the desk from the nun. "You got a call from Sister Daniela saying she needed help on a case of a missing child. Am I correct?"

"Yes, I got a message from Sister Daniela last night. I didn't answer, afraid that I would incur the resistance of the diocese. Sister Daniela was retired as a junior detective when she became a teacher, wasn't she? I come here seeking your advice."

The mother superior beamed. "I'm honored that you would come to me first, though I doubt you'll follow direction regardless of my opinion."

"I don't wish to get Sister Daniela into trouble."

"You're off the hook. Sister Daniela made it so that she and she alone is responsible."

"I have no idea why she's there, Mother."

"Oh yes, you were away when she left. Her sister lives in Filari and is undergoing chemotherapy for her cancer. The sister's husband asked Sister Daniela to come and help. While there, she wanted to be useful during the days her sister didn't need her. I believe she's helping the Mission Sisters in Siena. They run an orphanage within walking distance of the brother-in-law's winery. They needed a teacher. I assume the missing child's from the orphanage. I have no other details to share."

"But Father Sergio, the bishop's assistant, is surely going to want to interfere in this case. Aren't you afraid of his wrath?"

"This isn't a big deal unless you make it one, Sister Angela. As of yesterday, you and the students went on summer holiday, didn't you?"

"Yes, I planned to sleep in this morning, but I was concerned about Sister Daniela and her case."

"What you do during the three weeks of your vacation is your business, not mine. If you decide to travel to this village and take in some rest and relaxation, I can't stop you because I won't be aware of it."

Sister Angela smiled.

"I only ask that you keep your little red cell phone with you so I can call you in time to remind you to return and join your students in four weeks."

"Yes, Mother."

"I assume you usually book public transportation when you have holiday destinations in mind. That's important because getting you a driver might attract unwanted attention."

"I understand, Mother. I gather the ears in this office are agreed not to let this information go outside."

Mother Margherita's lips thinned—a bad sign that Sister Angela recognized immediately.

"Yes, you can call this office if you need to," said the mother superior. "I would suggest you leave the message that you want me to return your call and say nothing about the case or Sister Daniela. That way you don't have to talk about my secretary as if she's a spy. Do you understand?"

"Yes, Mother," said Sister Angela, thrilled that Mother Margherita seemed to be joining her in the conspiracy. "Would you like me to keep you informed about the details?"

"Good Lord, no. The less I know the better. If, however, you run into some sort of impasse, I might be a resource. That said I've never known you to run into one you couldn't break yourself."

"Then I'll reserve my tickets now," said Sister Angela standing. She felt much better, knowing Mother Margherita thought her a capable detective.

"So that she doesn't worry and return too early, please tell Sister Daniela that Sister Eloisa's becoming a strong teacher and that she must stay and take care of her sister. As for you, don't let this go to your head. I expect you back in three weeks to welcome your new students. I'm a teacher short and am not prepared to teach in addition to my other chores."

"What about…"

The lips thinned again.

Sister Angela, her hand on the doorknob, stopped and smiled. "I know what you believe I was going to say, Mother, and you're right. Think about it. If someone in the outer office had to do it herself, she might be more polite once she saw how hard we all worked." Sister Angela was out the door before the mother superior could answer about anything concerning her secretary, Sister Marcella.

Sister Angela had to hurry. She planned to visit Chief Detective Allesandro DiMarco before she caught the bus to Petraggio.

"Is he in?" she asked upon arriving at the station unannounced.

"Yes, of course," said the police constable on duty. He lifted the counter and gestured for her to enter. "He's in his office."

Sister Angela peeked through the open door and found him sitting at his desk, deep in thought.

"Hello, Allesandro," she said. "I'm on my way to Siena. I have a case."

"Ah, my favorite detective, Sister Angela," he said, standing. "What can I do for you? It's been quiet here. I suppose it could get busier now that school's out but probably not a murder or robbery. Maybe a drunk and disorderly call. That isn't quite up your alley, is it?"

"As I said, my services have been requested in Siena. A child, an orphan, has disappeared."

"They must have heard about your talents. Did Father Sergio call you in?"

"Sister Daniela's working at an orphanage in one of the villages. She called. It isn't official. It's actually my holiday. The diocese hasn't been consulted."

"Ah, winetasting. It can't be all bad, I suppose."

Sister Angela smiled. "No, it isn't all bad, but still—they're looking for the child in earnest. She may not have a family, but the nuns who run the orphanage are just as worried. I was wondering…"

"I'm looking it up, Sister." His fingers danced across his laptop keyboard. "It's Chief Detective Ricco Pagano. I'm afraid I don't know him. Would you like me to inform him you're coming?"

"That would be nice. I'm sure they have lots of support. Siena's much bigger than Montriano."

"And I'm certain they'll want you to reveal some of our winemaking secrets, Sister. They're in the Chianti Classico area. Our vintners are in direct competition with theirs. Keep our secrets to yourself."

"If I knew them, I would zip my lips. Too much alcohol might lead to loose ones, but without a car or knowledge of our methods, I can do little more than embarrass Montriano and the *scuola media*."

On the way back down the hill to the school, Sister Angela stopped at San Benedetto Church where she sat in the cool interior to pray for the sisters' success in locating the child. Making her way up the center aisle, she let her eyes follow the Stations of the Cross on one of the walls. Then she gazed the altar. To the right, the Virgin Mother drew in all her visitors. To the left, the white marble rendering of St. Francis of Assisi offered his services to protect the animals and all those poor souls who seek his blessing. Sister Angela took a seat in front of him and fingered her beads. She didn't have time to repeat all the prayers on her rosary, but she could whisper some of them. After about ten minutes, she felt energized and exited as quietly as she entered.

At the *scuola media*, Sister Angela walked to the office and grabbed her packed bag. Then she hiked down the hill to catch the bus to the terminal in Petraggio where she'd transfer to another bus on its way to Siena.

Finally seated on the train, the nun retrieved a bottle of cold water from her red-striped tote and sat back to watch the olive orchards and vineyards sweep by. She loved Montriano and Petraggio. The two hill towns were her home. She'd never leave them, but her detective work was also important. She loved watching the world go by. Unfortunately, she usually traveled because something happened outside of Montriano, and this was no exception.

Sister Angela had been to Siena once before. She knew the large cathedral in the center of the city. All the hills and roads seemed to lead the visitor to its front steps. But the group of nuns that worked in Siena lived in an old house closer to the Basilica. Sister Angela worried that the distance between the Basilica and Filari, where Sister Daniela lived and worked, wasn't supported by a bus. How would she get there? Would she have go into town to discuss clues with the police?

Some of her questions would be answered as she descended the steps of the bus across from the train terminal.

The nun heard a honk from a faded Fiat idling along the curb across the street.

"Sister Angela? Are you looking for someone affiliated with the *suore di missione?*"

Sister Angela waved and put her tote over the opposite shoulder. The driver leaned over to open the passenger door for the older nun. "I'm Sister Liona."

"I didn't expect you to have a car, Sister."

"We have to cover a wide area. You're here for the problem at the orphanage, aren't you? You couldn't get from here to Filari without wheels. We keep a car here in town," she said, pulling away from the curb without looking. A pickup behind her honked several times, but she didn't seem to notice. "It would be nice if the nuns at Filari kept one too. That's our next project—to get a car for the orphanage. We need it for our work."

"Are you all affiliated with the orphanage?"

"Oh no. Some of us at Mission House work at the food bank. Others concentrate on housing the poor. A few help the elderly. I specialize in legal aid. We're quite busy. Sister Carmela and Sister Natalia work at the orphanage. Most of the time they sleep there too. Sister Carmela stays there all the time. They aren't alone, though. They hire others to help out."

"Hopefully everyone's background is verified."

"Most have been there for years. Then there's the new one, Sister Daniela. I think you know of her. Most come recommended, and many are nuns."

"Where are we going?"

"To Filari. Sister Daniela has a room for you at her sister's house. I believe she wants to put you to work immediately. She said you'd insist on that."

Sister Angela smiled.

"Sit back and enjoy the rolling hills and rows of vines, Sister. It'll take a half hour or so to get there."

Chapter Three

Viviana delivered a glass of water to her grandmother's room and waited for more instructions. Her aunt took her arm, leading her into the hallway. Viviana carefully closed the door.

"What are you doing? You're no help here. I only suppose your mother feels shame for failing to come here herself and help out." Viviana's aunt continued down the hallway toward the stairs, and Viviana followed. "Leave it to Mara to take the easy route."

"My mother's in Roma. She'd lose her job if she left now, Aunt Lucilla."

"She's too self-important. What kind of woman leaves her duties at home just so she can work with the men?"

The two reached the bottom of the stairs and strolled into the small sitting room where Mara's younger sister sat knitting.

"What's the matter?" asked Clarissa.

"I was telling Viviana that Mara should be here. It does absolutely no good to send Viviana. What can she do?"

"You two want me to represent my mother while you go through the jewelry. My mother doesn't believe you should go over Nonna's things until her will's been read. I don't see what's wrong with her opinion."

Clarissa carefully put down her knitting and lit a

cigarette. The smoke curled toward the ceiling.

"Mara believes her mother has bequeathed everything to her," said Lucilla. "You know that. It's just like her to make *you* do the work, Viviana. She was always like that. When we were children, she'd sit on her throne and tell Clarissa and me what to do. Your *nonna* would smile and then explain that I was the eldest, and it was my job to mete out the chores. Then, when I was five…"

Viviana had managed to inch toward the door as Lucilla went on without stopping to take a breath. She quietly opened the front door and slid out onto the steps, taking a deep breath. She had to get away from the strong aroma of mothballs, stale cigarette smoke, and death.

Pulling her long, light-brown hair into a ponytail, Viviana began to walk down the long road toward town.

About a mile down the dusty road, Viviana realized she wasn't heading in the right direction. She visited her grandmother once or twice when she young but didn't remember how her father drove to get into the town of Corsa Pietra. On the next hill over, she could see it, its red tile roofs gleaming in the sun and the tall church steeple piercing the sky. But the road continued without turning toward it. She stopped to examine the situation. Behind her, the hill of her *nonna's* house descended into a valley where another road twisted up the opposite side.

Between her and that road, a grassy field introduced rows of grapevines. The neat lines led her eyes down the slope to another road and the river where a bridge would take her to the town. There didn't seem to be a fence. Perhaps she could cut across here to save her time. Stepping carefully through the yellowing grass, she entered expansive network of vines.

The grapes looked like they were ready to be picked. Perhaps she could try a few. She stopped and looked around in all directions. There was a house beneath a bushy olive tree about halfway down the hill. Tall cypress trees framed a long driveway less than a kilometer farther up the road she'd just traversed.

Viviana pinched off a bunch of grapes, popped one into her mouth, and started walking. After about five minutes she heard the noise. Spinning around, she came face to face with a rearing horse. She dropped the remaining grapes.

"You're trespassing," a voice boomed.

She covered her eyes so she could see the figure in the saddle.

"I'm sorry. I didn't know how to…"

"Don't you know that you damage the vine when you fool with the grapes that are this close to maturation?"

"Well, no. I didn't."

The man dismounted. He patted his horse's mane to calm it down.

"Do you own this land? It's beautiful. Your winery must be very successful." She noticed his strong tan arms and long legs.

He pushed back his black bangs like a little boy before taking the reins and starting to walk beside her. "Do you know anything about wine? If you're from around here, you should."

"Unfortunately…"

"Then you must stay and let me take you on a tour. It would benefit me and other growers for you to learn something in case you decide to take more walks. As it is, if you intend to make it to town, it'll take at least another hour. Then you have to turn around right away to climb the hill and get to wherever you're staying."

"Oh, yes. I'm staying at my *nonna's* about a kilometer up the gravel road. I don't suppose you know her."

"Uh, probably not. Look, why don't you change your plans? If you follow me, I can give you a tour and then take you into town."

"I don't want to interrupt your work."

"I'd already planned to go into town for some supplies."

"Is it that building behind the beautiful olive tree?"

"No. You can't see it from here. It's beyond that. We make Chianti Rufina wines. The winery's award-winning."

"I don't even know your name."

"This," he said with a sweeping gesture, "is Amarena Balda, and I'm Giulio de Capua. Amarena Balda is owned by the De Capua family, which consists of me and my brother, Ermanno. The winery's been here for over a century."

Looking like a large warehouse, an outbuilding stood on the other side of an even larger house. Viviana wanted to ask De Capua if he lived there with his brother, but she bit her lip.

"This is the building where we create our tasty wines. In spite of our size, we've won awards all over the valley."

The inside was a wide expanse of space at one end. A few tables and a desk in the middle formed an office and lab with a couple of laptops and a microscope. At the other end, rows of barrels surrounded a larger vat. Her gaze stopped at a door at the far end.

His eyes followed hers. "That's where we store our supplies."

"I know almost nothing about winemaking. Are there a lot of supplies?"

"Are you interested?"

"Yes, of course. I know that you grow grapes, crush them, and let them age."

"That would be great if that was all there was to it. I'd pick and crush the grapes in September and then travel the rest of the year. Unfortunately there's a lot of paperwork and politics involved too. Too much bureaucratic red tape. I hire more people to do paperwork than I do winemakers and experts on taste and quality."

"What do you mean?"

"In order to sell the finest possible wine, I have

to grow premium grapes and, using the best equipment and a special mixture of grapes and chemistry, produce the best-tasting product in the region."

"I thought you grew all the grapes."

He smiled. "I grow most of the grapes, but neighbors grow different types. I buy from them too. The other winemakers create varieties with different quantities of each grape. In addition, we might alter the process slightly. Each variance can make big differences in taste and texture. Alterations are necessary because the grapes are all grown in the same region and carry similar fruity tastes. My wine has a taste that's distinct from the wine my neighbor produces."

"Wow. I guess I really don't know very much."

"You must start by tasting the different products. I have some bottles over here."

"I've been winetasting before. A tasting room that has some atmosphere or something to make the consumer feel comfortable is a must. Do you have something like that here?"

"No. Not now. I'll have to ask you for advice when we build it, though. Come closer," he said, holding up a glass of his red wine. "Do you know how creating what we call *Chianti* is governed?"

"I know nothing, except how it tastes."

"It's quite complex. Our prestigious standard production, labeled as superior, has several flavors." He handed her a glass and filled it about a third full. "Hold it up to the light. What do you see?"

"It's dark red. I can barely see any light coming through."

"Now take a sip. Let it sit on your tongue. Does the taste remind you of anything?"

"I can taste a fruit. Cherry maybe? But it's spicier than cherry."

"What else?"

"There's a smoky flavor. Is that from the oak barrel?"

"Take some more. Does it really taste like oak?"

"No, maybe a campfire."

"What about a cigarette?"

"Oh, yes. I haven't had one of those since my early teens so I hardly think about it. There's a musty taste too, I believe."

"So now you know how it tastes. If you were explaining this to a customer, I'd recommend you say that it has a black cherry, tobacco, and earth flavors. We're in the Rufina sub region and are therefore included in the DOCG rules that regulate what we put into our wines and how long the wine must be aged. You just tasted Chianti following the rules for Chianti Superiore. Our finest Chianti is our *riserva*. The grapes must be eighty per cent Sangiovese, and all the grapes must be grown somewhere within the Chianti region. They once used quite a few white grapes in Chianti, but we no longer add them. To be competitive, only the best red grapes go into our wines. In our case, we grow over ninety per cent of our own grapes."

"Whoever handles the business end must be overwhelmed. The desk's messy. How can he or she pay all the bills when they're strewn all over the table?"

"He has his methods. My brother takes care of that so I can work on getting the best wine possible."

"Where is he?"

"He's on the road right now." He took her arm and turned her away from the surface. "He'll be back by the end of the week. I see that Serena, my sister, has texted me and asks if you want to come to dinner. They've set a place for you at the table. Perhaps we can go into town another time."

"So your whole family lives in the house?"

"My sister, my mother, and my brother. My father died about five years ago. We all take care of my mother now."

At the house, Giulio showed her where she could freshen up. When she returned, the family had already moved outside.

Signora de Capua sat at the end of a large picnic table. Viviana went up to her to thank her for the invitation. Then she looked out to see Corsa Pietra across the valley. Setting behind the hill in back of her, the sun made the hill town shimmer.

"It's beautiful," she said. "What a perfect view."

Giulio took her arm and led her to the bench next to his sister. On the way to his seat across from Viviana, he grabbed a bowl of pasta and carefully placed some on her plate. To one side, a dish of lettuce, tomato, and olives looked equally inviting. Then he poured her wine from the bottle on the table. "This is the *riserva*," he said. "Enjoy." Giulio turned to his mother and began to tell her about the successes and frustrations that filled his day.

"I'm Serena. Giulio tells us you might be working for us."

Startled, she looked back at Giulio.

"I was hoping we might work something out. I'm not even sure you're interested in doing the job I mentioned."

"I think I told you that I'm not from this area. I'm here because my grandmother's ill. My aunts felt I should represent my mother and help them with Nonna's care."

"Are you saying you can't stay here?"

Viviana hesitated, her mind whirling. She'd much rather have the job than care for her dying grandmother, but she'd made a commitment. How would she get out of it? "Let me see what I can do."

Every time Viviana took a sip, Giulio would refill her glass. She had no idea how many glasses of wine she had. "The meal was delicious," she said. "Please let me help you with the dishes."

"No, no," said Signora de Capua. "It will be dark soon. Giulio can at least see you back to the road."

Giulio pulled her toward the first rows of vines, and walked behind her as they trudged back the way she'd come. At the end of the first row, he took her arm, and turning her to face him, he leaned down to kiss her.

Viviana felt her cheeks grow hot but didn't retreat. When he rested his hand against her back, she leaned into him. Perhaps it was the wine or maybe the strong attraction to him that she felt from the first moment they'd met. She wouldn't resist.

Giulio lowered his hand and drew her up. She could feel his hardness just below her bellybutton and wanted to explore it further, but he pushed her away from him and stared into her eyes. "I hate women in trousers," he said, his voice gruff.

Viviana smiled. "Trousers are good protection for day one, don't you think?"

He took her hand and began walking with her again. "No. And they aren't very good for your job either. I want you in a dress when you deal with the public."

"Not business wear?"

"A skirt then. Just so the men don't think you're trying to be like them. No ponytail. Keep your hair down. Oh, and the shoes—wear heels."

"It sounds like you're trying to sell *me* instead of the wine."

Giulio laughed. "Damn right I'm trying to sell you. Once you get them to taste the wine, they'll get confused and end up buying the bottle."

They reached the road just as the moon began to rise behind hill town. He continued to walk with her, his hand gripping hers, and they talked about business and family until they were in front of her grandmother's house.

"So I might be bought. I thought you wanted me for yourself."

"I always take what's left over, Viviana. Rest assured I won't sell you. I'm keeping you for myself.

Chapter Four

Sister Angela hoped Sister Daniela was still at the orphanage. Fortunately, she found the young nun correcting papers in the basement classroom.

"I'm glad you came so quickly," said Sister Daniela, rushing to hug her old friend.

"This is Sister Liona. She drove me from Siena."

"Yes, I know Sister Liona," she said, turning to hug the driver. "She often drives people back and forth. We're grateful for all who assist us at Mission House."

"We'd like you two to come to dinner tomorrow night," said Sister Liona. "Do you think you'll be able to break from your investigation? I can pick you up when I retrieve Sister Natalia."

"No. I think I'll be able to borrow Michel's truck. I'll let you know if there's a problem. Sister Angela, I hope you can drive. It's much easier to drive around here than to call for help."

Sister Angela smiled. "I can operate a vehicle and have a perfect driving record. I'm just never offered a car. I hope your brother-in-law doesn't mind."

"We'll expect you at eight at Mission House then," Sister Liona said, retreating to the stairs.

"Thank you," said Sister Daniela. "We look forward to seeing Mother Faustine. Hopefully we'll have some news for her." Sister Daniela stopped to examine her old mentor. "I'm glad you're fit. Let's go up and get Sisters Carmela and Natalia. We must bring you up to date so we can start work first thing in the morning."

The two nuns and the cook sat at a table in the office just off a TV room and situated in the front corner of the old house. The afternoon sun shone through all four windows, making it the warmest room in the house. They stood when Sister Daniela and Sister Angela entered the room.

"Good afternoon, Sister Angela. I'm Sister Carmela. I'm the night administrator and discovered that young Pia was missing when the children rose the morning before last. This is Sister Natalia here on my right. She cares for the children during the day. She and I hunted for Pia, as did the police, yesterday morning. The two of us are aware of all the hiding places on the property."

"And the outbuilding?" asked Sister Angela.

"The garage, yes," said Sister Carmela. "It's no longer used for cars, however. We don't have one here. We store supplies in the garage. The woman at the end of the table is our cook, Sister Edita. She too went through many of the hiding places in the house yesterday."

"I noticed other doors near the classroom downstairs when I was taken to see Sister Daniela."

"Yes, one of them is the laundry," said Sister Carmela

"I assume you all checked the laundry room,"

said Sister Angela.

The two head nuns looked at each other. "Of course. Did you see anything amiss?"

"Oh no. I haven't been inside. I just wanted to know who does the laundry. I presume it's a job that takes most of the week to accomplish, but you haven't mentioned a housekeeper."

"The older girls do the housekeeping," said Sister Natalia.

"Not in the kitchen," said Sister Edita. "I keep the kitchen tidy."

"There are older girls in each room," said Sister Carmela. "The more mature ones are in charge of their rooms and wash all towels, sheets, and clothing on specific days."

"They take turns cleaning the bathrooms, both of them on the ground floor," said Sister Edita. "They have toilet duty once a month. It's all on a board in the dining room. The younger children have chores too. The common rooms and hallways are cleaned by the younger children. Some pickup and others vacuum."

"You have to be organized," said Sister Angela.

"They need time to study for an hour after their classes," said Sister Daniela. "I stay and make sure they've finished their homework before dinner."

"So efficient," said Sister Natalia.

A bell rang, and Sister Edita rose to answer the front door.

"Sister Angela, I presume. I've heard of you," said a man entering the room.

"This is Chief Detective Ricco Pagano," said Sister Natalia. "Ricco can explain to all of us what they've discovered."

The chief detective wasn't as old as his position implied. He had loose curls, something that added to his boyish face. He reached up and brushed his bangs to one side. His blue eyes lit up when he talked. Obviously the pressure of the job hadn't yet fazed him.

"The nuns call me Ricco because I was raised here at the orphanage—before it was just for girls."

Everyone sat down.

"I don't know what you've been told, Sister Angela, so I'll start at the beginning. Detective Sergeant Elmo Sacco and I arrived at seven-thirty yesterday morning. I believe Mother Faustine called the station at six-thirty."

"What time do the children usually rise?" asked Sister Angela.

"At five-thirty," explained Sister Carmela. "It may sound early, but it takes a lot of work to get them all fed before they start school."

"The program's awful," said Pagano. "I couldn't wait to graduate out of here. In the first year of freedom, I had to teach myself how to sleep in. Now my wife has to get me up because I sleep through the alarm."

Sister Angela smiled. "Who roused the children that morning?" she asked.

"There's a bell that goes off," said Sister Carmela. "It isn't that loud, but loud enough to awaken some of them. The roommates urge the rest of the girls out of bed."

"So by six yesterday morning, you all knew she was missing?"

"Yes. We didn't go looking for Pia right away, but Mother Faustine called from the house in Siena so I told her we were busy searching for Pia."

"Excuse me," said the nun detective. "Does the mother superior usually call so early?"

Sister Carmela appeared confused, but she looked that way only a few seconds. "No. She called because she wanted to tell me something before I retired. I go off duty by seven. I'd tell you what she told me, but I don't remember. I was so befuddled with the problem here that I guess I didn't really listen to her. Anyway, she called the police, and Ricco and Elmo showed up a half an hour later. That was important because we needed the help. With all the children up and about, it was hard to look for her and take care of the other girls' needs."

"What did you find out, Chief Detective?"

"We inspected the attic chamber where she slept. We interviewed her roommates. Then we examined the other rooms and questioned all the girls. Elmo dusted the doors for fingerprints. We checked the windows and everything else in all the rooms."

"And the garage?"

"Yes. I informed Mother Faustine that the garage was a fire hazard. We had to move a lot of supplies in order to uncover possible hiding places."

"What about footprints or tire tracks?"

"We made casts of any larger footprints. The child's footprints matched half the other orphans in the house. We formed casts of tire tracks in the area and recorded the tire marks from cars and trucks that regularly visit."

Sister Angela sat up. "What about the people

who don't come here regularly?"

"What do you mean?" asked Sister Natalia. "The girls would be familiar with people like the handyman or food delivery men. We aren't sure they recognized the culprit in this case."

"They *witnessed* the kidnapping?"

"Sister Daniela didn't tell you?" asked Sister Carmela.

"We always feel it's best if I learn the facts on my own."

"A few of the girls believe they saw someone enter the room and walk out with the child," said Pagano. "We don't see their stories as credible."

"I had them draw pictures of what they saw," said Sister Daniela. "I'll show you the sketches after dinner."

A young girl entered the room and served each guest a cup of espresso.

"How do you do?" said Sister Angela. "You are..."

"This is Grazia," said Sister Natalia.

"How old are you?" asked Sister Angela.

"I'm nine."

"Did you see Pia leave the orphanage?"

"I saw a shadow pass under the bathroom door when I was using the toilet."

"Going what direction?"

"Toward the stairs."

"Who did you think it was?"

"I didn't know," said Grazia. "I guess I thought it was one of the girls."

"I don't think you mentioned that," said Sister Carmela. "Did you tell one of the detectives?"

"No. Nobody asked so I didn't think of it."

"What made you look at the bottom of the door?" asked Sister Angela. "Were you scared?"

"Sometimes I'm nervous about people wandering around at night. Simone—she's one of my roommates—says the house is haunted. I worry a little about that. But that night I heard something— like someone was rattling the front door to see if it was locked. Maybe it was Evelina. She always checks it to make sure all the doors are latched before we go to bed. I looked down to see if she was going to return to her room. She did because she was heading up the stairs. It must have been Evelina."

"Did you see her shadow going toward the door before she rattled the knob on the front door?"

"No."

"What time was it, Grazia?"

"I don't know. I must have slept because I suddenly awoke. My blanket had fallen off the bed, and I was cold. I put on my socks and went down the stairs to the toilet so I wouldn't have to get up again."

"Is your room on the floor above this one?" Sister Angela asked.

"There's no sleeping chamber on this floor," said Sister Carmela. "Grazia and Simone sleep in one of the bedrooms on the next floor with four other girls. Evelina's room is also on the first floor up so she'd have climbed the stairs as Grazia described."

"Did anyone ask Evelina about being up?"

"I did," said the chief. "She said she didn't go down the stairs to check the door again after the lights were out. No one else mentioned they noticed Grazia get up. Any other questions, Sister Angela?

Elmo's written up what we found. I'll have him send you the report."

"I'll also need the reports on Pia. There's always the possibility that one of her family came to get her. How long was she here?"

"She came to us two years ago," said Sister Natalia. "That would make her four at the time. I'll ask Mother Faustine to provide the girl's background."

"Perhaps you'll allow Sister Daniela to show me around now before we head to her sister's for dinner. I'll want to see the crime scene and all the places that were already searched. Is that all right with you?"

The others nodded and rose to disperse to different parts of the large house.

"It's almost too quiet. Where are the children?"

"They've been studying," said Sister Natalia. "Evelina took them to the classroom. As soon as you two go downstairs, the noise will start again. Sister Edita, you're excused to prepare dinner. The car should be here soon for me to go to Mission House. Sister Carmela will take over here for the night shift. It was nice meeting you, Sister Angela. I'm sure we'll talk more tomorrow."

Sister Daniela, Susanna, Michel, and Sister Angela sat in the dining room enjoying dinner.

"I'm so happy you got out of bed to meet me, Susanna. Sister Daniela has talked about you for so long I feel as if I know you."

"And I'm glad I was able to rise. I hate it when I'm sick."

Michel put his hand on hers. "I'm so relieved you and the doctors are doing something about this."

"Dani helped me wash my hair this afternoon. I'm afraid I'm losing some of it. I hope I'm still attractive when I don't have any."

"I'm not afraid. You'll look beautiful no matter what," said Michel.

Sister Daniela placed the lasagna on the table. "Be careful, it's hot."

Susanna turned to Sister Angela. "Did you learn anything about the case today?"

"You mean from the police? Yes, I understand they're searching everywhere for the child. Volunteers are roaming the vineyards and fields."

"I know," said Michel. "I sent my workers out to lead police and volunteers between the vines. I needed someone to help me keep them from tramping on the plants in the middle of the rows because I need flowers to protect the grapes from insects and disease."

"I saw them," said Sister Angela. "A few volunteers must have had trouble stepping around the marigolds. Hopefully someone warned them about touching the vines. I'm sure the grapes are particularly susceptible right now."

Michel took a sip of wine before he answered. "It's a matter of priorities, Sister. Finding the child's more important than the business. We can repair any minor damage the search has caused."

"I noticed the vineyard between yours and the orphanage."

"Yes, La Barca's."

"He doesn't do as much for his rows. Everything looks more rustic."

"Don't let his methods fool you. He's always experimenting with flavor, and that's the game, isn't it?"

"How are his methods different?"

"He uses amphorae—clay pots. It's how they used to make wine as far back as 6000 BC. The clay manages to give both the reds and the whites a more beefy flavor. I prefer the woody tastes that my oak adds, but his isn't displeasing, and with some foods, it can be preferred."

"Do you know him well, Michel?" asked Sister Daniela.

"Not well, no. I have my family…"

"You mean he lives a different lifestyle?" asked Sister Angela. "I must make it a point to meet him."

"What about the drawings, Sister?" asked Susanna. "Do you think the children saw something?"

"Yes, they're all too similar for the likenesses to be a coincidence. Their caretakers will probably say that they must have talked among themselves before they drew them, but I don't believe the younger children would've been influenced by the talk. They must have actually seen something."

"Couldn't the child have walked out on her own?"

"Do you think no one would've noticed? I don't believe so. Yes, Pia could've gone to the toilet or climbed down the stairs sleepwalking. I don't believe she would've walked out and closed the door behind her. We should find out tomorrow whether her prints are around the front door or not."

"We don't know which door she or they walked out of either," said Sister Daniela. "They may have gone down to the basement first. I have to speak with the chief detective tomorrow morning. I want him to check the vent in the laundry room. I'm not sure what the detectives looked at down there. I can see several areas they might not have noticed."

"And what about the heavy mist that took place just before dawn?" asked Michel. "If they questioned tire tracks on my drive, they must have found footprints."

"I didn't know about the mist. I only heard about full moons and sunlight," said Sister Angela. "Needless to say, we still have work to do. I'd love to take you up on your offer to learn about how you make your wine, Michel, but unfortunately there's a time factor. The longer we go without discovering a clue, the farther away the child can be taken. There are two of us, Sister Daniela. Before we go to sleep tonight, we should decide what things we need to investigate first and then divide them up and actually accomplish them."

"I get up at six and turn on the espresso maker. I arrive at the orphanage at seven-thirty. When do you want me to knock on your door?"

Chapter Five

The straight rows of vines, heavy with grapes, made Sister Angela stop in her tracks. Even though the harvesting season was near, roses bloomed, capping the end each row, and marigolds still dotted the paths in between. Carrying a shoulder bag full of corrected assignments, Sister Daniela scurried to catch up with the older nun.

"Can you smell it?" Sister Angela asked her, slowing down as she drew near. "It's nearly time. Michel must feel the excitement in his stomach. Pretty soon the crusher will be humming."

"Hopefully we'll find Pia before that."

"So you want to elicit a detective's help to search the entire basement? I suppose one of your students will help you teach today."

"That's the plan, yes. And you want to interview everyone, right? I showed you the sketches yesterday. When we get there, I'll hand them over to you again."

"When school lets out, we'll go back to your sister's vineyard and take the truck."

"Yes. I made a dish last night and put it in the refrigerator, but I never left a note for Michel. He won't know how to heat it up. Before we leave, I'll write him instructions, and also remind him that I borrowed his truck."

Sister Angela waited for Sister Daniela to settle down her class and assign her a student. Then she and Allegra climbed the stairs and walked to the office next to the dining room.

"Hi, I'm Sister Angela. I was going through the sketches of the roommates and found that you had drawn this one," she said.

"Yes. That's mine." Short auburn hair fell just below Allegra's ears, framing her wide smile.

"I believe Sister Daniela put you in charge because you're the senior roommate. How old are you?"

"I'm fourteen. I'm the oldest in my room."

"And you drew this picture. Did you actually wake up and see the figure leaning over Pia's bed?"

"Yes. My bed's right next to hers."

Sister Angela stood. "Would you take me up there? I need to see where you sleep."

Allegra stood and led the nun up the two flights of stairs. Winded, the nun paused on the top landing.

"There's a chair right here inside the door."

"Bless you, child." Sister Angela looked up. "Which bed's yours?"

"Mine's here closest to the chair. Pia's is the next bed."

"So, what happened?"

"I was sleeping here on the bed. I was facing in your direction when I heard the floorboard squeak. I was asleep so it took a while for me to wake up, but when I opened my eyes, I was gazing at this wall."

"Was it dark?"

"Yes, but not very dark. The nightlight in the hall was on. The little ones like to have a nightlight because they get scared. Unfortunately, it also makes shadows on the walls and ceiling, and sometimes that frightens them even more."

"So you noticed the nightlight was on."

"I'm not sure, but it still wasn't that dark. I lifted my head and heard rustling and the squeaking of mattress coils. I was up on my elbow and turned my head to look at the others. The dark figure was crouching. I glanced at her back."

"Why didn't you ask what was going on?"

"Because her black costume was loose like a habit. I figured Pia was in distress, and the nun was comforting her."

"Did you hear conversation?"

"No—maybe very low whispering."

"Did the nun look up?"

"If she had, I would've seen the white of the wimple and know for sure she was a nun. Instead, I lay my head down on the pillow and dozed. When I awoke again, the sun was shining in through the window."

"Did you hear any noises as the two left?"

"No. I can't even say that the figure and Pia left together."

"Since you're the big sister here, who would you recommend I talk to next?"

"I think Terza said she saw something."

"Who else rooms with you? I have a sketch by you, Terza, and Cammeo. Are there others?"

"Yes, there's eleven-year old Elenora and nine-year-old Liliana. One sleeps in a bed across from mine, and the other in one next to her. Both said they didn't wake up."

"You don't sound like you believe them."

"I suppose I do. It's possible they slept through it."

"I'll have to talk to them. Sometimes fear can make them keep details to themselves. Will you return to the basement and have Sister Daniela send up Terza to speak with me?"

Allegra nodded. "We didn't talk among ourselves, you know. I didn't see the other sketches, but if they're similar, there's a good chance some of us saw the person here."

"Thank you, Allegra. The pictures are indeed similar. Let's hope we can identify the person who Pia left with?"

Sister Angela could hear Terza's confident footsteps on the stair treads. The noise stopped at the top landing. Even though she expected the young girl, the face peeking around the door frame gave the nun a jolt.

"Are you Terza?" she asked, pushing up her reading glasses to see the skinny little girl. "You're eleven, aren't you?"

"How do you know?"

The nun produced the child's drawing and showed it to her. "You wrote it on your picture, see?

Which bed's your?"

"It's on that side, near the window."

Sister Angela stood and walked over to the bed. "Your pillow's in the middle of the mattress. At which end do you usually put your head?"

Terza smiled. "It depends on how I feel."

"And when you saw the person in the drawing?"

"I was sleeping near the window."

"You actually *saw* this figure, didn't you?"

"Yes."

"Did you hear her coming?"

The child nodded her head. "I pretended to be asleep, though, because I was afraid Sister Carmela would get upset if she noticed I was still up."

"Has Sister Carmela ever been angry with you?"

"Yes. She holds my head to keep me from squirming. She's says I'm a top and need to be stopped before I disrupt everything."

"So the night before last, you couldn't sleep."

"I may have slept earlier, but I was awake when I heard steps on the stairs. They weren't loud."

"But it sounded like one person?"

"Yes."

"How did it sound?"

"Thump-thump-thump. Really soft."

"Could the figure have worn slippers?"

"No. It was like she wanted to tiptoe, but she wore big shoes so it would have been clomp-clomp-clomp if she didn't try to be quiet."

"You saw her shoes? I don't see them in the picture. You show a long habit that covers her shoes."

"Yes. Her skirt wasn't so long, I think. She had

dark socks pulled up her leg so the skirt must have been shorter."

"You also drew white cuffs and wimple. Are you sure you saw them?

"Yes."

"You saw hair?"

"She had bangs that stuck out of the front of her wimple."

"What color were they?"

Terza stopped to think. "I'm not sure I saw the hair."

"Did she have rosary beads hanging from her cincture or a cross on a chain around her neck?"

"I don't remember."

"Did you recognize her?"

"Yes. It was Sister Octavia."

"When was the last time you saw Sister Octavia?"

"At Christmas she was here."

"Did she walk around on her own at Christmas?"

"No, she sat in a chair most of the time."

"Did she have a walker or a cane?"

Terza thought about it. "She had a cane, maybe."

"Wouldn't the sound of a cane make her coming up the stairs sound different?"

After she left, Sister Daniela sent up ten-year-old Cammeo. Her blond curls bounced as she pirouetted through the doorway.

"And who are you?" asked Sister Angela.

"My name's Cammeo."

"Ah yes, I have the picture you drew. Where do you sleep?"

"My bed's on this side near the window. It's the one with the doggy."

"A well-loved doggy, I see. What side do you sleep on?"

"Sometimes I sleep toward the wall, but that makes me have nightmares so I try to remember to sleep facing the door."

"Can you see Pia and Allegra?"

"Yes. But I'm not sure how I slept when Pia left."

"I have your drawing here. You drew a woman floating in the air."

"She was a witch. "

"Did you sketch it because you actually saw her on a broomstick or is that part not what you remember?"

"Oh, no. I saw the broomstick."

"Tell me about what you saw."

"An old woman flew through the door. When her broomstick got to the window, it turned around, and she landed in front of Pia's bed."

"And then?"

"She gave Pia a magic mushroom and told her to come with her."

"You saw Pia eat something?"

"No."

"Did they both fit on the broomstick and fly away?"

Cammeo laughed. "No. She took Pia's hand and led her down the stairs."

"Did she leave her broomstick?"

"No. She took it with her."

"Did the witch ever look up and see you watching?"

"She had dark green eyes—like a swamp. They twinkled when she looked at me. I was frozen. I wanted to pull my blanket over my head, but I couldn't because she put a spell on me."

"It was too dark to see her eyes, wasn't it?"

"No, there was a full moon. It shone in like it was daytime."

"Could her broomstick have been a cane?"

Cammeo laughed. "No. Witches don't ride canes."

"So let me see. The witch flew in. That means you didn't hear her coming up the stairs."

Cammeo let out a swishing sound.

"But she did walk downstairs with Pia. Did you hear her shoes on the stairs?"

"Yes. The witch tried to make her shoes hush, but they didn't. I suppose she forgot to put a spell on my ears."

"You told Sister Carmela you had a dream. Do you still think it was a dream?"

"Uh-huh," the little girl, nodding her head up and down. "Witches don't exist. I must have dreamt of Pia."

"Who told you witches don't exist?"

"Sister Carmela. She told me the next morning. I must have had a dream."

The morning passed with little new information. Sister Angela questioned both Elenora and Liliana. Neither child remembered anything other than waking up and not seeing Pia.

Right before the break for lunch, Grazia suddenly appeared in the doorway.

"Good morning. Grazia, isn't it?"

"Yes."

"Do you sleep in this room?"

"No." Brushing aside her wavy black hair, Grazia took the nun's hand and pulled her up. "My room's one floor down. We can go down there now so you can see my things."

"We talked to you yesterday. Maybe you remember something new? How old are you, Grazia?"

Grazia didn't answer. She led the nun down the stairs to the first landing. "I'm in the first room here."

"I see. It's a lovely room. Which is your bed?"

"The one closest to the door. Last year, I failed to get up in time and wet the bed. They put me here so I could get to the toilet easier."

"But the night before last, you weren't in the bathroom when the stranger entered the house, were you."

Grazia removed her shoes and sat in the middle of the bed cross legged, her hands twisting the blanket. She stared at the nun with serious dark eyes.

Sister Angela sat down beside her. "I know

because of your sketch here." She handed the drawing to Grazia. "Tell me how you knew what the visitor looked like."

"I saw her."

"Why did you make up the story about seeing a shadow?"

"Because I was up late. Sister Carmela says that I'm not to leave my bed at night, but I can't sleep."

"So you didn't go down to use the toilet. You were up. Go on."

"It was a warm night. We don't have a window in our room so it gets hot. I got up like I often do and walked over to the window off the landing."

"Show me."

The little girl padded out the door.

Sister Angela followed. "It was dark in the hallway. How could you see to walk?"

"There was a full moon. It was like it was daytime outside. I walked to the window. There's always a chair near it. I opened the window and sat down."

"How long were you there?"

Grazia shrugged her shoulders. "I just stared outside. There was a barn owl. *Screech, screech*," she cried out. "They don't hoot, they roar like lions and tigers. It was scary. I tried to see where it was. The moonlight lit up the rows of grapes on the other side of the fence. Do you see the grapes, Sister?"

"Yes. The fence is about six or seven meters from the wall."

"She was there."

Dumfounded, the nun grew silent.

"She was standing when I first looked out."

"Was she on this side of the fence or in the vineyard?"

Grazia gazed in the direction of the grapevines, her brows knit. "She must have been on the other side of the fence because she wasn't that big. She saw me, and for a second, we just stared at each other. Then she backed up and crouched down between the rows. Maybe she thought I didn't see her from up here, but I did."

"Was her habit like mine or was it more like Sister Carmela's?"

"More like Sister Carmela's." Grazia seemed to avoid making eye contact with the nun and stared at the wall. "Her ring—the one that Jesus gave her when she married him—glittered in the moonlight. I couldn't look away."

"Come with me, Grazia."

The two descended the stairs and crossed the foyer to the front door. Sister Angela walked down the steps and turned to gesture for the little girl to follow. They walked around the side of the building, and the nun looked up to see the window.

"Okay, you stood to look out of that window, right?"

"Yes."

"And she waited behind that fence?"

"She stood more in front of the end of the row."

"In order to come into the house, she would've had to travel down this fence to the road," said Sister Angela.

"You don't think she climbed it?"

"You didn't see her leave?"

"No. I had to pee. I went downstairs to pee."

"And you didn't hear or see anything while you used the toilet."

"No. I went back upstairs."

"Did you look out of the window again?"

"Yes. She was gone, and I went to bed. I must have slept immediately because I didn't hear anything else."

"I want you to go back upstairs and look down at me. I'm not going to climb over the fence. There seems to be a gate near the road. I'll walk down the drive and come up on the vineyard side. I want you to tell me how well you can see me from there, and I want to find out if I can see you. Then we'll switch, okay?"

The nun hobbled down the drive. The gate opened easily, and she was able to make it back in front of the window without tiring too much. When she looked up, she saw Grazia bending over the window sill so she could gaze in all directions.

"Did you lean out that night?"

"Yes."

"Pretend I'm the nun. Was I here or closer to the vines?"

"Back just in front of the vines. I can see your face better because of the sun."

"So I get a good look at you, though your face was probably in the shadow because the moon wasn't directly facing you, right?"

"The moon was shining over the backyard. I could only view the moon from here when I leaned forward and looked up."

"And after seeing you, she retreated into the vines and flowers, like this?"

"Yes, the end vine."

"There must have been more shadows. How could you see her?"

"She was taller than you and wore a white wimple that glowed in the dark."

The two switched places. Climbing the stairs, Sister Angela could smell lunch and felt her stomach rumble. She watched Grazia walk toward the spot in front of the vines.

When Grazia looked up, she shaded her eyes. "I can't see you that well, Sister."

"The bright moon probably made it difficult for her to see you very clearly too. No wonder she thought she could hide from you by crouching among the vines."

"But can you see me?"

"Yes. I can see you very clearly, even when you duck down. We have to get to lunch or there might be nothing left. Be sure you secure the gate as you come back."

"Sister, do you believe me now?"

I'm afraid I do, child. And the sight of a woman in the vines at night would have scared me too.

Chapter Six

Sister Daniela marched the last of her students out the door and instructed them to begin their homework in the dining room upstairs. She turned and ran into Detective Sergeant Sacco.

"I was just coming to look for you," she said.

"Sister Angela told me you wanted to see me. What can I do for you?"

She hesitated. In her mind, she tried to form the question clearly. "I was told your team checked the laundry at the end of the hall the morning we reported the child missing. Is that correct?"

"Yes. *I* checked the laundry room myself. Has something changed?"

"Yes, uh no. Please follow me." She approached the door and tried the knob. "It's locked," she said, fumbling with the key ring in her pocket, trying to identify the correct key by feel. "I suppose Sister Natalia's still keeping the children out. Heaven only knows how many loads of wash will be waiting for us."

Finally opening the door, she reached inside to turn on the light. Sacco pointed his flashlight to allow her to find the switch, and soon, the lights buzzed on.

"Did you notice something that looked out of place?" he asked.

She led him to the vent on the side wall. "This vent," she said. "It has a screw missing on one corner, and the other screws are loose."

"Can you verify that it wasn't like that before the incident?" he asked, donning rubber gloves and pulling out the remaining screws. He dropped them into a plastic bag he pulled from his pocket. Then he removed the grate.

"Yes. I've noticed this grate often, though I rarely come in here—maybe once a week."

Sacco looked at her over his shoulder, his brows raised.

"It's filthy. I wanted to take it off and wash it. Look around the rest of the washroom. It's tidy. But the grate…"

Sacco flashed his light into the remaining hole.

Sister Daniela bent over to examine it. "Is it a venting pipe? Wait. Turn off the flashlight."

Sacco turned it off.

"Where's that light coming from?"

He handed her the flashlight, and she shone the light around the edges.

"No wonder it's dirty," she said. "There's no ventilation duct here. We're exchanging air with the wall. Look, the space is wide enough to crawl through."

"But nothing to support someone's weight. I don't think anyone crawled through there." Sacco stood up, picking up the loose grate.

"Light seems to be coming from the left. Did you see it?"

"I'll need a plastic bag for this evidence. I still think it's nothing. Maybe the light played a trick on you so you thought the screws weren't loose before."

"But wait. Come with me outside." She took his

hand and led him down the hall to the outside door. "Look at the basement from out here. The hallway's in the middle. What's between the back door and the far wall? There must be another room."

The detective sergeant ambled around the outside walls of the orphanage. Then he walked back inside. "There are small windows on the side until the level of dirt eventually covers the whole wall toward the front. But I would guess it's just dirt. The ground probably rises on the inside too. It's most likely only crawl space."

"Why wouldn't they at least dig deep enough to give this place more storage?"

"I don't know why. It was built more than a century ago. I can't ask anyone."

"There has to be a door. The kitchen's above it. What if they needed to fix the pipes?"

Sacco exhaled and wiped his brow. "Is there a plastic bag for this grate in the closet?"

"My guess is they'd put an entrance on the inside. Let's try the supply and electrical closets off the hallway. This is getting exciting, isn't it?"

"I'm Sister Angela from Montriano. You're Evelina," she said, "You're sixteen. Am I correct?"

"Yes, Sister, I heard you were helping the police."

The nun stood. She was full from her lunch and felt a bit sleepy. "Could you show me your room?"

The nun followed her into the room next door. "I sleep in the bed right here by the door."

"You're the closest to the landing. Did you see or hear anything that night?"

"No. I saw nothing. Unfortunately, I slept through the whole thing."

"In the next room, Grazia said she got up that night because she couldn't sleep."

"Yes, but she doesn't know what time it was, and I didn't see her. She often gets up at night, you know. Sister Carmela told her that she mustn't leave her room, but Grazia often has trouble taking direction. I suppose Sister Carmela's thankful she doesn't go down the stairs until she has to use the toilet."

"Did you hear from anyone else on this floor that saw or heard something?"

"No. I've asked each one of them. Grazia's the only restless one on this floor."

"Grazia mentioned that you have something to do with locking the doors at night. Tell me about that."

"I go around when we retire and check the doors."

"About what time?"

"We have to have our lights out by ten, Sister."

"And what do you do between dinner and ten?"

"Some of us finish homework, some play games, and others watch TV in the sitting room at the bottom of the stairs."

"So, at nine-thirty you go around and make sure the place is locked. What about Sister Carmela?"

"What do you mean?"

"Doesn't she check too?"

"She's usually busy doing work in her office."

"Where's her office?"

"It's off the kitchen. We don't disturb her. She has a bed in there. She sleeps here during the day."

"I thought she slept at Mission House."

"No, she attends services and plans for supplies. She's really pretty busy and stays here so she can work longer hours."

"So at nine-thirty or so the night before last, you went around the house to lock the doors."

"Actually it was closer to ten."

"You remember doing it?"

"Yes. I told the sisters and the inspectors that I did that. I remembered right away."

"At one point, Grazia told us she heard you check the door in the middle of the night. You say you were asleep."

"I was in bed by lights out and didn't awaken until morning."

"So when you lock the doors, what route do you take?"

"I lock and test all of the doors. I go to the back door off the kitchen first. Then I go to the front door before checking the one in a nurse's office at the end of the hall beyond the bathroom. That room's rarely used now as we don't have a nurse on duty fulltime. The door's always locked, but I check it anyway."

"And the basement?"

"I don't lock the basement. Sister Daniela's in charge of locking that one."

"What about if someone has gone out and come back late?"

"There are keys to the basement in Sister Carmela's quarters. We can borrow one if we need to go out and can't return until after ten."

In the afternoon, Detective Sergeant Elmo Sacco was called to another incident. He told Sister Daniela he'd return as soon as possible and asked her to wait for him to help investigate further. Sister Daniela wasn't one to wait for anyone, however.

In the classroom, Sister Daniela asked Allegra to come to her desk. "Allegra, I believe you prepared a special lesson plan for when I needed to leave. You should practice if you want to go to teaching college and become one like me. Could you help me now?"

Allegra smiled. "Yes, Sister, I'm ready."

The nun stood and talked to the class. "I won't be far so if I hear anyone making trouble, I'll be back in a few minutes. I don't think any of you'd do anything to jeopardize Allegra's future, would you?"

Sister Daniela stepped into the hallway and shut the door behind her. She walked back to the laundry room and, opening the door, reached in to switch on the light. Her eyes went straight to the gaping hole in the wall. Only Pia could've made it through the hole into some kind of closed-off room. Suddenly waking up from her thoughts, she grabbed a white apron from the wall and returned to the hallway. Rolling up her sleeves and removing her veil before slipping into the apron, Sister Daniela turned to the first closet along the wall opposite the classroom.

This closet contained four shelves that wrapped around the small, walk-in storeroom. A year's worth of cleaning supplies sat on each shelf. It would take her forever to move them and examine the wall behind the shelves. She started immediately, clearing two shelves facing the front.

I don't see anything here. There should be an opening on the back wall, but it's sealed. Maybe there's a pass-through near the floor.

The nun took out the cans and bags on the bottom shelf. There was no sign of an opening there either. Instead of replacing the supplies, she immediately moved to the next tiny room, the coat closet. It was summer, but winter would soon come, and every child would need a jacket to stay warm. Inside the walk-in closet, neat rows of boots lined the walls beneath hanging coats of all sizes. Stacked next to the entrance were umbrellas. On a high shelf, hats, socks, and gloves were piled high.

She smelled it first. Yes, these shoes had been in puddles and mud, but in addition, the strong scent of the earth seemed to permeate the stale air. The boots along the back wall were all lined up, but not so neatly as the ones against the side walls. A few had toppled over, but they didn't seem to affect most of the others. A wisp of air blew across Sister Daniela's face. She sucked in the air as a chill ran up her sweaty back. Stepping forward, she grabbed the pole full of hangers and pulled hard. The wall behind it pushed her backward. The opening widened.

"Who's there?" she whispered into the musty room. The small windows along the top of the far wall let light in, but the dust and dirt, displaced by the sudden opening, made it difficult for the nun to see anything.

Sister Daniela squeezed through the opening and felt her way forward. She scraped the foundation under her feet. This room wasn't a crawlspace. The cement floor proved that. At one time, it must have been part of a larger basement. She'd have to get the plans from Mother Faustine and see what it was used for before the closets and the classroom were added.

She inched forward and tripped over an object on the floor. The dust roiled again, and she covered her nose with her sleeve. She felt her heart in her throat. "Who's here?" she asked, but silence answered.

Sister Daniela turned and moved in farther. Perhaps she could open one of the windows to clear out some of the dust. Standing on her tiptoes, she tugged on the handle of the one closest to her. It wouldn't budge. She could see the loose soil against the pane as the ground rose outside. Perhaps the window was stuck because it was partially underground. She moved a few feet toward the back of the building and tried the next window. It too held fast.

Have these window ever been opened? she asked herself. Her head ached as she choked on the particulates she inhaled. *Maybe coats of paint have stuck the windows to their frames.*

She inched her way to the window closest to the back wall. This is the last one. Maybe I should go into the hallway and wait for Elmo. One tug and the window flew open, letting in the warm, humid breeze to replace the stale air.

Sister Daniela brushed her hands. *So this one opens. Is the window still too small for a skinny nun to crawl through?*

She took a deep breath and started to back away. Her foot caught on the edge of it. She fought to keep her balance, but her body was falling backwards too fast. She was halfway down when she realized the hard floor would render her senseless. To her surprise, she bounced. She'd landed on something soft.

A bed, she said to herself, trying to brush her arms, entangled in some sheets. Turning to get back on her feet, she ran into a lump lying next to her and let out a bloodcurdling scream.

Chapter Seven

At dinner, Sister Angela sat next to Sister Natalia. She looked across the table at several faces of nuns she didn't know.

"I noticed you two drove into town this evening," said Mother Faustine. "Where did you get that beautiful truck?"

"It's my brother-in-law's," said Sister Daniela. "Michel said we can borrow it in the evening. He uses it for work during the day. Sister Angela drove tonight. I didn't tell him she might drive it. I guess I'll have to confess that I let her drive before he finds out."

"And I did an excellent job, didn't I? Sorry we were late. Sister Daniela had to go to her sister's house to clean up after discovering some sort of room across from her classroom. I hope we didn't hold up dinner."

Mother Faustine stared at the younger nun. "Perhaps you discovered some clue about Pia's whereabouts."

"I'm afraid I did something stupid. I should've waited for the detective sergeant to return to help me, but I was too nosey. I discovered the entrance to some sort of secret room under the orphanage and went in on my own. Elmo reprimanded me, and I deserved it. I could've destroyed evidence. We now have to wait for the police to examine what was still there."

Sister Angela interrupted. "Perhaps I should've asked before we sat down, but I'd love to hear about what you all do."

Sister Liona smiled. "At the end of the table is Sister Julietta. She works at the food bank."

"I'm so excited to meet you, Sister Angela," said Sister Julietta. "I've heard all about you. I hope you can help us find Pia. What a cute child. Beside me is Sister Agata, who works with me at the food bank."

"Sister Agata's from Genoa," said Sister Liona. "Across from you here is Sister Sabrina. She helps out in a nursing home. Father Calvino at the cathedral is so glad she's there because she can call him in if he's needed. Next to her is Sister Trista. She and Sister Giana have opened a shelter for local homeless. It was needed. The government closed the last one a few years ago, and the poor had to make it to Florence or sleep in the streets."

"And you work in legal aid. You're a lawyer then."

"Yes," said Sister Liona. "There are good lawyers, you know. We aren't all selfish and greedy."

"Of course not. You who offer your services to those who can't afford an attorney are definitely not greedy. I suppose you do some drug cases. What else do you take on?"

"We work on immigration complications, thefts, and even murders. I've dealt with kidnapping within the family, but nothing having to do with a kidnapping by another nun."

"Ah yes, your very own crime," said Sister Angela. "Mother Faustine, can you tell Sister Daniela and me more about Pia? Her history would be helpful. How do we know we aren't dealing with a member of the family coming to steal Pia?"

"Heavens," said Sister Natalia. "Why would they steal her? All they have to do is ask for her."

"There's a procedure, is there not? If they wanted to raise her, they could just take her. But aren't there rules about when they adopt? Perhaps Sister Liona can tell us about that."

"Yes, there are a myriad of papers to be signed. The family would have to procure an attorney to help them through the process. I don't know if that's ever stopped someone who wanted to adopt, however."

"I'm not sure poor Pia has any family, though," said Mother Faustine.

Sister Angela turned to face the mother superior.

"The child was left on a doorstep of a convent when she was about two. There was no name so the nuns named her themselves."

"What doorstep?" asked Sister Angela.

"Pia was given to us by a group of Benedictine nuns at the Sacro Cuore della Francesca Convent in Castel Valori, north of Poppi."

"No one saw how she got there?"

"No. The child was alone. The nuns brought her in and cared for her."

"So you have no record of any relatives," said Sister Angela. "That opens the door to the possibility that a relative might be trying to retrieve her. You have no idea, then, if she is indeed an orphan."

"No. She was with the nuns at the convent for two years before they reported they had a child. Any investigation of an incident that might have resulted in her appearance on their doorstep would've gone cold."

"But that's not true, is it? We have history all around us. Marriages, births, and deaths are all recorded somewhere. That's a start. Computers have made it impossible to hide anything. A parent wouldn't leave a baby on a doorstep without a good reason. The circumstances would have to have been pretty dire to result in such an action."

"An unwed mother might have…"

"I don't have the statistics in front of me, but I'm afraid that in the last couple of years, few pregnant mothers have gone to the Church for help to find loving parents for an unwanted child," said Sister Angela. "They either keep the child and become single parents or offer to become surrogates to a family seeking a baby on the Internet." Sister Angela cleared her throat. "And this particular unwed mother kept the child for two years before she decided to abandon her."

Sister Daniela suddenly spoke up. "I can't imagine why a mother would leave a baby, unless she was in trouble and thought the baby would be safer with the nuns."

"Exactly, Sister," said Sister Angela. "And the fact that the nuns didn't report the child to the authorities makes this an interesting case. I must meet with these ladies in person."

"But first we have to wait for the police to figure out who might have used our basement as a bedroom," said Sister Daniela. "I'm not sure I'll be able to put it out of my mind when I return to the classroom tomorrow."

"What did the nuns say to you when they delivered the child two years ago, Mother?"

"I haven't spoken with them directly. Sister Liona and Sister Trista picked her up and brought her to the orphanage. There are so many rules. We have to follow procedure so a child's family can't come after us claiming we took the child. With all the problems in the Church, you can imagine what a relative might think. We know the Church doesn't collect children as future priests and nuns, Sister, but others might not be aware of that."

"In this case, however, we're open to scrutiny already," said Sister Liona. "We don't even know if Pia's an orphan."

"The nuns at the convent are liable here," said Mother Faustine. "They took in a child without reporting her. The police didn't know to investigate a possible crime."

"I suppose you're right, but Mission House hasn't conducted an investigation into Pia's circumstances over the last two years either," said Sister Angela. "You accepted a child who might still have parents and placed her in your orphanage. Surely Sister Liona understands what I'm trying to say."

"You have a point, Sister," said Sister Liona. "Mission House could probably fight culpability because law enforcement was involved in the transfer of the child to our facility. Unfortunately, we've opened ourselves to a fight if the relatives find out what happened. That fight would cost us money and reputation. I believe we should tread carefully when investigating this crime. Sister Angela may solve the crime but involve all of us in legal entanglement that obliterates all the good our organizations do."

"You're right, Sister Liona. I must work with the police to find out what happened. I can't do it without them. I'll keep you all informed about my findings. But you must know that my primary purpose will be to find Pia. If we don't find her, no matter what we reveal to those involved, the Church may be negligent in the eyes of the world.

Sister Angela sat in a comfortable chair and let one of the other sisters serve her coffee. "The dinner was delicious," she told Sister Liona who sat down beside her.

"I know you didn't want to discuss what happened today during dinner, but can we discuss it now? People are dying to hear about what Sister Daniela found."

"I suppose, as long as Sister Daniela does the talking."

The other nuns grabbed chairs and put them around the room. Sister Daniela was given an easy chair near Sister Angela.

"Again, I want to apologize for being late. I took the time to bathe and change my habit before we came. I washed it out, but it's difficult to clear out all the dust in that little room."

Mother Faustine handed a coffee to Sister Daniela before sitting in one of the free chairs. "Please, what made you try to go into that dirty crawlspace to begin with?"

"I noticed when I came into work in the basement the morning following Pia's disappearance that the back door was unlocked. I was alone and went looking for my students. They were lined up along the walls on the ground floor. I found out Pia was missing then. We decided the children who may have seen Pia's departure should come down to class and draw pictures of what they witnessed. While my older students supervised the art lesson, I stepped out and locked the back door. Then Evelina and I decided to check the laundry room at the end of the hall. It was empty, though it's usually in use most of the week."

"What made you think of the laundry room?"

"I don't know. I guess we should've left it to the police, but the police weren't accustomed to seeing it on a daily basis. We went in and discovered that the grate on a vent in the back corner looked as if someone had tampered with it. Today I decided to have Detective Sergeant Sacco accompany me to the laundry room so we could check it out further."

"I don't understand," said Sister Liona. "You said the door to the outside was unlocked when you came in. I would assume the kidnapper entered and exited through the back door."

"Perhaps. One of the children saw a nun in the vineyard next door that night. The old nun could easily have entered through the back door after she walked to the gate near the road and then hiked to the basement door in the rear of the orphanage. But where did she come from before that?"

"I'm not sure that helps us," said Sister Liona

"It's just that I had a feeling there was more. The detective sergeant and I soon discovered there wasn't a duct in the wall behind the grate."

"Could the nun and Pia have crawled through the space?" asked Mother Faustine.

"Probably not. It was too tiny. But when I turned off the ceiling bulb, there was light shining through the hole. That wall's in the middle of the house. Where was the light coming from? We went outside and noticed windows along the far wall. They weren't big and half of them had soil pushed against them from the hill rising to the front of the house. Even though Elmo tried to convince me it was just crawlspace below that part of the house, I decided there had to be another entrance. I scoured the cleaning closet, removing most of the supplies. When I didn't find anything, I left them on the floor and moved to the cloak closet. I confess I have to clean up the supply closet tomorrow morning before class. The cloak closet was neat but not perfect. I noticed that boots lined up against the back wall were pulled forward. I moved the jackets and found that I could open a door by pulling on the rack."

"Why didn't we know about this?" asked Mother Faustine.

"It wasn't in the plans," said Sister Natalia. "We've tugged on the rack dozens of times, at least twice a year, depending on the season. Nothing ever opened up for me."

"Perhaps nothing opened because it was well sealed before that night. I could feel air brushing my cheek. That meant the secret door wasn't really shut tight when I entered."

"What did you find?" asked Mother Faustine.

"The room wasn't as bright as I thought, though some light was shining in through two of the small windows. The second the door opened, a cloud of dust and dirt rose like a tornado. If the culprit was in there, she must not have been inside long because it would've been difficult to breathe. I struggled to get a window open to let out the dust. All the panes were stuck except the one at the back wall. I tugged so hard, I fell backwards onto an old mattress. Talk about dust—it whooshed up around me. I turned to get up and ran into an object behind me."

The group fell into an eerie silence.

"Well?" asked Mother Faustine.

"Elmo heard me scream and came running. He saw the cloak closet door open and entered through the secret door. The dust was already beginning to settle. I pointed to the mattress. It was a pile of clothing. Elmo called for a team. They're collecting prints and materials in the room."

"But as you already told us," said Sister Liona. "The room wouldn't have been so dusty if someone had recently been in there."

"We must wait for test results to determine if the items in the room are related to Pia's disappearance. Someone had used that room at one time or another. I didn't even get to examine any of the evidence so now we have to wait."

"You sound disappointed, Sister Daniela. You were frightened and understandably so," said Mother Faustine. "You could've been hurt."

"If I hadn't screamed, I would've been able to examine the evidence before Elmo found me. And if it had pertained to the child's kidnapping, we'd be a step ahead in the case. I wish I'd kept my wits about me."

Sister Angela smiled. "I'll try to talk to Ricco tomorrow or the day after. I may need a ride into town if anyone's going my way."

"I'll ask Michel if you can use the truck," said Sister Daniela.

Chapter Eight

The children gathered in the dining room for lunch.

The two nuns sat outside on the grassy slope when Chief Inspector Pagano approached. "I hope you're all right, Sister Daniela. You should've waited for Elmo before you entered the room."

"Did you find the nun's habit?" asked Sister Angela.

"Nothing black. There were sheets, a blanket, and a towel in the pile on the bed next to Sister Daniela."

"It felt like more than that," said Sister Daniela, playing with a tiny flower growing out of the lawn. "I thought it was a body."

"You couldn't see. That place was dusty."

"What are you going to do now?" asked Sister Angela.

"We'll take what we've found back to the station and examine the items. There might be DNA among the sheets. There was no pillow so we have no pillowcase, but you never know."

"And your opinion?" asked Sister Daniela.

"The dust was so thick I doubt anyone had been in that room for years. Do you think this nun suspect could've slept there the night of the abduction? Her habit wouldn't have been black when she approached the victim. As for her white headpiece—it was probably bigger than yours, Sister. You two wear more modern ones. Vatican II changed everything."

Sister Daniela touched the edge of her veil. "It's a good thing I removed it before my search. I didn't have to scrub it this afternoon."

"I'm so glad you were able to bathe and don a fresh habit earlier," said Sister Angela. "How long do you think it will take to get the DNA back from the lab?"

"About a week, assuming we can find something to test. Then we have to match it to someone in our database. Odds are, we have no nuns in there, but you never know. Sometimes they're arrested for protesting in government buildings."

"A week's too long, Ricco. The child will be long gone."

"I agree. We can't wait around for the results. We have to find another lead."

Sister Daniela walked into her classroom to teach until the final bell that would send her students to study hour on the first floor. Thank you for the help, Allegra."

"Do they think Pia was in there?" asked Liliana. "Did the witch make her stay there?"

"No," said Sister Daniela. "It's just an empty room. We don't know where she took Pia. I'm changing the subject. I need to assign some homework."

From inside the classroom, Sister Angela stared

through the window at the fence and the vineyard next door. She'd have to find out more about the vintner. What was his background? Did he know the nuns personally? Suddenly she stood and walked out the door. Someone had just passed by the window. She had to find out who he was.

Sister Daniela must have been too busy to notice. She continued answering questions and handing out new assignments.

Sister Angela spied a new picnic table on the grass and sat down on the bench. Not a minute later, a man appeared from around the corner with another bench.

"Who are you?" she asked.

"Gavino Abiati, the estate manager."

"I didn't know the orphanage had one. How long have you been here?"

The young man removed his gardening glove to swipe away a curl that was stuck to his forehead. "I took over my father's business when he died about ten years ago."

"Do you go inside?"

"Yes, of course, though I usually enter through the basement door when it's open."

"Do you have a key for when it's locked?"

"Yes, of course." He pulled up his t-shirt and showed her the dozens of keys hanging from a ring on his belt loop. Please don't ask me which one's for this door."

"I take it that means you rarely use it. Is one of those keys for the nurse's room off the deck above us?"

He unclipped the ring and handed it to her. "If you're asking had I been in the basement earlier today, the answer is *yes*. The door wasn't locked. I needed the bag of fertilizer that was stored in the supply closet. I passed the cloak closet. Someone had actually broken into the basement chamber. I hadn't seen that room since I was a kid."

The nun's ears perked up. "Are you saying you knew the room was there?"

"Yes. It was my grandfather's room. He used to sleep in it. There was another chamber where the classroom is now. It wasn't as big, but it had a table and sink with a stove. There was a toilet off the living area."

"When did that change?"

"My grandfather died in the seventies. During his lifetime, the nuns weren't here. The building was a rooming house for veterans. There were quite a few boarders in here."

"Did the former residents do a lot of damage to the grounds?"

"No. They were pretty respectful. My grandfather used to remind me that they'd been through the war and that everyone was working hard to recover from it."

"So did the former owner block off that room after you grandfather died?"

"Pretty much. My father didn't want to live down there so the owner had him board up the door. Then the nuns moved in and wanted the extra space. They had my father build the closets in front of that wall. Then they instructed him to take down a wall or two and create a huge classroom."

"Wait. Go back. Did you know about the secret door?"

"Yes. I helped him put in that door."

"Did one of the nuns give you permission?"

"Since the wall had been boarded up before they came, I don't believe the nuns knew a room existed back there. My father only put in that secret door because he was positive the nuns would change their minds and ask him to increase the space even more."

"Did you ever open it? I can imagine how much fun it would be to pretend it was a castle or a prison."

"No. My grandfather died in that room. It sort of spooks me out."

"So you'd never come back here that night to get in through the basement door, I suppose."

"Of course not. There's no one in the basement at night. It's dark in there. Did you think I was that nun who broke in and stole the kid?"

"It crossed my mind. You didn't, did you?"

"No. The nuns bring me tea and cookies before I leave every evening. I wouldn't want to ruin that. They didn't mention that I might have done it, did they?"

"So your family has managed this property for decades. Are there any other secrets we should know about? How about the fence over there." She pointed to the side yard. "The one outside the classroom windows."

"That was put in before my father retired to Naples."

"Was it because the nuns didn't want the children to run all over the place?"

"No, I believe La Barca wanted it put up. I guess he was afraid the children would crush his vines. I used to help myself to some of his grapes when I was young so I suppose he was right to fear a number of children might do even more damage."

"La Barca?"

"Martino La Barca owns that winery. He's okay, I guess. I don't know him well, but no one complained about him."

"Oh yes. I think someone else mentioned his name. Do you think his wine has a good reputation? His vines don't look as healthy as others in the area."

"I don't know. His wine's good enough. He isn't a showy guy, if you know what I mean. He doesn't become friendly with his neighbors. The nuns might know him better. I'm not sure. I really should get back to work."

"What are you doing?"

"I'm putting out the picnic tables. The nuns want to have a barbeque with the kids. I don't know why they decided to put them out this late in the season."

"I heard there was going to be a fundraiser in a week or so," said Sister Angela. "Perhaps they need to make money to pay for their activities." The nun walked back inside and to find Sister Daniela. She stopped when the gardener cleared his throat.

"Just remember to return the keys to me as soon as you checked the room on the deck above us."

She waved the ring at him and smiled.

"Mr. Abiati told me the story of the secret door. I'm not sure we found anything that can help us with the case."

Sister Daniela looked surprised. "Mr. Abiati?"

"Gavino, the estate manager."

"Ah, I don't know him that well. What did he say?"

"That his grandfather, estate manager number one, lived down here until his death in the 70s. The room across the hall was his bedroom, and your classroom was his kitchen and living room. Estate manger number two, Gavino's father, wasn't interest in raising his family in the basement so the owner had him close off the room. According to Gavino, that was okay with him because it was spooky. When the nuns came, they had the Gavino build the closets along the wall on one side and tear down the living-area walls across the aisle to create the classroom. Gavino's father decided on the secret door because he didn't trust the nuns. He thought they'd change their minds and want him to make the area bigger. Evidently, no one ever told the nuns the room was there."

Sister Daniela sat down. "So Mr. Abiati doesn't think anyone has been in there for years. That's strange. The bed and stuff on the bed was just left there? I swear I've heard noises coming out of there on occasion." She stood and grabbed her bag.

"Stop right there," said Sister Angela. "You can't

drop a bombshell like that and then just walk out. You're perfectly aware the pipe for the furnace passes through that room to that side of the house. That must be the noise."

Sister Daniela smiled and opened the classroom door. "I'd love to get home and take a bath. I sure hope Michel and Susanna have leftovers so we can just heat up something.

Because you're from Montriano, Sister, you must know that the wines in both areas are only subtly different," said Michel, leading the nun between the rows of vines. "The grapes we have here are Sangiovese." He reached down to pluck a bunch from one of the vines. Flipping a grape into his mouth, he closed his eyes as if in prayer. "These are fine grapes and just about ready. Please have one or two. Don't throw away the rest. I'm sure Dani and Susanna would love some too."

"They're very nice," the nun said after tasting one.

"The Sangiovese grapes are extremely sensitive to our weather and our soil. The aromas seem to be different, depending on what we put into our soil. The sandier the soil the more flowery the wine smells. Limestone creates a fruity fragrance with a hint of tobacco. But prevalent in all the Chianti Classico wines is the scent of violets and irises. Every Chianti Classico wine must contain at least eighty percent Sangiovese grapes."

"And the taste?"

"The flavor's dry and savory with a level of tannin that makes the taste soft and velvety over time. The color must be ruby red.

"What makes up the other twenty percent?" asked Sister Angela, trying to keep up with his long stride.

"First of all, the grapes, whether Sangiovese or not, must be grown in the Chianti Classico designated area in this part of Tuscany. There are more rules— lots of them. That's why I can't produce everything by myself. My partner takes on making sure many of the other rules are documented for the *Denominatzione di origine controllata*. The wine in Montriano is grown with separate rules, though I'm not aware what they are. Here I use other native grapes from the area, though I don't always grow them. The Canaiolo grapes or the Colorino are sometimes used. There are other varieties that I don't reveal to anyone. Let's go into the winery and check out what happens after our fruit's gathered in a few weeks."

"I saw the crusher when I was waiting for Sister Daniela one morning."

"The first step is de-stemming. Then we crush the grapes. The juice, together with the skins, is put into these containers for fermentation. The temperature must stay below thirty degrees Centigrade for about two weeks. The fermentation will push the skins to the top of the liquid and form a mass or cap. We then break the cap and push it downward to squeeze out the flavor. Mind you, the chemical results must be checked at least twice a day. Then the wine's pressed and put in barrels to ferment again. During this time, bacteria transform the aggressive malic acid into a softer lactic acid. The wine's then racked to clear it of the sediment. It must age for at least two years in the oak casks and then another year in the bottle to get a DOCG label, assuring the buyer that it meets the taste and grape standards of Chianti Classico."

"Oh my, I *am* getting a taste of the results, aren't I?"

"Of course. Over here in the corner are my casks and bottles of Chianti Riserva. To be a reserve, the wine must age at least two years longer than a standard Chianti. This is the type of wine that should be oxygenated before service. I have some at the house that was opened before dinner. Perhaps Susanna and Dani can join us. I believe Susanna has some aged cheese and crackers to go with it."

The two crossed the field and entered the house. Sister Daniela came running down the stairs when she heard the nun. "Sister Natalia contacted me," she said as soon as she caught her breath.

"Did they find the child?" asked Sister Angela.

"No. Perhaps my news isn't as important as I thought. Let's eat first. My mouth's watering. I haven't tasted the *riserva* before. I guess family doesn't count."

"That's not true," said Michel. "I just thought we might need a bigger group to drink the whole bottle."

Thy sat down and quickly emptied it.

Sister Angela finished off the cheese and turned to face Sister Daniela. "Now, what have you learned?"

"I heard they found hair at the scene but don't know how old it is. It'll take at least a week to get it tested."

"Where? It could have been anyone's."

"In the closet where the hangers hooked to the pole. If the nun didn't enter that chamber, she might still have known about it and tried to get inside." Sister Daniela bit her lip.

"Or someone wanted a coat and inadvertently got the hanger caught in her hair."

"I want to hope it belongs to the old nun and that helps us find her."

"But a week's too long," said Sister Angela.

"If she didn't stay in the basement room, that must mean I left the basement unlocked, doesn't it?"

"Either way, I suppose the old nun had to get in through the basement to get to the room. But your possible slipup is still jumping to a conclusion," said Sister Angela. "The nun could've possessed a key or had one made. Someone on the inside might have let her in. There's the door of the old nurse's room that doesn't have a key at all. The old nun could've entered through an open window. Did anyone check the windows?"

"But how did the kidnapper get in or out without leaving prints?"

"Gloves."

"Did the children notice the nun wearing gloves?"

"The gloves could've been clear plastic or skin tone. Please don't blame yourself until we collect additional information about the perpetrator, Sister. I'd offer you more wine, but I'm afraid we already drank it.

Chapter Nine

Viviana smoothed her skirt and spun around in front of the mirror to see how she looked from behind. Her aunts scrambled to inform her mother that Viviana had no intention of taking care of family business first.

The young woman received the call early the morning following the job offer. She hadn't even had time to think of what to say to her mother.

"Hello, Viviana. What happened? Lucilla called me last night and told me you were serious with a young man, making out with him on the front porch for all the neighbors to see."

"Lucilla never saw me do anything, Mamma. The man who walked me home yesterday was my new boss. He offered me a job. I was just thinking how I can manage to get something to wear for it."

"So you took the job?"

"No. I plan to take it. Aunt Lucilla and Aunt Clarissa expect me to wait on Nonna all day while they discuss her jewelry without me. Poor Nonna can do better than having me keep her company. If you hoped I'd secure some of the jewelry…"

"Don't be ridiculous. I'll come and do that myself. I have to get vacation from my job first. It may take a few weeks."

"I don't have a few weeks. I need money for a dress and shoes for my new job at a local winery. It's a big opportunity for me."

"I understand, Vivi. I'm sending you some money. I hope Nonna can hang on until I get there."

Viviana twirled once more in front of the mirror. The four-inch heels were the perfect touch. Giulio would love them. Her cheeks grew hot. Would she be able to work beside him without feeling the need to touch him?

Her shoes packed into a bag, Viviana hiked up the road, turning left at the ornately-carved sign at the entrance to Amarena Balda. For the first time, she noticed a couple of trucks with workers carefully unloading supplies outside the building with the tasting room at one end. The doors to the office and winery were open, and Viviana walked in.

She was acquainted with no one. A man at the desk looked up. "Ah, you must be Viviana. My little brother has talked about you incessantly since I returned. My name's Ermanno. Giulio mentioned you might be perfect for the tasting room."

"I'm afraid I don't know where the tasting room is. Are you still setting it up in the little office at the front of this building?"

"Yes, but that's only temporary. Excuse me if I seem scattered. I always return to this—all the paperwork's been strewn over the desk. I have to make sure the invoices have been paid."

Viviana tried to peek over the edge of the counter, but Ermanno managed to cover the papers with his arm. "I have worked in several offices. If you need help…"

"Thank you, but I think I can handle this. No one's supposed to organize my invoices because that's my job. Once one of my brother's fellow vintners tried to pay some of the suppliers and actually paid them more than once. We had a difficult time getting the monies back. That's why only one of us is in charge here. Ah, Giulio has returned."

Propped against the desk, Viviana was busily trying to change her shoes when he walked in.

"Viviana, look at you," he said. "Let me help you with those shoes. I love the dress, and your hair," he said, putting his nose close to her head and inhaling. "Come, let's see what we can do with the office."

Giulio felt his brothers stare. "Ermanno and I are looking at plans to expand the tasting room. You can be in on that too, if you wish."

"We'll see how this goes first," said Ermanno, pushing a stack of papers into a folder. I suppose, Giulio, you'll want us to offer tours next. Who do you have lined up to conduct the tours?"

Giulio glanced back at him, a tiny smile on his lips. Then he helped Viviana take the first few steps on her new shoes. "There you go. The entrance is right over here."

Giulio closed the door behind them and laughed. "My brother's very private. I hope he didn't say anything to offend you."

"No, he was quiet polite." She looked around the small room. "You haven't done anything to it."

"I thought you wanted to tell me how it should look."

"Someone has to take some of the junk out. I think we should paint the walls—maybe have them textured. You can build a counter here in the middle. We wouldn't want the customer to get the idea he can pour himself more. That way, I'll stay on this side with the alcohol. I'd need a sink or something to clean the wine glasses."

"So we have to do a lot."

"I'd have dressed more appropriately had you mentioned I needed to do everything myself."

He leaned toward her.

"Why don't I go home and change into other clothes," she continued. "I can return after lunch and help move the garbage out of here."

"I can get someone to do that."

"What about the other ideas? Do you want me to pick out shades of paint for the walls?"

"Why don't you come back tomorrow in your work clothes? I'll have this place cleared and the counter built. We can go from there."

"I could stay and help with the paperwork if you'd like."

Giulio hesitated. "Ermanno's here. He doesn't like others fooling with the invoices."

"Even just filing them? He looked like he could use the help."

"I think you should let me prepare your office for you."

"It would be nice to meet my mother when she comes. I'll be back tomorrow morning then."

Mara Mioni drove up the short drive to her mother's house.

Viviana ran out to meet her.

"I thought you had a job."

"I do," said Viviana. "The tasting room wasn't ready so I'll go back tomorrow." She took her mother's bag from her. "You told me it would take a few weeks before you could get off."

"I thought you needed me so I just took the time off. How's Mamma? Is she doing well?"

"Not really. Nonna stays in bed. I open the shades for her every morning. If I don't get a chance, they stay shut all day. I also make sure she takes her morning pills. I didn't today and noticed she hadn't yet received them."

"I'll have to talk to my sisters about that. Did you and your aunts get any business done? That's why I sent you here."

"No. They only want me to clean and do the chores. If they have meetings, they don't tell me."

Mara sighed. "Oh dear. I guess I'll have to stay awhile. It's a good thing I had some vacation saved up." She carried a small bag up to the house, letting her daughter struggle with the bigger trunk.

Mara stayed with her mother for nearly an hour before reappearing in the sitting room. "Hi Clarissa, Lucilla. Where's Viviana?"

"She had chores to do. She wanted to make sure your room was ready."

"I'll go help her," said Mara. "What time's dinner?"

"When Viviana decides to make it. We usually eat at eight, but since she has a job now…"

"Since she has a job, I recommend one of you takes over a few of hers. Clarissa, you have a car. You can shop for food. Lucilla, you can cook. I know you can. You're a good cook. I think I'll take Viviana into town and make sure she has enough outfits for her new job. We can get groceries tonight. Lucilla, please make us a list."

"We can have a meeting tonight, Mara, if you're interested."

"I'll be there," she said, starting up the stairs.

"So you have one dress and a pair of shoes," said Mara, sifting through the items crammed onto the rack. Don't you think you'll need a few more things?"

"Yes, Mamma. I would love more than one dress. Giulio, Signor de Capua, wants to make sure I look like a lady. I need to wear high heels."

"I saw your dress. It was hanging on your door. I understand that a sundress might be nice in the hot weather, but don't you want something more business-like? And those shoes—what about something a bit more practical? Are you leading tours?"

"No. They're hiring someone else to do that."

"I always find that it's wise to volunteer to help out when there aren't others to do jobs that might benefit the company. What if they don't get someone in time? It would make you look good if you do the first tour."

"I volunteered to help with the filing, but they said no."

"This is a nice skirt. It makes you look smart. You'd appear like a real business woman in this and a blouse."

"We have no air conditioner there. I would be too hot."

"You can wear the skirt with a lighter blouse. Look at these colors. Aren't they beautiful?"

"Maybe the skirt's okay," she said. "We'll have to take it up though. People don't want an old lady serving them wine."

"What about these sandals. Will they let you wear sandals?"

"These over here are nice. The wedge is attractive, don't you think?"

"I'm not sure you need to be attractive, Viviana."

"It's a sales job, Mamma. Of course I have to appear attractive."

The next day, Viviana appeared at the winery in work clothes.

"We got someone to apply plaster to the walls. It should be dry now," said Giulio. "Ermanno insisted on getting the paint. I think he got a deal on it. It'll do, won't it?"

Viviana smiled. "Yes, it'll do. I'll paint while you build the counter."

"I bought a cabinet. I'll assemble the pieces and then top it with marble. I also found some stools. The counter will be high enough so the tall stools will work. You might want to find some material for the cushions, but that can wait."

"What's that crate?" she asked, pointing to a box in the corner."

"That's a small refrigerator. We can get hors d'oeuvres or munchies to serve with the wine. The sink will go into the shelves that I plan to build behind you."

"Wow. I see now that you and Ermanno are serious. I can get some plants or flowers." She picked up a can of paint and climbed the ladder.

He looked up at her. A boyish grin crossed his face. "Ermanno was impressed with you."

"Was it the shoes?"

"The whole package. You'll have to promise me you aren't attracted to him, or I won't finish the shelves."

She bent down and brushed his face with her free hand. "There's no comparison," she said. "I'm the loyal type." Then she took the roller and began to cover the wall with Ermanno's paint.

Giulio took her to the house at lunchtime. The two made sandwiches and sat in chairs overlooking the valley to eat them. Giulio washed his down with milk, and Viviana laughed when the milk formed a mustache. He wiped it away. "Back to work."

"What about your job? Don't you have to check the aging wines?"

"I have an assistant doing that. We should be finished tonight. Then I can hang out the tasting sign I made and go back to my other work. Before you leave tonight, you should take home a manual that gives you information you're supposed to know. You'll start on Monday."

"What about the rest of the week?"

"Read the manual. You'll need to study it. There's a lot you have to know so you can answer questions."

"Did you get someone to give tours?"

"No, but we have plenty of people who can do that."

"So I can wear my shoes."

His voice softened. "Definitely wear the shoes. And if they hurt you, you can take them off. There's nothing more appealing than to watch a woman remove her shoes. The tasters would love to see that."

Viviana smiled. Did she have him hooked? She was beginning to think so, but there was work to be done to make certain he didn't get away. She looked out over the valley. After all, this is where she wanted to spend the rest of her life.

Chapter Ten

The morning was sunny and hot. It was only nine when Sister Angela entered the police station, but the offices were already busy.

"I'm looking for Chief Detective Pagano," she said to a uniformed policewoman scurrying down a long hallway.

"He's in his office," she said. "Follow the hallway to the desk, and they'll tell you where he is."

"Thank you, dear."

Pagano's office had glass walls so he was easy to spot. He waved at the nun and held open the door for her. "I suppose you're here to help investigate the child's background. The mother superior at Mission House called ahead and gave me the details. The nuns in Castel Valori took the child in just a few years ago. I suppose that means the newspapers in that area were already online. Poppi and Arezzo are two that might be found on the Internet. We have a man on holiday. If you'd like you can use his desk and computer up front. I don't think he'd mind. Do you know how to browse?"

"Yes, of course, but you'll show me how to get on, won't you?"

"Elmo sits up front. He can serve as a resource if you get into trouble."

Pagano led her to the desk and got her started. She looked over her shoulder at Detective Sergeant Sacco, talking on the phone. He seemed very busy.

Sister Angela went directly for the maps, intending to identify all the towns and villages around Castel Valori. Then, beginning with the smaller ones, she looked for online news feeds. Nothing. After an hour she sat back, defeated. Sacco approached and asked if she needed refreshment.

"Do you have any orange soda in your machine?" she asked.

"Of course. It's my favorite too. I'll get you some. Are you having any luck?"

"No. It seems most of the smaller regions have no online news. Perhaps they have no crime."

"I'd start by putting in the specific story, if you know one. Do you have any names?"

"Well, I have the convent name where Pia lived for the last few years."

"The stories about the smaller hill towns often end up in papers in Florence and here in Siena."

"But is it a worthy news story if a child was dropped off at a convent? I'd say the story's a local one and therefore not picked up in larger papers."

"That's possible. Then I'd dash to the library. They have news stories for the local papers on microfiche."

"That's an idea. Perhaps I can try a bit longer here and then go to the library. It seems this might be a more difficult job than I thought. What about police issues?"

"What do you mean?" asked Sacco.

"Did the local police investigate a baby being left

on the convent steps? They probably did, even though they failed to act at the time. They might have investigated the circumstances. How does one get that information?"

"I can call them. If they failed to remove the child from the convent, it might be considered a cold case. They may not want to admit to that, though."

The nun smiled. "But they might admit their failure to me. I think I'm going to have to set up a visit. Perhaps you can tell one of the detectives that I'm coming and would like to talk with him."

"That sounds like a good plan. I'll get your orange soda first, Sister. You're going to need your strength."

Having ordered news content for the required date from the reference desk at the library, Sister Angela settled into a chair in front of a table holding up a large microfiche machine.

"The event took place four years ago," she whispered to herself. "Let's look at stories about a week before the child was delivered to the nuns."

The first paper she found was a regional newspaper that included Castel Valori, Val d'Alsa, and Ascedo. She scanned the front page for news. Most of the stories involved local businesses and their offerings. One had to do with a family feud. There was also an armed robbery of a produce market. She couldn't think of any tie to a missing child. She scanned the obituaries and then moved on to the stories the next day. After over an hour, she increased the search radius to include villages a bit farther away. Again, she searched the local news a week before Pia's appearance. Lunchtime came and went, and her stomach began to growl.

Perhaps I need a meal. I fear they'll ask me to leave if my stomach gets any louder. Outside the door, she spied a lunch cart and let the scents of food lure her across the street.

"Hello, Sister," said a voice.

"Hello, Sister Liona. I was just trying to decide what I was going to eat for lunch. What do you recommend?"

"I didn't realize the nuns had revealed our secret eating place the other night. I always recommend the pizza, but Sister Agata would tell you the focaccia is superb. What are you doing in town?"

"I'm trying to figure out the event that led to discovery of Pia at the convent's front door."

"Oh, that might be difficult. Perhaps you should ask the nuns for more information."

"Mother Faustine indicated the nuns knew very little about where the child came from. I figured I'd look through the events of the week before I went to see if something might have precipitated the deed."

The legal expert bit her lip. "It could've happened earlier than that. I mean, the decision must have been very difficult to make. Families tend to chew on their particular problem for weeks or more before finally making the decision."

"You're right, of course. It could've been as simple as that."

"I believe the nuns would go to the parish priest and question him about recent confessions," said Sister Liona. "Presumably, he wouldn't reveal the details. But he could've counselled the parents about laws regarding leaving an unwanted child. The nuns were probably satisfied they could keep the child."

"That's true. There might not have been third-party episode that led to the convent at all. But failing to let the state know they had the child was wrong because the relatives weren't given a chance to intervene. I believe the nuns would've involved the authorities much earlier if they thought they could avoid having a child raised in an orphanage."

"Ah. Perhaps you're right, Sister Angela. The child should've been raised by a loving family who knew the parents. But I'm not sure the police ever found answers because they sent Pia here. You might also acknowledge the orphanage was an excellent place for the child to end up."

Sister Angela smiled. "You have a point, Sister Liona," she said. "But the orphanage in Filari lost the child, and I don't think she's in a good place now. It's incumbent upon us to find her and send her to a loving home, whether it's a family related to her or the larger family at the orphanage with whom she has shared her childhood so far."

Sister Angela checked in at the police station before returning to Filari.

"I'm leaving for home," said Pagano. "Would you like me to give you a ride back to the orphanage?"

"Oh, no, Chief Detective. I have the truck. I hope it's still where I parked it. It would be a shame if the police towed it because I left it in a restricted space or because it wasn't straight enough."

"What did you find out here or at the library? Were there any occurrences in the region that caught your attention?"

"There were lots of stories about events there during the time of Pia's discovery. Unfortunately, I haven't a clue which ones might have contributed to the drop off."

The chief detective picked up his lunch box and accompanied the nun to the exit. "Tell me some of the stories, and I'll give you my opinion."

"Let me see. There was an avalanche in the hill above Alceda. Three people were killed in addition to injuries. Then there was an armed robbery of a bank in Castel Valori. At least two thieves dressed up in masks. There was a ten-car pileup on the autostrada near Poppi. Three people were killed there."

The two stood on the curb outside the station.

"One paper reported on three different domestic disputes two weeks before the drop off. And there was a single car accident on one of the back roads where the driver was killed. There were no passengers."

Pagano scratched his head. "None of them seem promising, but at least you'll sound like you did your homework in preparation for meeting with the police."

"And the nuns. I plan do that in person."

The chief detective looked up. "Where's your car?"

"It's the truck. I parked it right across the street, and it's still here. Please give my regards to your wife, Chief Detective."

"And good luck with your investigation. We'll continue to search through the local vineyards for Pia and our old nun."

Sister Angela pulled the truck up the drive next door to the orphanage. She heard someone in the large building near the house and walked up to its open entrance.

"Good evening, Sister. What can I do for you?"

"I'm looking for Signor La Barca."

"I'm Martino La Barca. Are you from the Mission Sisters next door?"

"I'm visiting them, yes."

"I'm so sorry they've lost a child. When I heard, I checked all around, but I found nothing."

"I'm staying with Michel Matta and his lovely wife. He mentioned that you were an authority on the use of amphorae in making wine, and I was wondering if you might have a bit of time to tell me about it. I know you're busy, but if there's a better time…"

"Please, I can tell you now. My wife's visiting her mother, and I'm on my own for dinner." He took the nun by the arm and led her inside.

A long row of strangely-shaped clay vessels stood upright in a row in the center of the chamber.

"It looks like the aliens have landed," she said.

"During the Bronze Age, the Greeks used pots called *dolia*. They buried them in the ground and fermented the grapes that way. The Romans had open pots. They spread olive oil over the top of the wine and emptied the amphora from the bottom. Still serving as a lid until the pot was empty, the oil on the top would spread over the surface as the wine level went down."

"But yours have lids."

"More recent history has shown fermentation in terracotta can yield new and very fine wine characteristics." He patted the one closest to him. "I moved away from oak and steel because I was looking for a less-aggressive medium to ferment and age my wines. Whereas in ancient times amphorae were the natural vessel of choice, now it's a conscious or a philosophical decision to use clay jars. I swear by them. There's a marked difference between wines fermented in wood or steel and those aged in terracotta. We need that—variety, I mean."

"These don't look that old. They're works of art. How long do you think it takes to make one?"

"It takes months for the local artisans to deliver one. They're local to Tuscany. Terracotta amphorae cost more than wood or stainless, but they're worth it. They're free standing. We don't bury them anymore, and they have removable lids.

"Do you produce Chianti?"

"Yes, and I follow the rules set down by the DOCG. I grow several rows of the Sangiovese grapes that I use in the Chianti. I also had some Cabernet grapes. That's what the *controlatta* requires for both Chianti and Chianti *Riserva* so I'm able to use the label. But I also produce Pinot Noir and Riesling. The wines have a beefier taste and are preferred when eating strong food like game meats. I have a bottle of Riesling open, if you'd like a taste."

"I certainly didn't expect such hospitality. I would love a glass."

He poured some into a tumbler and handed it to the nun, standing near the exit door of the wine hut.

"You look at the orphanage every day. Do you get along with the nuns?"

"They haven't been any trouble, Sister. They're quiet."

"I imagine the children aren't so quiet."

"The sound of children doesn't bother me. At first, my wife was disturbed by it. She and I decided to put off having children. The nuns, however, made my wife welcome. Once she was able to make friends with some of the children, she enjoyed waving to them."

"I hadn't heard that. How did she get to know them?"

"She was their cook for three or four years. She trained Sister Edita."

"I noticed the fence. Did you think they would trample the tender grapes, Martino?"

"We feared some of them would wander into the fields and hurt themselves."

"Did that ever happen?"

"No. We put in the fence pretty quickly."

She sipped the wine and savored the unusual flavor. "Are you aware there was a witness the night of the kidnapping?"

"I heard they saw a nun. Is that what you mean?"

"One of the girls saw a nun on your side of the fence."

Martino's brows shot up. "She thinks it was one of us?"

"No, she said it was a nun standing at the end of your vines. She didn't see how she got there or where the nun entered the orphanage. She and I walked along the fence to see how well the child would have been able to see the nun. The moon was full enough so that they could see each other."

"Please show me where she stood."

The nun handed the vintner her empty glass and carefully led him down one of the rows to the end. "It was right below the window up there."

La Barca checked the vines directly behind the nun.

"She supposedly hid by sitting down near the end of this row."

"I see, I see. There are a few broken branches here. She must have sat directly on them. Did the eyewitness say how big she was?"

"The nun was taller and thinner than you are. She wasn't able to hide very well because her head was evidently still visible above the vine."

"Has anyone in the neighborhood seen a woman with a young child?"

"Did you know Pia?"

"I'd seen her in the yard. Whenever the children were out, I'd try to wave to them too. That must sound nefarious, Sister, but I felt for them. I just wanted to make them feel liked."

"Perhaps you and your wife could adopt one of them. If you decide not to have them yourselves."

"My wife and I are too busy trying to get this place going before I go broke. We're still young. Maybe someday."

The nun suddenly realized she hadn't yet eaten. She grabbed her rumbling stomach. "I really should get the truck back to Michel before the wine hits me," she said. "Thank you for the taste. It's magnificent. I'm sure your winery will do well." She headed back down the row until she got to the driveway. As she struggled to turn the truck around near the house, she glimpsed in the rearview mirror and saw La Barca running toward her. Completing the U-turn, she stopped and rolled down the window.

"Sister Angela, Sister Angela. I found something among those vines," he called out, almost breathless. When he got to the window he revealed what he held.

"What is it?" she asked. She watched as the small crumpled object began to bloom in his hand. "Wait," she said, looking for something in the truck with which to take the object. "We shouldn't be touching evidence." She found a box of tissue in the glove compartment and let Le Barca place it on a tissue.

"Was it on the vine with the broken branches?"

Still trying to catch his breath, he coughed. "No," he finally said. "It was on the ground at the bottom of the vine."

I wish I'd seen it myself, the nun thought. "It's almost the same material as my habit," she said. "The old nun must have torn her habit on the vines. And you didn't see any rag cloths around the winery here? She may have wanted to dispose of her habit on your land."

"I've never seen any cloth like that around here, Sister."

"I'll have to get this to the police, Martino. Good job. This verifies a witness's testimony. If you find anything else, let me know."

Chapter Eleven

Strolling through the busy Siena police station the next morning, Sister Angela ran into the chief detective.

"I didn't know you'd be back so soon, Sister," he said.

"The terminal's just down the road. I had someone drop me off here, and I plan to walk there when my train's due. But I wanted you to have this." She slipped the baggie from her red-striped tote. "Last night, I talked with Martino La Barca at the vineyard abutting the orphanage."

"Yes, I interviewed him already."

"I showed him where Grazia saw the nun on his side of the fence. The child said the old nun tried to hide among the leafy shoots."

"We didn't check out that story. I should've done that."

"Yes, because there were broken shoots on one of the vines closest to the orphanage. After I walked away, he kept examining the bush and discovered a piece of torn material that had fallen to the ground." She slipped the swatch of black fabric out of her pocket. "It looks like part of a habit, doesn't it?"

"Is it the same material as your habit?"

"No, mine's a lighter material. I belong to a community that's comfortable with Vatican II, remember? Most of the nuns at Mission House are younger, and they wear the same type of habit I do. But some of the older nuns choose to wear the older style."

"You're saying that this fabric's what the old style was made from, right?"

"Every community's different, but this fabric's common. I have to warn you that La Barca held the fabric tightly in his hand when he tried to catch up with me. There may be no readable DNA because of that. But at the very least, the existence of material does seem to corroborate Grazia's story."

"It could be bad news for the vintner, it adds him to the list of suspects."

"I'm surprised, Chief Detective, that he wasn't on the list already."

Unable to secure a taxi or bus outside the terminal in Castel Valori, Sister Angela stopped at a cart along the tiny village's town center and bought an apple.

"Pardon me," she said to the vender. "Can you tell me where I might find the Sacro Cuore della Francesca?"

"Yes, Sister. Continue through town. Just down the road from where Castel Valori ends, you'll find a large gray building on your right. That's it."

"Thank you." The nun said, beginning down the road, slowing to window shop each time she passed a store.

At the end of town, the road narrowed. Dried

grass and bushes crowded the edges. On the downside, the golden shoots ended, and rows of grapes took off into the valley below. To her right, gravel drives navigated the hillside, framed by tall cypress as they approached farmhouses. Sister Angela stopped to let a strong breeze, carrying the songs of birds perched on the vines and trees, cool her face. Then she continued her dusty trek. Rounding the bend, the building the vender described suddenly came into view. The outside walls were a dirty-gray plaster that had chipped away, revealing mortar and brick. Faded red-painted wood framed the windows. She urged her legs up a slight slope and then took ten steps to a flat piazza. A marble archway framed a thick wooden door. Sister Angela reached up and pulled on a rope until she could hear the bell ring inside.

The trip on the train had been easy. Siena had a large train terminal with plenty of windows where she could get her ticket. She carried a thermos of coffee with her, balancing a paper cup while she retrieved biscotti from her tote. The rows of grapevines and olive orchards whizzed past the windows. Ancient hill towns looked down on more modern villages.

A few minutes passed before she heard someone inside unlatching the door. "I'm sorry for taking so long," said a nun in a long white and gray habit. "We were attending sext, our noon service. I didn't hear the bell because of the chanting."

"And I'm sorry for interrupting your service," said Sister Angela.

The middle-aged woman smiled. "I'm Sister Concetta. What can I do for you?"

"I'm Sister Angela. I called…"

"Oh yes. The prioress mentioned you were coming. Please sit down here while I fetch her."

Sister Angela glanced around.

"I'm sorry we have so few chairs. The ones we do have are only fit for a penitent. The others are being reupholstered for the first time since I arrived. Reverend Mother was worried that we might need the money for some catastrophe in the future, but fixing them could invite more to call. Visitors would be appalled by the worn furniture."

"I don't mind," said Sister Angela. "I could use a glass of water, however."

Mother Patrizia entered the room with a cold bottle for their guest. "How do you do, Sister Angela? We've been so worried about Pia and would like to help anyway we can. Why don't we retire to the room behind the kitchen? The chairs are much more comfortable. I'm sure some of my sisters would love to speak with you too, but I don't want to overwhelm you. Do you plan to return to Siena tonight or would you like a cell?"

"I brought no luggage with me so I'd like to catch the train, Reverend Mother. My schedule says it leaves at seven. That gives us plenty of time to talk about Pia's past, doesn't it?"

The two women sat down at the long table. The room was surprisingly cool.

"Do you have air conditioning in the cells too?"

The prioress smiled. "No. We have small fans, though. If all the cells had air conditioning, I fear I might not be able to rouse enough nuns to come to the chapel for the morning service. Does the orphanage have air conditioning?"

"The orphanage has air conditioning in only a few of the rooms, but I'm staying with a nearby family. They do have air conditioning. I sleep like a baby and am becoming quite spoiled." Sister Angela removed a notebook from her tote. "Let me see," she said, donning a pair of reading glasses. The reading glasses were something new. It irked her to finally admit she might need them on occasion. "The story the Mission Sisters told me about Pia is that she arrived when she was two. Is that correct?"

"Yes, but we aren't aware of her exact age because we didn't know who she was. The doorbell rang, and she was on our doorstep."

"Was she in some sort of cradle? I keep imagining baby Moses in a tiny basket floating down a river…" She hesitated. "But Pia wasn't a baby. She was a toddler. Why didn't she just get up and run away?"

"I'm sorry. No, she wasn't on the doorstep in a cradle. She was beside the doorstep, crouched down and crying. It was raining, and she seemed thoroughly miserable."

"Did she tell you her name? Did you even ask her for it?"

"No. She said nothing to us at all. She didn't speak for weeks. She wanted to drink from a bottle, and she cried like a baby. The first word out of her mouth was 'Mamma.' She was here for two years. It took several months to coax anything out of her that could be attributed to a two year old."

"When she did talk, did she give you her name?"

"Again no. We called her *Pia* at the beginning. It was my idea. It means *pious*. I thought the name would help her when we prayed for her. Several months later, we stopped and asked her for her name, but by then, she called herself *Pia*. Whatever she knew about her past was washed away. I'm so sorry. We loved her dearly, but evidently not one of us knew much about children."

"And that brings me to a question that may seem disrespectful, considering you're my superior. Please don't take offense."

"You must want to ask me why we kept her here for two years."

"If I don't, someone else will."

"The police have questioned us already. At first we kept her because we believed her mother or other relatives would change their minds and come to retrieve her. As the weeks passed, we decided to go out and ask around the town if they knew of a family situation where the child no longer lived in the home. We were thinking that a villager might need help economically or that a mother might have needed protection from her husband. A few more months passed. By then, we'd become thoroughly attached."

"And how did the authorities find out she was here?"

"It was a lovely day. One of our sisters felt sorry for Pia because we had her inside most of the time. The nun took her for a walk, and someone saw them. She reported her to the parish priest in the village. The police came to take Pia away. It was heart wrenching, as you can imagine. Pia put up a fight too. There were tears enough to produce a waterfall down the front steps. I asked the police to return in a few days so we could prepare her better. We called around until we found the Mission Sisters. They saved the day. They came to pick up Pia. The child was confused and upset a bit because they wore black habits while we wear white ones, but she calmed down by the time they put her in the car. We took much longer to recover, though."

"Was it Mother Faustine who came?" asked Sister Angela.

"No it was Sister Liona. She's a lawyer, you know."

"Let's go back to the beginning. Someone rang the bell, and when you answered it…"

"We heard the bell. Sister Baptista actually opened the door," said the prioress.

"I went to the door and opened it," said Sister Baptista "There was no one there, but something told me to step outside." Her petite figure gracefully rose and left the room. "Follow me. I'll show you."

Sister Angela walked with the younger nun out the front door.

Sister Baptista pointed to a spot beside of the steps. "She was there," she said. "Just a tiny baby crouching against the steps, trying to get out of the rain. She was sopping wet, poor dear."

"When you say tiny baby you didn't mean she couldn't walk on her own."

"She could walk. She could even run, but we didn't know that at first. I carried her into the convent and dried her off."

"Did she say anything to you?"

"No, but we already told you she didn't give us her name. That's when we began to call her Pia. She must have liked the name because she responded to it right away."

"I presume she also ate solids."

Sister Tiberia giggled from a folding chair inside the door. "None of us knew she could eat solids. We must have fed her milk for a week before we realized she was getting very hungry."

"You fed her milk from a bottle?"

"Yes," she said. Sister Tiberia was loftier than the others and looked as if the she was about to tip her perch. "The others sent me to the store down the road. I bought a couple of bottles. They had the nipples turned upside down, and it took me a while to figure out how they worked. I also bought a large carton of milk. When I went to pay for the items, the sales clerk looked confused. I told him we had a kitten without mother at the convent."

Sister Oriana continued. "Pia went through several liters of milk right away. When she didn't stop, we tried to give her cereal. She liked that so we tried other foods too. She thrived with us. It almost broke my heart when the police threatened to take her away if we didn't find her a place to live. I know Sister Giana of the Mission Sisters. She and I were childhood friends. She told me about the orphanage."

"And how did you hear about Pia's disappearance less than a week ago."

"The police told us," said the prioress. "They wanted to make sure we kept an eye out for her, and we did. But when you think about it, she'd only be five or six now. Would a six year old be able to navigate her way to this convent? Even with assistance from the Blessed Virgin, she wouldn't know how to make it back here. We're devastated. Even though a few years have passed, it feels like it was just yesterday that she left us. I suppose that now she doesn't even remember us."

"Did she have a certain cell while she was here? Does it still have a few things that belonged to her?" asked Sister Angela.

"She came with almost nothing. She didn't even have a coat to protect her from the rain. She took everything we gave her while she lived here with us."

"You've heard nothing else about someone in the area having lost a child?"

"No," said Sister Tiberia. "Perhaps someone who was passing by noticed us and left her on our doorstep."

Sister Angela thought about the little-used regional carriageway in front of the old building. *Not likely*, she said to herself. "Perhaps I should talk to Father Montez. Someone may have revealed problems and mentioned them in his confessional."

"I've asked him that," said Mother Patrizia. "He tells me he wouldn't reveal the details of anyone's confession to us. But he might tell you if someone had talked about anything that had to do with the case."

"Well, that's all I have to ask you," said Sister Angela. "I'll call you if I learn anything new. My train leaves at seven, and I want to talk to the police on the way to the terminal. I'd better start back now."

"Can we give you any nourishment before you go, Sister?" asked Sister Baptiste.

"No, I'll be fine," she said as she stopped once more on the steps to look at the spot where Pia had crouched in the rain. Then she closed the door and started down the steps to the dusty road.

She had walked about twenty minutes in the blazing sun when it suddenly hit her. *Who rang the bell?* She turned to look back at the convent, but it was well out of sight. *Would a two year old be able to reach the doorbell? Of course not. Someone was with her. Someone has to know the story of how Pia got to the convent.*

Chapter Twelve

The rhythm of the tracks nearly lulled the nun to sleep. Was it the fact that she was returning with little new information? Maybe her blood sugar was low. She'd failed to take the time for decent meal. She rummaged through her tote and pulled out the apple she bought from the cart in Castel Valori. Then she settled back to think about what had happened.

On her way back into town, she'd stopped at a market and purchased an orange soda and a yogurt. Why hadn't she accepted the nuns' offer of a meal? She sat at a table on the large piazza in the shade of an umbrella, whipping in a wind that began to blow up.

She stared at the church at the far corner of the piazza, its grand Romanesque style sported an imposing quadrangular bell tower. The prioress had explained that the church was built for an order of Augustinian hermits in the thirteenth century and had been visited by Martin Luther in the sixteenth. She suggested that Sister Angela examine the large collection of art inside.

I'd love to, she mused. *But unfortunately I'm still on duty.*

Feeling refreshed, Sister Angela stood and crossed the piazza, entering the church at the side door and sitting in the pew just inside. She saw the priest kneeling at the altar in front of the statue of the

Virgin Mary but dared not interrupt him. After a few minutes, he crossed himself, stood, and spun around to approach the visitor.

"How can I help you, Sister?" he asked. "Do I know you?"

"No. I'm looking for Father Montez."

"I'm Father Montez. Do you have a question?"

"I'm Sister Angela from Montriano. I'm investigating the disappearance of Pia, the toddler that lived at the convent here in Castel Valori. Do you know who I'm talking about?"

"I've spoken with the police…"

"I plan to talk with the police before I leave."

The priest slid into the pew beside her. "I'm afraid I know very little, Sister."

"Tell me how you found out she was with the nuns at the convent."

"One Saturday, a parishioner came to the confessional and said she'd seen one of the nuns with a child. I can't tell you who it was because…"

"I understand—your vows."

"Not only that, but I didn't recognize the voice. She must not have come to church often because I would've recognized her voice."

"Do you think she was from out of town?"

"Sister, I know you're aware of the problems concerning young people coming to church."

"She was young?"

"I honestly don't know. I'm just saying that while ninety-five percent of the townspeople are baptized Catholics, a much smaller percentage actually participate in the Mass or sacraments beyond baptism or extreme unction. I can only tell you she told me she'd seen a nun with a small child. My first inclination was to ignore her observation. We have lots of nuns in and around Castel Valori, and those nuns have nieces and nephews who come to visit them. But prayer kept bringing her insignificant gossip back into my mind. I decided to pay a visit to the convent—just in case."

"Did you tell them you were coming?"

"Of course, I gave them a few days to make sure they were ready for a visitor. I don't think they receive many. Then, at the designated time, I rang their bell. They served me coffee, and we talked about the church news. I didn't go inside farther than their parlor, and all was quiet. I asked to use the facilities, and one of the nuns showed me the way. It was there that I noticed it."

"What gave them away?"

"There was a paper towel laid out for me, and I washed my hands and dried them. I turned to find a wastepaper basket near the sink—the kind you opened by pushing down on a lever with your foot. I was never the athletic type, Sister. I once tried the trick with the football where you sort of kick it and it pops back up so you can balance it on top of your foot. I couldn't balance it. I kicked it into my face, breaking my nose."

The nun listened to his amusing story, amazed that he'd be so honest.

"I pressed the pedal on the trash contraption and somehow broke it, dumping over its contents. I quickly bent over to pick up the paper and such and found a diaper. Well, it was actually a little girl's pair of panties, Sister. I was shocked but still held onto hope that there was an innocent explanation."

"I see. What did you do?"

"I stood the can upright. I'm afraid I couldn't find the broken pedal that had managed to escape the wrath of my foot. Then I carried the panties into the foyer. I've never seen so many distraught faces in one room before. I asked for one of them to get the child."

Sister Angela had her hand over her mouth.

"I asked if they had some sort of permission to have the child at the convent. They explained she'd been left there. They said they didn't know what to do with her. The nuns were aware they'd crossed some sort of line. I told them I'd go to the police. When I left I felt terrible. The child was very young, but she seemed to be attached to them. She'd evidently lived with them awhile."

"Did you work with the police to find a place for the toddler?"

"No. It was out of my hands. The Church didn't need another scandal. We have too few parishioners as it is. This is an expensive church to keep afloat. Our income's shrinking."

"Have you tried to charge tourists for the privilege of looking at the beautiful artwork here?"

In a grand gesture, Father Montez gazed in all directions. "I can't even get tourists to come in when it's free."

Sister Angela leaned against the headrest and closed her eyes. The click-clack of the tracks was relaxing, but her mind still raced. Had the police sergeant taken her seriously? If so, his face didn't show it. Detective Sergeant Este Turo listened to some of the nun's theories as she sat across the desk from him. He was young with short light brown hair and green eyes. He was so still Sister Angela had to force her gaze from his as she spoke.

"I looked through the papers at the time that Pia was dropped off at the convent, Detective Sergeant. There were events in the area that could've produced a situation where a child might become parentless. I assume each incident was thoroughly investigated." She looked for a response but he gave none. "For example, there was an avalanche in the hill above Alceda."

"Yes," he finally said. "There were three deaths and even more injuries. The hillside was scoured. There were no other bodies, and no one else was reported missing. Don't you think we would've heard that someone was missing by now?"

"There was also a bank robbery here in town. Could there have been some sort of kidnapping with that?"

"No. The robbers were captured."

The nun squirmed. "Certainly you're sure they were the ones involved. They wore masks. Were the masks found?"

"Yes the masks were in the getaway car. They drove their own vehicle so there was no other driver."

"But…"

"Okay, I see your point. There may have been another suspect waiting for them, but neither suspect revealed such a partner. Most of the time, this type of criminal makes sure he isn't the only one taking the blame. All the money and goods were recovered."

"Not if the additional partners were relatives."

"You're correct, but you have to admit, Sister, that it's a stretch to believe an armed thief would commit an unrelated kidnapping or murder."

"There was also a car accident close by."

"We do have accidents…"

"But this one was different. The newspaper revealed that the car had a dent that indicated the driver had been forced off the road."

"Yes, if I remember correctly, the driver died. Hit-and-run accidents aren't uncommon. There was no evidence that there were other passengers in the car. Do you think the offender got out of the other car, stole the child, and then delivered it to the nuns? I suppose that's possible. The other driver could've felt guilty and feared harm would come to child, but why take all the evidence of the toddler's existence? There would've been some sort of car seat, toys, or blanket—items the nuns didn't find on the child. The story isn't very convincing."

The nun looked at her notes. "There was a pile-up in Poppi with three people killed."

"That's a bit farther away. I believe the Poppi police looked into that one. I don't see the connection. Maybe you should ask *them*."

The nun sat back. "What theories do you have, Detective Sergeant?"

"We believe the child was probably left because the parents no longer thought they could take care of her. We checked around Castel Valori and found no one who would've done that. We collected DNA but found no relatives."

"Therefore you believe someone outside the area left her at the convent because nuns would be able to care for the child."

"It could also been someone from outside the country."

The nun's brows shot up involuntarily. "That doesn't ring true to me, Detective Sergeant. Why would nonnatives feel the child would be safer among people of a different culture?"

"I'm talking about refugees of some sort. You know Italy's a gateway into Europe, Sister. Suppose a refugee feared he or she would be deported to the home country. What's safer than dropping off an anonymous child? Italy wouldn't expel a child, especially when the authorities didn't know which country she came from."

"I see. You're saying that the refugees are escaping from some sort of war-torn area. I understand how difficult it might be to track such a child. What I don't understand is what interest someone may have in the child now. You're aware Pia was kidnapped. Perhaps the parents came back and tracked the child to Filari. Worried they might be captured and deported again, they stole the child instead of asking the nuns at the orphanage or the police for their child back."

"I'm not included in the search for the child. I don't know what theories the Siena police have. Your conjecture's just as good as any other."

The nun stood. "I really must get the train," she said. "I do hope when I return we can work together on finding her."

"Are you planning to return, Sister?"

"I believe the kidnapping in Filari's related to the original drop off at the convent here. Finding out more about Pia will help us uncover where she is. Perhaps she isn't an Italian citizen, but she's still a beloved child. I'm not ready to let any six year old end up in the hands of criminals. I also believe you have more interest in the case than you reveal." She smiled. "I look forward to working with you, Detective Sergeant. Here's my email address. I'd appreciate it if you'd give your files a peek and send me other things that might have happened around Castel Valori that didn't make the papers."

The detective sergeant stood and shook her hand.

The nun roused when she heard the train horn. She shaded her eyes to see what she could out the window. On the hillside, a few lights twinkled. Was the train slowing? She stopped the conductor as he passed her seat. "Are we entering Siena?"

"No, Sister, there's something on the tracks ahead."

"Is it common for this train to stop when something's on the tracks? I hope they aren't bandits."

The conductor smiled but also continued to appear concerned. He vanished through the door at the end of the aisle.

The train remained in one spot for nearly thirty minutes. Sister Angela gestured to the coffee lady, who pushed her cart down the aisle.

"Are you still serving espresso?"

"Yes, Sister. It's late, but we can serve you coffee."

"Please. Do you know how long we're to wait here? I've someone picking me up at the terminal in Siena. I hope she doesn't give up on me."

"There's something on the tracks. It's very hush-hush."

"I hope it isn't a body or anything like that."

"They haven't told me anything. It could be a bomb for all I know."

The nun stood to open the window. She leaned out and looked toward the locomotive. She couldn't see anything. The coffee lady returned in five minutes with an espresso.

"Ooh, a cookie. How delightful?" said Sister Angela. "Have you heard anything more?"

"They've cleared whatever it was. We should be moving again in about five minutes."

"Are the police there?"

"Yes," the coffee lady said. "Two policemen came onboard and asked the conductor a few questions. The engineer would've been the only one who saw something though."

"I didn't see them come through."

"No, they disembarked and walked toward the front of the train again. I think they wanted to know if anyone boarded the train when it stopped."

"I didn't see anyone new in this car. I suppose the conductor would be the person who remembered everyone." The nun took a sip of her coffee. "Why would the police be involved? It would have to have been something important."

"You mean they must think it's something to do with terrorism?"

"I would've loved to speak with them myself. If it was a body, what did the body look like?" Sister Angela asked, mostly to herself.

"You have a strange obsession with murder, Sister," said the coffee lady. "Most of the human victims who die on the tracks are suicides."

The nun nibbled on her cookie and smiled at the coffee lady. "You're right. It was probably a cow or some other animal. I don't know why we would automatically think it was something more frightening." She handed the coffee lady some coins. "Thank you for the refreshment. Hopefully we'll get a tailwind that thrusts us into Siena on time."

Chapter Thirteen

Empty cup in hand, Sister Angela descended the stairs and headed for the kitchen, shading her eyes from the sun that shone directly through the large windows.

"Good morning," said Sister Daniela. "Do you need more coffee? I have breakfast ready for you. Don't take too long. I still have to be at work."

"Thank you, Sister. I appreciated you coming to pick me up at the terminal last night."

"Aside from the train being late, I couldn't wait to speak with you about what you found out."

The older nun sat down at the table, and Sister Daniel poured her some juice. "I told you about the commotion on the tracks last night, didn't I? I forgot to ask if you'd heard anything about it when you were waiting for me outside the terminal."

"No. They said nothing. Only that you were late." She placed the honey on the table beside the butter. Then she set a basket of hardboiled eggs in front of Sister Angela.

The nun positioned an egg in the cup and began to crack it with her spoon. Sister Daniela handed the older nun a plate with a croissant and finally sat down beside her.

"I might have to go into Siena and find out what the police know about it," said Sister Angela. "What if it has to do with our investigation?"

"I don't want to think about it. The idea of anybody being hit by a train makes me tremble."

"I had other things to talk to the chief detective about too. I want to speak with him face to face. Perhaps he's already considering the questions." The older nun drew a long sip of her cooling espresso. "Ahhh," she said. "The taste of espresso is a joy only second to that of Michel's *riserva*."

The two nuns trekked past La Barca's Vineyard toward the orphanage.

"I don't know if I told you, but Martino gave me a tour of his winery. It's quite unlike Michel's. The wine tastes different too."

"Do you like it better or worse?" asked Sister Daniela.

"Just different. In my mind I can taste Martino's going with strong meat—like game. We also found a piece of nun's habit."

"What? Why didn't you tell me on the ride home last night? Isn't that the story Grazia told you? Did she really see a nun in La Barca's vineyard?"

"Last night I concentrated solely on telling you what happened during my visit to the convent. Yes, it looks like Grazia really saw a nun. Martino evidently didn't know anything about it until I mentioned the story. We both went to the spot where she saw the nun and looked around. He found a swatch of a nun's habit. I was hoping to talk to the chief detective today. Maybe I can request a ride into town from

Sister Liona."

"You should've told me. I would've asked for the truck."

"I'm sure Michel would love to have his truck for work. I'll find a way to talk to the chief detective."

Sister Daniela removed the keys from her pocket and let them in through the back door of the orphanage.

"We have a meeting in ten minutes," said Sister Natalia, peering around the classroom door. "Ricco and Elmo are coming to update us on what they've found,"

"You go ahead," Sister Daniela told Sister Angela. "I have to wait for my students so I can put someone in charge."

Sister Angela followed Sister Natalia up the stairs and took a seat in the office off the TV room. Sister Edita entered and placed carafes of espresso at each end of the long table and a plateful of cookies in the center. The nun resisted the temptation to look at them, though the smell of fresh-baked cookies made her stomach rumble.

Soon after the nuns gathered around the table, the two detectives arrived. Sister Carmela rose and poured each man a cup of espresso and added cookies to their plates.

"Welcome back, Sister Angela. I hope your trip was successful," said Pagano.

The nun smiled. "Maybe you can start by telling

everyone about the swatch of cloth."

"Yes. Unfortunately, we didn't learn much. The results of tests will probably show nothing, except maybe something from Martino La Barca."

"For those of you who haven't heard," said Sister Angela, "Martino found a torn piece of nun's habit below one of his vines. That seems to verify the story Grazia told about seeing a nun in Martino's field from the window upstairs the night of the abduction."

"I sent a team to investigate the area. They found nothing else and no footprints."

"What about my footprints? I was there. What about Martino's footprints? He was all over that vine."

"There were prints like someone had pulled a rake around the whole section of vines. Any evidence that people had been there was erased."

"Oh my," said Sister Angela. "Did they ask Martino about it?"

"Yes. He responded that someone who worked with him took a tractor to the area without consulting him."

"Why did someone need to do that when the harvest's around the corner? Perhaps you should bring that worker in?"

"I plan to bring both the worker and La Barca in," said Pagano. "We also had a time look for footprints on the orphanage's property again. If the old nun had trudged to the back of this building to get in, there would be footprints, right?"

"Presumably," said one of the nuns.

"Well, we couldn't find any."

"Abiati," said Sister Angela. "The gardener was

preparing for a picnic outside the classroom. Perhaps he did something to smooth the dirt. You should probably question him too."

"I'll see that he's interrogated. Did any of the children hear a door shut?"

"If it was at the back of the house, I doubt they would have heard it. It's another floor down with a thick door at the top of the stairs."

"That might mean the front door was never used," said Pagano. "After all, I believe it was locked the next morning, wasn't it, Sister Carmela?"

"I didn't verify that. In the confusion, anyone could've unlocked the front door."

"I also have a group checking into child sex rings in this area," said Pagano.

"Good Lord, we don't have any of those, do we?" asked a visibly-shaken Sister Carmela.

"We can't identify where the organizations originate. As far as we know, they don't have to exist in one place. All they need are a few people to infiltrate an area and seize a remote property. They pass the children on to the next level of the organization and ship them off to a destination."

The nun groaned. "You don't think…"

"As the days pass with no sign of the child or the old nun, it's a possibility we have to face." Pagano turned to Sister Angela. "What did you find in Castel Valori?"

"I spent several hours with the nuns at Sacro Cuore della Francesca. They told me about Pia. They didn't know where she came from and were ashamed of their error of keeping the child there. They greatly admired the team of lawyers that handled the child's transfer here. I had questions I mentioned to the Castel Valori police."

"What do you mean, Sister?"

"As you know, the toddler was left at their doorstep. One of the nuns mentioned she heard the bell that someone was at the front door, whereupon she walked out and saw Pia crouched down beside the steps in the rain. I assume Pia was less than meter tall because that's the average height for a two year old. I didn't ask the nuns whether or not they thought she was large or small for her age."

"She was about average height and weight when she was here," said Sister Carmela. "I imagine they didn't know that much about young children."

"Then let's accept that she was a meter. If you were that tall and stood on the front step, would you be able to use the bell? I stood at the door and rang the bell when I first arrived. The door was very thick and there was a crucifix where the door knocker would've gone. If anyone rapped on the door, no one inside would've heard it. A little rope stuck out the door just about the right side of my head. I reached up and pulled on the rope and heard the tinkle of the bell inside. No child could've reached that rope, and a young child wouldn't have known that the rope led to a bell."

"What are you saying?" asked Sister Natalia."

"I'm saying that someone would've had to ring the bell that called the nun to the door. Someone purposefully left the child there. We have a witness. We just have to find him or her. I went to the local priest and inquired about confessions he'd heard about the case. He told me he knew no one in the parish that confessed to leaving a child or asked for help feeding the family. He did say something concerning the woman who informed him about the child kept by the nuns."

"Could she have left the child?"

"She reported it after two years had passed. I believe she saw the child with one of the nuns on a walk and thought the situation incongruous. Father Montez couldn't identify the penitent's voice so I was unable to investigate that further."

Soon after the meeting began, Sister Daniela quietly entered and sat down at the table. "Speaking of the gardener, he's in the yard now if you, Chief Detective or Elmo, want to question him."

Pagano nodded for his detective sergeant to detain Abiati. "What did the Castel Valori police say?"

"Not much. I presented the news stories to Detective Sergeant Turo. He told me the incidents had all been investigated and that there was no evidence a child was involved. Of course, at the time he wasn't informed that a child was missing because she was living with the nuns at the convent. We have DNA. Unfortunately we no longer have a crime scene to match it to. I really need to find witnesses."

"I suppose Turo didn't offer to help you hunt for anyone."

"No. I don't blame him. The trail has reached a dead end. What about your theory concerning sex trafficking? How do you investigate that?"

"We have a few reports of missing children in the area. Some are probably runaways. Most of the children are teens or older so our first hunch is the children left voluntarily. In this new light, maybe we should start treating them as possible kidnappings. I'll have a team go back to the families with open minds. Perhaps we should recheck computers, friends, and actions. If we can identify someone having something in common with those who disappeared, we might discover a sex ring operating in the area."

The group dispersed, and Sister Angela followed Pagano out the back door to find Sacco holding Abiati. They located the detective sergeant sitting atop the picnic table. Abiati was raking the lawn on the side of the orphanage. When he saw them, the gardener stopped and approached them.

"We have a few more questions, Mr. Abiati," said Pagano. "I had my men check for footprints along the vineyard side of the building. We suspect the old nun walked down the drive and around the building to enter through the basement and that she and Pia left through the same door. My men found no footprints, however. Can you tell me if you've done anything to the side yard that might make them disappear?"

"It's been nearly two weeks," Abiati said. "Every Friday, I rake the soil in the gardens. It keeps the dirt from clumping on that side of the house. I probably ruined the evidence myself. I'm sorry. I'm not used to crime scenes. My job's to keep the grounds neat and tidy. It irks me that I, in any way, might have helped the old nun who took the child."

"And in the last few weeks, you never saw

anyone on the other side of the fence at all—either someone you know or someone you didn't."

Leaning his rake against his shoulder, Abiati stopped to think. "I saw La Barca out there a few times."

"What was he doing?"

"Actually, he's come out to this section pretty often lately. I guess I figured it's because the grapes are nearly ready, and he's checking them."

"You rarely saw him before a few weeks ago."

"That's right. I noticed his truck come and go up and down his drive, but I didn't often see him."

"What was he doing when you saw him?"

"The last time was in the last couple of days. He came out with a rake and cleared the area from the fence to his vines. I waved at him and heard him say something about the weeds under his breath."

"Was that odd?"

"Well, no. I do it on this side of the fence all the time. It wouldn't strike me as odd. But now that you mention it, I'd never seen him do it before. Weeds always grew along the fence before that. I was exasperated because the seeds from the weeds always seem to blow back through the fence and grow on my side. That's why I rake all the time—to keep them from germinating."

"Did you ever see him digging in the area?"

"Come to think of it, yes. It was the evening before last, just as I was putting tools away after my shift. He was shoveling around the end of one of the rows. I don't know why. I guess he knew what he was doing."

"Very deep?" asked Sister Angela.

"Like he was trying to dig up the end vine."

"My team didn't mention anything about digging," said Pagano.

The chief detective walked to the side of the building. Sister Angela and Abiati followed.

"From here you can't tell where he was digging," said Sister Angela. "He must have tamped it down pretty well."

"Which row?" asked Pagano.

"I come out of the basement shed right here," said Abiati. "It must have been two or three rows back toward the road."

The nun and chief detective looked at each other.

"It sounds like we're going to have to bring him in," Pagano said, taking out his phone.

"I had planned to return to Castel Valori as soon as possible," said the nun. "But under the circumstances, I think I might like to find out more about what Martino's been up too."

"I'll wait here until my men arrive." He gestured to the detective sergeant, jumping down from the picnic table. "Elmo, can you please drive Sister Angela to the station?"

"Do you want us to get you lunch, sir?"

"Why don't we wait until after we've questioned La Barca and see what he has to say about the recent upgrades to his property. After that, I might be able to keep something down."

Chapter Fourteen

Sister Angela sat in a chair in the corner of Pagano's interrogation room. A table was set up for the chief, his detective sergeant, and the suspect.

Pagano suddenly rose. "While we wait for Elmo to bring the witness, why don't I ask someone to bring in water? Would you like anything else?"

"No thank you."

Within minutes, La Barca stumbled into the room, and he and Sacco sat down.

"You know why you're here, don't you?" asked Pagano, fiddling with the recorder.

"I suppose it's because I found the piece of cloth."

"It has more to do with the fact that when you found the cloth, you immediately covered up any other evidence in the area."

"I told your officers that one of my staff…"

"We have a witness who said he saw you rake the dirt yourself. You lied to us so you wouldn't be a suspect in the kidnapping of one of the orphans next door. Why did you rake the area?"

La Barca's hands began to shake, and he hid them under the table. "I always rake beyond the rows before we pick the grapes."

"You always rake a certain area that just happens to have evidence of a crime?"

"The weeds along the fence are starting to die. It's easier to pull them in the fall."

"But the weeds continue to grow along the fence all the way to the road. Why only do the middle section?"

"The nun—Sister Angela—showed me the window where there was an eyewitness who described the kidnapper. When we were there, I noticed the weeds. Onlookers from the road might think I was being inattentive. I started in the middle section because I figured police would be examining the place and notice it. I didn't even consider the police would need to comb the area for more evidence."

Pagano let out a long sigh.

"Do I need an *avvocato*?"

"Yes, I'm just trying to make up my mind whether to keep you or to let you go."

"On what charges?"

"You lied to us about who raked."

"I only did that because I didn't want everyone to know my vineyard isn't as successful as those around us."

"How many people work for you?" The chief detective slapped down a piece of paper and pencil on the table in front of the suspect. "I want their names and the names of your suppliers—anyone connected with you and your operation. We'll come back in a while with my decision."

The interrogators left the room. The nun poured water from a pitcher into a paper cup on the table before she too walked outside the door with the cup. The three reconvened in Pagano's office.

"Well, what do you think?" asked Pagano.

"I don't think he's giving us the whole story," said Sacco. "I just don't believe him."

"I have to confess I did see him glance around the area when we were at the last vine," said Sister Angela. "Maybe he was embarrassed. Let's ask ourselves why he'd claw through the vine to find the cloth if he were guilty. Was he trying to pin the kidnapping on the old nun because he'd heard the stories a witness had told? That's a possibility. I suppose you already figured that out because you asked him to write down the names of his suppliers."

"I don't think he'd lead us to the truck that took her away by writing it down as I requested. I'll send out a team to get molds of tire tracks when we go back there to investigate."

"What about the wife?" asked Sacco. "Do you think she's in on it? We should be out there now."

"I have a car in front of the vineyard. If she comes out, they'll call us."

"He told me she was away visiting family," said Sister Angela. "Someone should check on that too."

"So you both think he's guilty."

"I'm not sure," responded the nun. "Do you think he sold the child for money?"

"It sounds like he needed cash to keep the operation going. The quicker we find out who did it, the more likely we are to find her alive. We can't just sit here. I'm afraid La Barca's just going to have to sit it out in jail, Sister. Hopefully he'll be out in time to pick his grapes. But that'll probably only happen if we find the child."

Sister Angela stepped outside and bought herself a slice of pizza from the cart along the curb.

Not long afterward, Chief Detective Pagano joined her. "I was going to offer you lunch. You moved too quickly."

Sister Angela smiled. "One of the nuns told me the food from the vender at this cart's good. I had some the other day, and it was delicious." She sipped on an orange soda. "Has anyone seen Martino's wife?"

"No. You said you were there for a tour. Did you see her then?"

"He said she'd gone to visit relatives. If your scouts don't see her, maybe you should find out where she is. She might be involved, you know."

"I'm well aware of that. I should have asked him when we questioned him. Next time I see him, he'll have his *avvocato*—a definite obstacle to our efforts to find her."

"There's another angle to this."

"What?" asked Pagano.

"Does she exist? Before you go looking all over for her, you might want to check and see if he actually has a wife."

"Well as soon as we're finished with lunch, we'll all head over to the vineyard. Maybe she'll be there."

The nun took another bite of her pizza. "Do you think the *avvocato* will beat us there?"

"A good *avvocato* will want his lunch first. Then

he'll head over here to talk to his client. We have a bit of time before he figures out where we are."

"Moving to another part of our investigation, I was on the seven o'clock train from the mountains last night."

The chief detective stopped mid bite and swallowed hard. "The one that was stopped?"

"Yes. They never told us what that was all about. Did we hit a cow?"

"No. Someone stuffed a large burlap bag full of tires and hay and threw it across the tracks. The train conductor thought it was a body. I suppose it looked like a body from his vantage point. My men figured there might have an explosive inside so they had to get the bomb squad out there. It wasn't a bomb." He turned to face her. "You were on that train? I wish I'd known. One of my crew might have offered you a ride into town."

"Why would anyone do that?"

"Block the train? Do you think it had to do with your being on it? Again, who in Castel Valori did you talk to?"

"Let me see. I saw nuns, a priest, and the police. I don't think any of them would let it slip that I was an investigator assisting you. I doubt it had anything to do with me. Is it related to the case? I'll have to think about that. Was there any other reason someone would want to delay the train?"

"What did the priest say? He knew of no one who might have left the young child on a doorstep."

"No. He only had the warning from a woman that a child might be living at the convent."

"That person could have known the child was

there because she was the one who placed the child there. You mentioned the bell at the convent—that someone would've had to leave the child and ring the bell. What did the woman the priest saw look like?"

"It was in the confessional, so Father Montez didn't actually see the woman. She said she witnessed the child out walking with a nun. You may be right, but the priest wouldn't be able to identify her so there doesn't seem to be a way we can find the woman to question her."

The two finished their lunches and placed the plates and cups on the counter.

"We should have a team waiting for us. Why don't we see what we can find at the vineyard?"

The hot sun slipped behind a line of clouds just as Sister Angela emerged from Pagano's car. *Relief from the heat*, she said. *Thank you.*

"We need to get this going before it storms," said Pagano to one of his detectives. "Have your men start digging."

"Where are you digging?" asked Sister Angela. "What do you suspect?"

"We have to check the area where La Barca tried to cover evidence."

"You think we might find a body buried there?" she asked.

"I don't know. Didn't one of your orphans see the old nun? You reported La Barca discovered a piece of evidence in that area."

"Well yes. I would've concentrated on the vine where the swatch was torn off."

"Then why did he have to rake the area from there to the fence? We could've scanned it for footprints. Do you think he did it innocently?"

The nun and chief detective walked down the aisle between some of the grapevines in the direction of the raked area. *But a body is a leap. Do the police think Pia might be buried there? Possibly, yes. Probably, no.* Sister Angela remembered walking over the area when she was with Grazia. At the time, neither of them noticed any turned or loose soil. *Could the old nun have come back and buried Pia later?*

Her thoughts were interrupted by a policeman rapidly approaching. "There's no one in the house. I left the papers on a table, sir."

"Is there evidence his wife still lives there?"

"Yes, there are clothes in the closet. It looks like a woman lives there. But the kitchen's a mess—like she isn't there now."

"He could've been telling the truth," said the nun. "She might be visiting relatives."

"Or she could've left him. Check for address books. Is there a computer?"

"Yes, a laptop. I'll bag that."

"What about a cell phone?"

"He brought that with him to the station."

"Call in and get someone to find her number. If she's visiting relatives, they'll be communicating."

The two continued to the end of the row. Several men marked the area with twine and had already begun digging. The nun walked up to the vine on the end. La Barca had lovingly trimmed the broken branches. She reached under the remaining ones and pushed them aside, checking them as her eyes followed the vine's twisty trunk to the ground.

"I'm sure La Barca already checked under there," said Pagano.

"Look down here, Ricco," she said. "The ground's been watered down."

"What do you mean?" He pushed aside the branches of the vine next to it. "This one's dry. Why would he only water one?"

"Because a bucket of water would tamp down dirt that has been recently turned."

"When you finish there," he said to one of his men. "Take out this vine here."

"Please remove it carefully," Sister Angela said. "These vines are worth quite a bit of money. La Barca's going to need the money to pay his *avvocato*."

The chief detective and Sister Angela made a quick tour of the house.

"Do you see anything of interest here, Sister?"

"The bed's still made. It looks like he's been sleeping on top of the spread. Her drawers are partially empty, like she planned to come back."

"Or left in a hurry."

"Her toothbrush isn't in the bathroom. Everything looks as if she'll be gone for a short time. There are more suitcases in the hall closet. Are they empty?"

"Check these," he said to one of his men.

Sister Angela gazed at Pagano.

"What?" he asked.

"If your men do find a body, it might not be Pia's."

"Let's go to the winery and see what Elmo's discovered."

She followed him into the next building.

Detective Sergeant Sacco approached them. We've found nothing new here. It looks like it's a business. That's all.

Someone in a white lab coat, now smudged with dirt, approached from behind them. He carried a plastic bag.

"We found something."

"What is it?" asked the nun, pulling the bag toward her and tipping it for more light.

"It's a frock," said the man in white. "A black frock."

"Where did you find it?"

"We were digging out that vine you asked us to remove, and the shovel got caught on it. We left the vine where it was."

Pagano smiled. "I didn't want another body anyway. Good job."

"Sir, over here!" Another voice echoed through the cavernous chamber.

Sister Angela and Pagano rushed to his side.

"I removed the lid from this clay pot," said the young assistant inspector. He tilted the amphora so they could all take a peek. "It looks like this isn't just wine. I see a something bobbing, don't you?"

The nun let out a sigh, grabbing the beads tied at her waist. "It isn't Pia, is it?" she asked.

"Empty it," ordered Pagano.

Elmo and the assistant inspector overturned the amphora and carefully let the wine spill out over the tiles. "We're going to have to find a better way to empty the others," Elmo said as he laid the earthen vessel on its side.

The man from the lab who had followed them with his bag removed his muddy gloves and replaced them with clean ones. He crouched down, reached into the amphora, and carefully tugged. "Lift the bottom slightly so I can get a better grip."

Under her breath, Sister Angela continued her litany of prayers. The chief detective pulled out a handkerchief and placed it over his nose.

"Here she comes," said the lab tech.

The form slipped out of the top and onto the white tiles, gooey with congealing red wine.

"Who is it?" asked Pagano.

The nun looked down at the body. The knees were tucked up, and the arms crossed the upper torso. "It's in the fetal position. Pull it apart, if you can. It's a man. There are his shoes. Tug on those. Elmo, pull him from the other end—under his arms here. Can you straighten him out?"

Elmo reluctantly placed his hands under the man's armpits and held on while the lab tech yanked the feet.

"Look, Ricco," she said. "He's taller and thinner than he looked at first. I know you can't do it here, but if you removed the frock from the plastic bag and placed it over his front like he was trying it on, you'd see what the children saw."

"You think our frock is a habit?" he asked, still

looking a unsure.

"And I think our body's a part-time old nun who likes little girls. Now we have to make sure this is the only body. If Pia isn't here, we'll need to figure out how our dead man relates to our vintner and why he took Pia."

Chapter Fifteen

First it was the picking season. Viviana busied herself trying to keep up with the tour buses that lined the long drive. The tourists crowded into the small tasting room, asking her to pour them more as soon as they finished savoring a particular wine. The crushing season was even more hectic as she rushed to clean the tasting goblets between customers. She couldn't leave a bottle on the tall counter Giulio built for her because it would disappear among the throngs. Empties speckled the drive, revealed only after the lines of buses had left.

She didn't see much of Giulio. He was busy making sure the grape juice fermented and turned into the kind of Chianti he wanted. She often arrived before six, hoping to catch a glimpse of him before preparing for the masses of visitors that would soon overpower her. But the only thing she saw were the trucks, delivering supplies the vintners would need to produce the wine.

Just as quickly, it was over. The season was coming to an end, and the number of buses and cars slowed. She finally had a breather to find him.

"He's gone," said Ermanno, stooping over his stacks of receipts.

"What do you mean? Where'd he go?"

Ermanno bent down and pulled an empty bottle from a cupboard under his counter. "We don't let customers drink the whole bottle—at least not for free. I don't want to find any more of these on the property. You'll reimburse me for this one."

"Where's Giulio?"

"He's on the road. He's making appearances to introduce the restaurants and stores to our wonderful wines. You don't get a great reputation by hiding out." He never looked up from his papers.

"When's he expected back?"

"In a couple of weeks."

"It's slowing down now. Is there any work I can do to keep me busy through the winter? Remember I can file or track things for you."

Ermanno looked up. "Our mother needs a companion. If you're not busy, you can check on her. Serena has a job in town, and Mamma shouldn't be left alone."

Back in the tasting room, she sat at the counter and sulked. Why didn't Ermanno want her near the business? She'd have to wait for Giulio to return and ask him to find something more for her to do.

Giulio returned home for Christmas but didn't stay long. Relief from Viviana's long hours of caring for relatives, however, was changing. Her aunts decided to send Nonna, whom Viviana had continued to tend to after work, to a nursing home closer to Roma while her aunts continued to live in the house.

One morning in January as Viviana was leaving for work, Clarissa asked, "Why are you wearing pants?"

"Because it's too cold to wear a dress. My boss is out of town. I can wear whatever I want when he isn't there. These aren't just pants. I pulled up leggings on the outside to keep me warm too."

"Do they have you working with the grapes? What kind of job do you have?"

"No, it hasn't changed. We have fewer customers this time of year." Just as she said it, she had an idea. Maybe Ermanno would let her box up cartons of wine for the online customers. At least the physical labor would keep her warm.

Spring arrived early with the bud break.

On her way to work, Viviana found Giulio in the fields examining the vines. "You're back."

Giulio smiled, but not for long. "What are you wearing? I can't believe Ermanno let you come to work like that."

"Didn't he tell you? I'm caring for your mother. There weren't enough visitors for winetasting. He decided to take over that job."

"No he didn't tell me. We should be getting more visitors in a few weeks. I'll make sure you go back to that job. You have to start dressing to do yours. I won't have you looking like a boy." He touched her arm, and she shivered.

"Where were you all this time?"

He smiled. "My big brother doesn't like to schmooze. He sends me out to do TV appearances and cooking programs."

"You must get a lot of attention from the ladies."

"You shouldn't be jealous. It doesn't suit you. You do perfectly well when you're in a dress and heels. I was surprised you lasted the whole season without being hoisted onto one of the buses and taken to New York."

"I have to get to the house," she said. "Ermanno gets angry when I'm late."

"I'll talk to him. He mentioned that he wanted to put tables and chairs outside the tasting room this year. We can accommodate more tourists that way."

"I'll be a waitress too? Next you'll expect me to serve them food."

"At least I'll be able to watch you work when you come out of the tasting room."

Viviana didn't speak with him again until the tiny star-like blossoms began to drop from the vines. She'd begun to wear dresses again, just in case he was around. A few buses grew to several, and she was beginning to get busy.

One warm evening Giulio entered her tasting room and asked to savor some of the wine. When she put a bottle on the counter, he grabbed it. "C'mon, I have dinner waiting."

She smiled. "Thank you for hiring someone to take care of your mother. It's good to be back."

"I have a picnic basket for us in a quiet corner with a view."

"I must put up this picture first," she said. She removed her heels, climbed onto one of the stools, and stepped from there onto the counter. "This isn't very steady," she said. "Don't let me fall." She bent down to pick up the picture and hammer at her feet.

He held her ankles. "You've got good balance."

When she was finished, she squatted and sat on top of the counter, her bare feet dangling over the side facing Giulio. He reached down and rubbed her feet. His hands traveled up to her thighs, and she felt her cheeks flush. "Help me down so I can get my shoes."

He led her past the farmhouse and shed to a clear spot on the ridge overlooking the river. The shed blocked any view of them from the farmhouse windows. Beside it, a picnic table sported a checkered tablecloth and basket. He placed the bottle of wine on the table. On the river side, the village shimmered with lights.

"Your table," he said. "Sit down and let me take your shoes before you break a heel. He got down on a knee and slid off her shoes, lingering to kiss each bare foot.

"Are you sure you want to eat?" she asked, sitting at the table.

"Of course," he said, climbing over the bench to sit beside her. He removed a dish of oil from the basket. Then he grabbed a loaf of bread and tore off a piece, dipping it into oil before taking a bite. The oil rolled down his chin, and he wiped it with his forearm. "I have vegetables in here. They taste great when you dip them in the oil too." He offered some to Viviana.

She dipped her bread into the oil and took a bite, the oil dripping down the front of her blouse. Giulio laughed and opened the top button of her blouse, leaned forward, and licked the tops of her breasts.

Viviana visibly shuddered.

Giulio watched her but said nothing. He grabbed a cherry tomato and bit into it, the juices collecting in the corners of his mouth. Then he leaned forward and kissed her on the mouth. She responded by inching toward him, continuing the kiss as he pulled his leg over the bench to straddle it. They parted, and he tore a pepper into two pieces. He reached into the basket and pulled out a sauce. He dipped each piece and handed her one of them. With the sauce that remained on his hands, he reached over and wiped them above her bra. Then he leaned forward and licked the spots, caressing her breasts with his free hand. He moaned.

Wishing he'd do more, Viviana didn't pull away, but she was beginning to doubt she'd be able to stop him. He climbed off the bench, quickly put away the food, and removed the basket from the tabletop. Then he scaled the table, and lying down on his side, gestured for Viviana to join him. She rose and held his hand as she carefully stepped onto the bench and stood above him. He slid to one side and patted the table beside him. He pointed at the sky.

"The stars," he said. "They're beautiful tonight."

Viviana lay on her back and looked up. The twinkling sky reminded her of the ceiling of her childhood bedroom. Papà had stuck glow-in-the-dark stars to it. Then he left Mara and her. Where was he now? Did he ever think about her?

Viviana had unconsciously lifted her knees and felt Giulio's hand slide along her thighs, slowly inching up her skirt. She closed her eyes and felt his hand lift the leg of her panties. Her knee dropped to the side so he could explore the fleece that protected her secrets. She felt the rush of dampness and tried to pull her knee back up, but he reached over her and yanked her panties over her knees to her ankles. Should she tell him to stop now?

If he wasn't liking what he felt, he didn't let on. He explored her further until her back arched. He smiled and pushed her legs down, the panties hanging off of one foot, and pulled her on top of him. She moved with him, as he drew up her chin to kiss her lips.

"You're so beautiful," he whispered in between kisses. "I don't deserve you." His breathing became rough.

Straddling him, she sat up. He urged her back as he unzipped his jeans and pushed them down. She knew what he was doing, but tried not to look when he placed her hand on him. The heat of it surprised her as she caressed it. Then he pulled her down and rolled them both over, nearly pushing her off the edge. But he didn't drop her. He drew her back under him and tugged her knees up again.

Realizing that it was too late to tell him she didn't want it, she lay there as he made his way into her. He slowed, asking her if she was all right, and when she saw his beautiful, concerned eyes, she lifted her feet and let him make her move to his rhythm. She grabbed his shoulders and felt her resistance escape through her fingers. And just as her body tensed, the stars seemed explode. Giulio thrust once more, and she consumed him until they were one. She clung to the sensation for long seconds before she realized how heavy he was.

She nudged him, and he slid off of her. "You're wonderful, Viviana."

She smiled. "You're pretty good too. Is there anything else in the basket?"

Their relationship had changed. Viviana's dress became less businesslike and more revealing each day. She even moved differently, watching Giulio over her shoulder as he passed by. Less than a week later, he asked her to dinner again. This time he had spread a blanket on the ground, making it even easier to move around.

After four or five encounters, they stopped. The sun stayed later in the sky, making it more difficult to hide in the dark.

The flowers on the vines had disappeared, replaced with tight bunches of young grapes. Tourists were beginning to show up, making it difficult for Viviana to flirt with Giulio, who was much busier trying to produce bottles of his product.

Viviana was late to work one day, and Ermanno made a point of chastising her for her laziness. She tried to ignore him, but it ate at her throughout the day.

As the last tourists found seats on their tour busses, Giulio suddenly appeared at the door with more bottles. "I figured your stash was low. It's getting busy. We should talk about that idea to have tables outside. The ambiance would be good," he said, moving to the back of the room to place the wine where she could get it.

"Ermanno yelled at me today."

"Yeah, he said you were late." He put his hands around her waist and pulled her toward him. "I hate it when we're too busy to see each other." He kissed her on the nose.

"I wasn't that late."

"No problem. He won't do anything about it. He needs every hand he can get, and you're really good at what you do. I thought I could take you into town, and we could grab a bite at the restaurant near the church."

She smiled. "I guess we need to talk anyway. I'm not sure we did that during our picnics."

He laughed. "We learned a lot not talking to each other. And I enjoyed it. Do you have more comfortable shoes you can wear into town?"

"It doesn't bother you if I wear low heels? That's good because I have another pair in my purse."

At a quiet restaurant, as Giulio seated her at the table and began to talk about their plans for the tasting room.

"It's going to be more work."

"Maybe two or three at first," he said. "With umbrellas, of course. Let's see if you can handle two or three. No food. Just tasting. Or they can buy a bottle and enjoy it there."

"As long as the empties aren't taken out of my salary."

He poured her some wine, but she put her hand up to stop him. "You don't want wine?" he asked.

She gestured to the waitress and asked for water.

Giulio froze while pouring wine into his own glass. "Is something wrong?"

"Yes, dear. I have something to tell you too. You're such a good farmer. You're able to produce more than grapes." At first she couldn't bring herself to look into his eyes, but the silence finally made her look up.

He stared at her, his gray eyes showing little but love and concern. She felt herself exhale.

"We'll have to do something about that."

What did he mean? Was he asking her to take care of the predicament? The rush of a giant wave suddenly made it difficult for her to hear him.

"We have the wine and tables and chairs already. I know Mamma and Serena would love to help you with the wedding. We don't have time for a honeymoon, but we should plan the ceremony soon so we don't let it run into the harvest."

She stared back at him. Finally understanding, she smiled. "That would be fine. The answer is *yes.*"

Chapter Sixteen

Sister Angela cleared her throat as she and Pagano sat down at the table, waiting for someone to bring in the suspect. The door finally opened, and La Barca was dragged to a seat at one end.

"Have you found my wife?" he asked.

Pagano looked up. "I've just received a report. Yes, your wife has been found in Triesa. Apparently she left you about two weeks ago. Again you tell us lies."

"Carlota can verify that I usually kill the weeds along the fence right before harvest."

"Did your wife help you in the winery?"

"Yes. She didn't work all the time but filled in when we were shorthanded."

Sacco entered and walked directly up to his boss. "I have Signor La Barca's list of workers and can take a few men out to help me interview them."

"How many are there?"

"Five."

"Does that include the suppliers?"

"Yes. Not too many to tackle in one day, sir," he said, heading for the door.

"Signora La Barca must have helped you much of the time," he said, turning to face the winemaker. "I'm surprised you could run the winery with so few people."

"Workers come and go. I'll need to hire more in a week or so to help with the harvest."

"Who's checking the aging Chianti to see when the wine's ready?"

"It depends which amphora you're talking about. Each year's wine's aged in different areas of the winery. The wine that's been aged the longest has charts. Winemakers, usually myself but sometimes assistants, also do tests on the resting wine at least once monthly. That's why I hire people—to help perform tests that include ones for sugar content, acidity, sulfur, and percent alcohol."

"How do these charts indicate who checked the wine in all the amphorae?" asked Sister Angela.

"Every person who touches an amphora has to mark what actions he or she performed and initial the chart."

"That includes all the amphorae?" asked the nun.

"Yes. Once fermentation has taken place, the wine's poured into a clay vessel to be aged."

Pagano leaned forward. "Evidently, the last person to initial the sheet on one particular clay pot was your wife exactly two weeks ago."

"Carlota went to her family on the twenty-seventh of last month. She must have checked the wine just before she left."

"I suppose if your wife tampered with that particular amphora, she wouldn't have signed her initials." He handed the chart to La Barca. "Can you verify that these are your wife's initials?"

La Barca carefully studied the initials. "They look like hers."

Sister Angela interrupted. "Martino, why exactly

did Carlota leave?"

The vintner sighed. "She complained for months before she left that I worked all the time. She threatened on several occasions in the last few weeks that she'd run off with one of the workers." He looked up at Sister Angela. "I didn't believe her because she didn't seem to pay attention to any of them. I guess she wanted more from me. I was too busy to give her more attention."

"What do you mean?" asked the nun.

"She thought her life would be easier—marrying a successful winemaker. It was a fantasy, of course. All the winemakers I know work many hours."

"How long have you been married?"

"Three years."

"And no children?"

"We'd planned to have children, yes. But the winery struggled to make money. Our nest egg never grew."

"Perhaps Carlota left because she was afraid you didn't want children."

"She might have complained about waiting," said La Barca. "I thought she'd come back sooner so I didn't touch her things. I figured she left them because she planned to return. I told you she was with her family, but I didn't know for sure. Did she say she planned to return?"

Pagano squirmed. "We didn't ask her that. We may have to bring her back though."

"Why? Does she need to verify her initials? Why don't you take the chart to her?"

Pagano looked up, seeming to scrutinize the prisoner's face. "You don't want her here? Are you trying to protect her or do you think she witnessed the crime?"

La Barca's body visibly stiffened. "What crime? Did you find the orphan?"

The nun followed his gaze to the chief detective.

Pagano appeared uncomfortable. "Your wife seems to have been the last one to check the wine in a clay vat that was broken into."

"Carlota would've reported there was a breach in one of the amphorae. An amphora holds a lot of wine. The loss could be staggering."

"She wouldn't have been able to test for sugars or check for its acidity," said Pagano.

"Are you saying she signed the chart but didn't do the work?"

"No, Signor La Barca. I'm telling you that the wine had been dumped out and replaced with a dead body. This chart suggests your wife was involved in a homicide."

The guards removed La Barca when they heard yelling in the interrogation room. Pagano ordered espresso and cookies for the two remaining interrogators and sat across from the nun at the table.

"The fact that Carlota initialed the chart doesn't mean she murdered the old nun," said Sister Angela. "The chart actually indicates the acidity level. If she went to the trouble to dump out some of the wine and replace the space with a body, she wouldn't have signed it, let alone tasted it."

"Perhaps I just wanted to stir things up."

"And what does Martino's response tell you."

"That he probably wasn't acting. He didn't seem to know about the body. I hoped he'd try to defend his wife, but he seemed surprised by our discovery."

"That chart tells us our old nun was murdered about a ago," said Sister Angela. "If Carlota signed the sheet and then left immediately, there was only Martino left to man the winery at night. Our interviews with the workers will shed more light on that."

Sacco entered with a report from the medical examiner. Before reading it, he reached for one of the cookies. Sister Angela and Pagano waited for him to swallow.

"The victim was stabbed with a small knife. He was dead when he was stuffed into the amphora. About three-quarters of the wine remained in the amphora so his head was submerged, but there was no wine in his lungs."

"I suppose we still don't know the victim's name."

"No. There's nothing in the report."

"Elmo, you went through the clothing on the body," said Pagano. "Was there nothing in the pockets?"

"No," said Sacco.

"Which would be unusual. Someone must have emptied them to hide his identity," said Sister Angela. "There was a partner."

"How do you know?" asked Sacco.

"Because someone had to have taken Pia from him. Until we discover the child's body, she's still out there. The question is who took her and why?"

"Tomorrow I'm going back to the convent," said Sister Angela at dinner. She buttered a piece of bread. "I need to find out where Pia came from. There has to be some connection to her kidnapping."

"But the old nun's here," said Sister Daniela. "The connection's to the winery next door to the orphanage."

Taking a sip of Chianti, Sister Angela turned to face Michel. "Suppose you've just signed the chart above one of your barrels. If you'd murdered someone and stuffed him inside the barrel, would your have signed it?"

"Probably not. I'd have to cut up the body to get him into one of my barrels."

"So Carlota La Barca most likely tasted the wine and signed the chart and went home. At dinnertime, she found that her husband was running late so she made her decision. She'd depart and go home to her parents. That leaves her husband home alone. Sometime during the week, someone murdered Pia's abductor and, when all was quiet, dumped out enough wine to hold the body."

"Why do you say that?" asked Michel.

"Because if the killer hadn't dumped out some of the wine, the wine would've spilled over the top and stained the clay vessel."

"Would you know that, Sister?" asked Sister Daniela. "I wouldn't know to dump some of it out. I would've made a mess of the amphora."

The mature nun gazed at her friend. "You're right. We must conclude the killer knew something about the winery."

The nun looked over at Susanna who sat dreamily next to her husband. "Are you feeling all right, Susanna? You haven't said a thing. Aren't I giving you a chance to speak?"

"I'm fine. I just don't understand why you wouldn't check the other workers. It sounds like a local abduction and murder to me. Aren't you all making this more complicated?"

Sister Angela smiled. "You're right. But while we're rounding up and interviewing the workers and suppliers, some of us can be following other leads. I believe the kidnapping somehow involves the child's past."

"We don't know anything about her past, do we?" said Sister Daniela. "I thought that was a dead end."

"I'm not so sure. That's why I need you, Sister Daniela. Someone should be following what's happening with the investigation here. I don't think La Barca or his wife was involved, but neither has explained how the nun's habit was buried under the vine and why Martino watered down the dirt over the hole it was buried in or why he raked the entire area, covering up any evidence we could've used to find Pia."

Sister Daniela suddenly sat up. "You'll have to speak with Mother Faustine, of course. Someone will have to take over in the classroom."

"That might pose a problem. Do you think one

of your students can help out there?"

"I'm willing to do whatever Mother Faustine tells me to do. You know that. I'm always up for investigative work."

After a call from the chief detective, Sister Daniela drove to the station in Siena. She, Pagano, and Sacco convened in the interrogation room and sat around the table to enjoy a morning coffee. The break lasted only five minutes before Pagano asked Sacco for a report.

"We have five workers—all temporary. I thought La Barca said he had a fulltime winemaker helping him, didn't he? None of these qualifies as a winemaker."

"He probably only wanted to convey that his establishment was professional," said Pagano. "He has a propensity for lying. Did the workers have any records?"

"No. We were able to look up each one. They have all worked in this or that winery all over the valley."

"So we've established what? The old nun never worked there, right?"

"No. Our victim wasn't one of the workers."

"And La Barca's workers are all clean. Did you interview them?"

"Yes."

"Were their stories all the same?"

"No. They weren't there together. Some worked

for a while months ago. They worked and then quit before others replaced them. They explained their jobs differently. Some tended the grapes while others followed the winemaking procedures."

"That's not good enough," said Pagano. "I want to talk to them, even the ones who worked previously. Each probably realized that a body wouldn't be discovered right away and also knew to empty an amphora just enough so the wine inside didn't overflow. What about the suppliers?"

"We're still tracking them down."

"Were they regular to La Barca's winery? Had all been paid? Do any have records of some sort in the database? Have we checked who delivered dirt or chemicals to the vines? I can see someone standing among the vines watching the children next door."

"That's just it," said Sister Daniela. "You're finally talking about Pia. Someone probably killed the old nun and absconded with Pia. We need more connections. We should be working on the old nun's identity. Then we can find out who's associated with the victim."

"We sent off his fingerprints and dental records looking for a match," said Sacco. "No response yet. He may not be on our radar. You're correct, Sister. We need to match the workers and suppliers to the victim, but they could've worked together anywhere. What we need is a break."

"If you don't mind, I think I'll go back to ground zero."

"What do you mean?"

"I think I can help best if I see all the evidence you've collected from Pia's abduction. I want to see all fingerprints, footprints, and tire tracks. I believe I heard there was nothing in the murder victim's pockets or in the habit pockets. I want to see the evidence and satisfy myself that there's nothing about the clothing that's remarkable."

"What about La Barca's wife?"

"You know where she is?"

"Yes, she's in Triesa. It's not far from here. I have the address."

"You want me to interview her? You'll have to fill me in."

"A little more than week ago, Carlota La Barca left her husband," said Sacco. "He says she was visiting family. That's where her family lives. We got him to admit that perhaps she left to break up the marriage."

"A little more than week ago is when the abduction took place," said Sister Daniela."

"Yes. We suspect she was in on it, or at least helped plan it and that La Barca sent her away so she wouldn't be blamed for anything."

"You want me to see if she was involved."

"I want you to use your powers of observation," said Pagano. "She might roll her eyes or shed a tear. Hell, if she sneezes, I want to know about it. We don't need to waste more time on her if she's innocent."

"I understand."

"I also want to find out what she knows about our murder victim."

"Wasn't he killed after she left?"

"But he might have been around the scene before the murder. We need a name. To get that we'll have to have details about his life so someone else can identify him." He slipped a photograph from his pocket and jotted an address on a piece of paper. "Here's Signora La Barca's address and a photo we found in the farmhouse. I'd give you her cell number, but she might be a runner. I don't think you should warn her that you're coming."

Chapter Seventeen

Sister Angela slowly ascended the steps in front of the convent and lifted her arm to ring the bell. While she waited for one of the nuns to answer, she turned back to admire the view. The smell of ripe grapes wafted up the hill. They were almost ready. The musty smell lingered in her nostrils.

"Hello, Sister Angela," said Sister Tiberia. The tall nun bent down to grab Sister Angela's bag. "Let me help you with this. I can't believe you carried it all the way from the terminal. Come in. Come in. It's so hot. Please come through to the kitchen. I have some cold juice waiting for you. After you rest and hydrate, one of us can show you to your room. The fan's on, cooling it down so you'll be comfortable."

The nuns gathered in the front room before dinner to listen to Sister Angela's plan.

Tiny Sister Baptista continued to knit while Sister Concetta pulled more chairs to the center of the room. "I love our refurbished furniture," she said. "It's so comfortable."

"Please update us," said the prioress. "We've heard nothing since you left."

"Let me see," said Sister Angela, wriggling deeper into the soft cushion of her chair. "The police have arrested the winemaker who lives next door to the orphanage."

"They know who kidnapped her?" asked Sister Baptista, stopping her knitting needles mid stitch.

"No. Signor La Barca did some clearing of his vineyard right where there might have been proof the kidnapper was there."

"What proof?"

"Signor La Barca himself found a piece of nun's habit. If you remember, the children identified the kidnapper as a tall nun. But then he raked the area around it and watered the particular vine that hid the swatch of nun's habit so no one would be able to find more. He lied when the police questioned him about it."

"Why did he do that?" asked Sister Oriana, who had entered the room after taking out the bread baking in the oven.

Sister Angela didn't answer right away. The aroma that filled the front room was heavenly.

"I'm serving the bread at dinner," Sister Oriana said. "So the police arrested him because he lied?"

"Not exactly. They arrested Signor La Barca because he was the only suspect in the death of the old nun."

"The old nun died?" said Mother Patrizia.

"A man's body was recovered from one of Signora La Barca's amphora."

"What's that?" asked Sister Concetta.

"The winemaker aged his wine in large clay pots."

"I thought you said the old nun died," said Sister Tiberia.

"The old nun who kidnapped Pia turned out to be a tall man in disguise."

"Maybe he tried to hide in the clay pot, and someone poured wine over his head," said Sister Concetta.

"They discovered the habit in the same area where Signor Barca found the swatch. The medical examiner theorized that the man had been killed before he was hidden in the amphora. Signora La Barca was the last person to check the wine in that vessel. It was only then that Signor La Barca admitted his wife left him. The police have now found her, and my assistant, Sister Daniela, is going to Triesa to interview her."

"What about Pia?" asked Sister Tiberia. "Her kidnapper's dead, and the police have arrested his murderer. Did the police look in all the pots? Did Pia get away? Perhaps she's with the wife."

"Sister Daniela will check on that."

"Then why are you here?" asked the prioress. "You should be in Triesa too. They're so close to finding her."

"I don't believe the case will be that easy to solve, Reverend Mother. I have some investigating of my own to do here around Castel Valori. In the morning, I think I'll visit the Detective Sergeant in town about how his investigation's going. Maybe he can help me go over some of the unsolved cases that went on near here. If he won't help me, then I'll just have to do it myself."

"But if Sister Daniela finds something in Triesa, she'll call you won't she?" asked Sister Concetta.

"Of course. She'll call me tomorrow evening no matter what she's found. I have my little red mobile here in my pocket. She can get hold of me anytime."

Sister Oriana served them soup and bread for dinner. Sister Angela was hungry. She couldn't wait to slather butter on her piece of homemade bread and, when served, sat back to enjoy every bite. The nuns handed Sister Angela a second piece to dip in her soup. She was quite satisfied when she felt the buzz of the phone in her pocket. They all looked up.

"Excuse me," she said, walking back to the front room before answering it.

"Hi," said Sister Daniela. "I'm here in Triesa."

"You haven't approached her yet, have you?"

"No. I'm in my hotel room. I just wanted to let you know that I arrived safely."

Sister Angela smiled. "Was there anything new when you talked to Ricco and Elmo at the station before you left?"

"Only that the old nun wasn't one of La Barca's workers. Why would he kill someone he never met?"

"That doesn't mean he didn't know him. The old nun could have worked for Martino at another time or knew him in another context. Perhaps it has to do with his wife."

"Maybe La Barca killed the old nun because he suspected his wife was having an affair with her—I mean him," said Sister Daniela. "Elmo also said they interviewed all the current workers and all their stories were similar. That indicates to me that either they're all telling the truth or they rehearsed their stories and are all guilty."

"But no one seemed to know the old nun or even noticed the children next door."

"No. Tomorrow they're interviewing suppliers. Someone must have noticed the victim. How did the old nun get around? Did he have a car? If so, where is it? In fact, I asked the chief detective and Elmo a lot of questions, but they answered almost none of them. I'm sure I exhausted them. That must be why they decided to ship me off to Triesa."

"They sent you to Triesa to do a very important job," said Sister Angela. "Not only must you approach Carlota without scaring her off, but at the same time, you have to get into her house and make sure she doesn't have Pia there."

"The police didn't mention that. Of course we have to find that out."

"I suggest you get Carlota to trust you. Buy her an espresso or something to relax her. You can ask her a few questions about what went on."

"That's sort of what the chief detective and Elmo suggested. I'm not to tell her about the murder and our suspicions about her right away. I thought I might talk to her about her relationship with her husband and why she came to Triesa. I have to see if someone has told her about what has happened with her husband and what's going on in Filari before I go into any of the detail."

"And if you can't get her to take you home with

her, you must go to the police in Triesa and get them to check the house."

"I understand. This is exciting. I'm glad you let me get involved in the investigation."

The nun hung up the phone and hesitated. *Me too, Sister. I'm afraid Mother Margherita's going to take away my veil herself if she ever finds out that I've put you in danger. I'm going to have to repeat three mysteries on my beads tonight.*

Sister Daniela sat down at a table in a café along Via del Corso in Triesa. *Via del Corso's the main street in Triesa*, thought the nun, smiling. *Actually, it's the only street in Triesa.*

Suddenly, she heard a name and turned to look at the counter.

"*Due cornetti per favore,*" said the customer.

"Si, Signora La Barca. *Altro?*"

"Signora La Barca?" the nun asked nearly turning over the cup of espresso she was sipping. "Carlota La Barca?"

The woman took her bag from the cashier, spun around, and stared in the nun's direction.

"You probably don't recognize me. I'm the teacher at the orphanage next to your vineyard."

"Ah, one of the nuns," she said, looking as if she wanted to run.

"Please," said Sister Daniela, gesturing her to the other chair at her table. "Let me get you a glass of water."

The woman hesitated.

"How are your parents? Your husband indicated that there might be an illness."

Slowly Signora La Barca approached the table. "My parents are well. What else did he tell you?"

"Perhaps you haven't heard the news from Filari. Much has happened."

"Why are you here?" Carlota asked.

"We're looking for a child who disappeared from the orphanage."

"I don't understand why a runaway would come here. Triesa's a small town."

"Please sit down. It's a long story."

Carlota finally slid into the chair, and Sister Daniela gestured for the waiter to bring water.

"I suppose you weren't planning to come back," said the nun. "That's fine. I understand the difficulties of marriage. Was your husband abusive?"

Carlota looked stunned. "Never. He's a gentle man. Just not a good businessman. What news do you have for me? Is he all right? Has he lost the vineyard yet?"

"Actually I believe it has little to do with business. Do you know this man?" she asked, removing a photo from her pocket and placing it before her guest.

Carlota studied the photo. "No. What's wrong with him? He looks sick."

"He's dead."

Her face paled. "My husband's all right, isn't he?"

"He's in jail for the murder of this man, Signora La Barca."

Carlota glanced around to see if anyone heard what the nun was telling her. "Maybe you can tell me more on the way home. News spreads fast in small villages."

The nun took a last sip of her water and went to pay the baker.

Carlota was already outside when she finished. "How's the orphanage involved in this? How do you know my husband's a suspect in this man's death? Why are you really here?"

"I told you why I was in Triesa. The dead man was disguised as a nun. A child was snatched from the orphanage by an old nun. We have witnesses to the kidnapping."

"If you have witnesses, how was Martino involved?"

"The body of the man was discovered at your vineyard."

"Who is he?" she asked, failing to look at the nun directly. "Was he in our house? Did Martino tell you that he knew him?"

They two woman stopped in front of a small house along the same street.

"We haven't identified him yet. His body wasn't found in your house."

"Please come in," said Carlota. "I have juice or more coffee."

Sister Daniela hesitated. This was her chance to see if there was evidence of Pia in the house—but was she safe? Carlota seemed to be sincere, but was everything just an act to get her inside? Was Carlota a murderer?

She looked into the young woman's brown eyes. "Thank you. I don't want to bother your parents."

"They aren't at home. They have a gift shop in

town and are working during business hours. Please. I want to hear more."

Sister Daniela acquiesced. After all, Sister Angela always told her to go with her gut. The younger nun's gut was in turmoil. Was that telling her something or did she actually need juice or coffee to settle it down?

Carlota led the nun to the kitchen door. Sister Daniela followed silently, listening for any noise that indicated movement in another part of the house. Suddenly she stopped. Something shattered on the hardwood floor around the corner.

"Gattina!" said Carlota, her voice loud. She went around the corner of the short hallway. Sister Daniela followed and discovered the bits of glass at her feet. A black cat lay on his back on the book shelf nearest the hallway.

"Mamma will be so disappointed," Carlota said, picking up a good sized chunk of a crystal object. She stood up. "I'll clean it up later. Please, let's go into the kitchen so I can pour you a drink."

Sister Daniela sat down at the table.

"So let's see if I understand. Martino's been arrested. Are the police checking on others at the winery?"

"Yes. They're also investigating suppliers."

"The murder victim was a man who kidnapped a child at the orphanage dressed in a nun's habit. Who was it?"

"It was Pia."

"How terrible. I know that one. So you came here looking for the child?" She paused. "Oh my God, you must suspect that I'm hiding her. You *wanted* me to bring you here."

Sister Daniela froze, realizing that Carlota was smarter than she thought. "I considered that, yes."

"You think I was in on the kidnapping."

"Possibly in on it, yes. You *do* have ties to the murder, Signora La Barca."

"The house is open to you," she said. "Now that you're here, go ahead and search. You must be closer to the investigation than you told me."

"I never told you I wasn't working with the police. That said, I'll go through the house before I leave, but perhaps you should hear the whole story."

Carlota fell into her chair as the espresso maker hissed and chugged.

"The body of the old nun was found in one of the amphorae."

Carlota looked at her in disbelief.

"He wasn't wearing the habit. That was found buried among the vines. But the children described someone tall and thin. The body fit that description."

"My husband would've noticed the wine stain. If you dump something like that into a vat of wine, the object would displace the wine. The escaping liquid would have stained the terracotta on the outside of the amphora."

"And it didn't. The culprit would've had to empty the amphora and then place the body inside."

"Then he didn't drown."

"No. He was stabbed before being stuffed inside."

"So the murderer knew the amphorae are big enough to hold a man and that it would have to be emptied first. You're looking for someone who knew the industry. The number of wineries that use clay vessels is limited. There aren't too many people who are expert enough to know about them. What about the child? I assume she wasn't found at the scene. That bodes well that she's still alive."

"Yes. One other thing that you should know, Signora La Barca."

"Please call me Carlota. I believe you know me better than you do my husband."

"The chart for that particular amphora was initialed by you just before you left. Is that possible?"

"Yes. I often checked the aging wine. I even add necessary chemicals when needed. I see now why you might suspect me. How long had the body been in the amphora?"

"According to the coroner, the man had been murdered just over a week ago."

"And that's the same time I left my husband." Carlota stood. "I see you've finished your espresso. You said you needed to check the house. Please do that right away. I assure you the *gattina* and I are alone here today. I'll finish my espresso while you're examining the rooms and basement. If you have any questions, I'll be here with my coffee."

"And the shop? Are there places there where a child could be hidden?"

"We can go there when you're finished here."

The nun wanted to apologize for the inconvenience. Her news must have been terrible for Carlota to hear. But she had to remain professional—for Pia.

Chapter Eighteen

Sister Angela sat in a chair across from Detective Sergeant Este Turo. His dark, brooding eyebrows seemed incongruous with his graying hair.

"I don't know what you mean, Sister. The avalanche in Alceda wasn't in my district. I stay out of investigations under the jurisdiction of Inspector Sbarra. I'd have no idea what they found in Alceda."

"I'd like the files, please. This is an investigation concerning the kidnapping of a child. Time's an issue. Perhaps you'd like me to call Chief Detective Ricco Pagano in Siena."

Turo leaned forward in his chair, his arms stretching clear across the desk. "I understand your problem, Sister, but if I request the files now, it'll take the police at least a day to find them and have them delivered here."

"I believe it would be more fruitful to approach Inspector Sbarra myself."

"As you wish," he said, starting to stand.

The nun remained seated.

Turo sat down again. "I'm sorry. I didn't know you needed something else. I'm afraid..."

The nun looked him in the eye. "The nuns at the convent don't have a car. At least they haven't offered me one."

"Are you saying you need me to come with you? If so, I'm too busy to leave the station."

"No, no. I need a car so I can go to Alceda."

A pile of letters plopped down on the detective sergeant's desk, and Turo looked up.

"Some of these need to be taken care of soon," said the young man standing beside the nun's chair.

"Sister Angela," said Turo. "May I present Silvio, my aide."

"I didn't know the police department had aides," she said, looking the dark-haired youth from head to toe. "How old are you?" she asked.

"I'm sixteen," he said.

"Silvio?"

"I'll be sixteen in a couple of weeks, Uncle Este."

"Is your motorbike working, Silvio?" Turo asked.

"Yes. I have it outside."

Turo gestured for his nephew to face the nun.

"You have wheels?" asked the nun.

Silvio turned to his uncle. "I'm being paid for this, right?"

"Yes, it's official police business. I want you to stay with Sister Angela as long as she needs you."

The nun rose to leave with the boy, but stopped. "Please call ahead and ask for the evidence to be ready for me," she said to Turo. "I'll give the inspector your regards."

Outside, Silvio mounted his motorbike and patted the space behind him. "I'm afraid she doesn't go too fast. We drive on the side of the road. It's illegal for anyone to hit us." He handed Sister Angela a spare helmet. "You wear the red one so drivers behind us can see us."

Sister Angela pulled the helmet over her veil. Then she gathered up her skirt and put her leg over the back wheel. Looking down, she could see the drawbacks of Vatican II's modified habit. Hopefully she could hang onto Silvio's waist with one arm and hold her skirt down with the other, imagining the wind blowing her skirt over her face. "I don't think any car will fail to notice us," she said in his ear.

The small bike jerked and then rolled forward. Sister Angela could feel the eyes on the pair of odd bikers, passing through town.

About forty-five minutes later, Silvio pulled the motorbike into a small parking lot.

"Are you all right, Sister?" asked Silvio. "You were very quiet, especially on the hills."

Sister Angela slid off the back wheel but didn't straighten up right away."

"Are you sick?"

"No, Silvio. Let me hold your arm and try to stand up properly." She handed him the helmet.

"That's better. You look normal now."

I wish I felt normal, she said to herself.

The two entered the station, and Silvio asked for the inspector.

"He's not here," a policeman said. "But we have the boxes on the desk over there. You can go through them."

"What if I have questions?" asked Sister Angela.

"Agent Cira has the desk next to the boxes. He's at lunch. He'll be back shortly."

"Does he know about the case?" asked Silvio, suddenly sounding protective.

"He's the one who investigated the avalanche at the ski slope. The inspector knows less than he does."

Sister Angela settled into the desk chair, and Silvio pulled another up beside her. The nun slowly sifted through the documents. The officer's report was on top.

"What we're looking for is anything having to do with a child," Sister Angela said. "People were hurt and killed during the avalanche. Did any of those people have a child they may left in childcare? Did the police have to deal with surviving relatives?" She handed him a short stack of papers. "These are police interviews. Scan through them and let me know if there's anything about children in it."

"How old?"

"The child would have been two."

A half-hour later, the nun and boy began to place the documents back into the first box. Agent Cira had returned and taken a seat at his desk. The nun rose and introduced herself and Silvio.

"What do you want to know about the avalanche?" Cira asked. "There were three deaths and several injuries. Many were sent to the hospital or checked out at the scene and then released."

"We're looking for the children that were in the daycare that morning."

"That's in one of the boxes," he said, rising. He opened the second box and leafed through the documents that neither Silvio nor the nun had yet examined. "Here it is."

Sister Angela scanned the names and email addresses. "Do you know the ages of any of these children?"

"If it's not on the sheet…"

"Did you check to see if any of the victims was a parent of any of these children?"

"No. We interviewed the caretakers at the daycare, and all the children ended up with a guardian."

"Do you mind if Silvio makes a copy of this?"

"You're going to double check my investigation?"

"No, not at all. There was a toddler left on the steps of a convent around the time of the avalanche. I'm trying to find out who might have left her there and why."

"The avalanche was four years ago, Sister. Don't you think the relatives would've missed it by now?"

"Until recently, that child's been sitting in an orphanage. She disappeared a few weeks ago. Perhaps the relatives turned up and took her back."

"Not likely."

"In my investigations, I leave nothing unturned, Agent Cira."

"Is that all you wanted to see?"

"This is all I needed," she said, slipping the copy into her red-striped bag.

Walking out into the hot sun, the nun paused. "Have you had lunch, Silvio?"

"No. There's a panini place about a hundred meters up the road," Silvio said, slipping on his helmet."

"I'll see you there," she said, beginning to walk in

the direction of the sandwich shop.

"Wait, I can give you a ride, Sister."

"No thanks," she said, knowing the inevitability of having to straddle the back wheel would come soon enough.

Having told Chief Detective Pagano that she'd found nothing at the home of Signora La Barca's parents or their shop in town, Sister Daniela was ready for another adventure. "She really didn't seem to be hiding anything," the young nun explained. "She left her husband because the vineyard wasn't doing well. She hadn't planned to leave permanently but instead left it open."

"What did she say about La Barca?" Pagano asked.

"She described him as a gentle man that wasn't abusive. She just couldn't stay around to watch him run the vineyard into the ground."

"And the amphora?"

"Claiming she probably did sign it the day she left her husband, Carlota told me that the wine would've stained the clay on the outside if someone had put the body in there before she checked it. She also explained that the person who hid the body had to know about the pots to do it cleanly. What do we do next?"

"You did a good job, Sister. But it's too dangerous for you to help us on the next part of the investigation."

Elmo suddenly appeared at the door. "All set for eight tonight."

Sister Daniela's eyes grew large. "Where are we going?"

"We have a suspected sex ring doing business in Lutrasa."

"It's too dangerous to take Sister Daniela," said Pagano. "Sister Angela would kill the both of us if we let her come along."

"Nonsense," she said, trying to stand as tall as possible. "I promise I'll stay out of the way. I'd be able to comfort Pia if we found her."

"She's right. She could come with me," said Sacco.

"You must be exhausted," said Pagano. "You've done so much already."

"I'm fine. I'll call my sister and make sure she knows I'll be late. Maybe I should change into trousers."

Pagano looked her straight in the eye. "You won't need them. You'll be in the car."

The operation involved several cars. One by one they parked along the perimeter of the dirt drive. Pagano and Sacco both sat and waited for everyone else to be in place. Sister Daniela used a flashlight she'd been handed to look at her watch. It was nine-thirty.

Suddenly Pagano flashed his headlights and began to progress slowly up the bumpy drive. Sacco drove his vehicle close behind. After about half a kilometer, they stopped. Sister Daniela scanned the area ahead with Elmo's night vision binoculars but couldn't see anything beyond a sandy hill in front of them.

"What next?" asked Sister Daniela just as Sacco opened his door to step outside.

"The chief and I are walking in. You stay in the car." He put out his hand for the binoculars. "You won't need those. I will."

She handed him the binoculars and watched the two men move off the drive and head over the hill. As soon as they were out of sight, she got out to listen. It was quiet. Too quiet. She grabbed the flashlight from beside the passenger seat and pushed the door until it was almost latched. Then she took off in the direction the two policemen had taken.

She couldn't make them out when she got to the top of the hill. But she did see lights. Beams shone through the windows of a little farmhouse, perhaps another two to three hundred meters in front of her. She started down the slope in the direction of the lights when something caught her arm and turned her around. The rays of another flashlight prevented her from seeing who was there.

"Elmo told you to stay in the car."

"I know, Chief, but I figured you might need more help."

"We can't take her back now," said Sacco.

"Then you're responsible for her. If anything happens, it's your head. Do you understand me?"

"Yes, sir."

Sacco took Sister Daniela by the arm and

dragged her forward, trying to keep up with his boss. After about a hundred steps, the nun removed his arm and followed him. "Keep down," he said.

They were close enough now to hear noises from inside the farmhouse. Sacco pointed, indicating the nun should take cover behind a nearby boulder. This time Sister Daniela acquiesced, sensing everyone could hear the thumps in her chest. She peeked around the boulder to watch Pagano approach a window and glance inside while Sacco made his way to another viewpoint.

The chief retreated to a pile of logs a good ten meters from the house and talked into the walkie talkie clipped to his sweater. The response was almost instantaneous. Sets of several headlights sent beams into the night sky as the patrol cars climbed the hill and then descended.

Sister Daniela heard the sound of breaking glass and turned in the direction of the house once more. Shots rang out. She covered her ears. Sacco snuck up behind her and pushed her head down as he took aim at the window.

"The girls," she said. "Don't shoot the victims." More gunshots drowned out her voice. She couldn't hear his response.

It was over far too soon. The manpower provided by the police backup team was too much for the two men in the farmhouse. They emerged from the building with their hands over there heads.

Officers ran inside. Seconds later, they gestured that the house was all clear. Sister Daniela was the first to stand and join them.

There were only a few girls inside, though the

police were trying to uncover doors to a basement or hidden rooms. The two girls she saw were probably fifteen or older. They didn't show fright or elation that they were being rescued. They must have been drugged.

"No other rooms," said Sacco, standing by her side. "There might have already been a pick up some of them because there are two other rooms with empty beds."

Sister Daniela looked at him. "Were the other beds warm? Is there evidence that others had been here?"

"That's not our job. There's a team to do that. We're done here."

"What about these girls?"

"An ambulance is on the way. We have to move the cars out so they can get close enough." He took her arm.

"Pia isn't here," she said to him.

"No. I don't think we're going to find any evidence that a child's been here. These were probably street girls. Easy snatches, if you know what I mean." He tugged on her arm again. "C'mon. We can try to find another ring tomorrow. I'll drop you off at your sister's on the way back to Siena."

"Do you think we'll ever find her?"

"Maybe Sister Angela's having better luck."

Chapter Nineteen

After lunch, Silvio let off the nun in front of the station. "I could wait and take you to the convent,"

"No thanks you, Silvio," she said. "I believe I need to walk. I'd like to meet you here tomorrow afternoon; however, I might only be able to ride side saddle."

Silvio laughed. "I'll be around," he said. "I'll be doing odd jobs for the detective sergeant."

The nun walked into the station to talk to Turo before she left for the convent. She needed a hot soak in the bath.

"Hello, Sister. I take it you found what you needed."

"I probably could've interviewed more people, but the box of evidence was helpful. I must return to the convent and contact people using email."

"Do you want me to get Silvio to take you to the convent?"

"No, I can walk." *Barely,* she said to herself. "I'll be back tomorrow. I've more investigating to do."

"I'm surprised you're telling me. I thought after your previous visits you'd want to continue using your stealth approach."

"I no longer feel you're going to run from me if I make an appointment. Tomorrow's investigation is more local."

"Then perhaps you should give me a heads up so

I can get you evidence before you arrive."

"It's about the bank robbery."

"Same dates?"

"The same time period as the avalanche. I read there were a few calls about domestic disputes. I didn't write down the locations so I believe they were here in Castel Valori."

"Anything else?"

"Yes. There was a ten-car pileup on the autostrada near Poppi. I don't suppose you do the detective work for Poppi too."

"Actually that would be the *Polizia di Stato*, the *Polizia Stradale* division. They patrol the autostrada and the train system."

"Where are they?"

"There's an office in Arezzo. I can have Silvio take you."

"I'm afraid I'd have trouble traveling that far on the motorbike," said the nun, squirming. "And finally, there was a hit and run accident in Val d'Alsa. Where's that?"

"That's the next village just on the edge of town. My team takes care of that village. I think I remember that accident. I'll see what I can find on that too.

After requesting a report from Arezzo and various files from Turo, the nun headed outside to talk to Silvio. Silvio handed her a helmet. "Where are we going?" he asked.

"To the bank."

"That's across the piazza. I can see it from here."

Sister Angela smiled. "I know. I thought you might like to see what I do to investigate things instead of only providing transportation."

"Yes I'd like that, but why don't we walk?"

She handed back the helmet, and the two began their trek across the piazza.

The bank had just opened after their lunch break. Sister Angela asked to see the manager, who graciously led her to his desk. "Detective Sergeant Turo mentioned that you'd probably want to talk with me about the bank robbery four years ago.

The nun sat, and Silvio pulled up another chair. "I'm glad he mentioned it," she said. "I know it's a long time ago."

"I have notes on it. I was required to file papers with several agencies."

"Did you catch the culprits?"

"Yes. Most people inside the bank at the time were witnesses. It was easy identifying the thieves. There were two of them. They wore masks, but several people recognized their voices."

"And where are they now?"

"In jail. They got ten years each."

"You're saying there were two men. What about the driver in the getaway car?"

"They had motorcycles. There was no third person."

"Can you tell me more about the criminals? Were they married? Did they have families?"

"They were Croatian. I have no idea if they were married. I don't believe any families showed up at the trial. They'd robbed several other banks in Tuscan villages in the weeks preceding this particular one. A boat was evidently moored in the Adriatic. The police speculated they planned to make the hits and then head over the tiny mountain roads to the coast. They would escape to Croatia in their boat."

Sister Angela and Silvio left the bank disappointed.

"You can see, Silvio, that we must ask a lot of questions to proceed."

"It's the same at the station."

"Speaking of the station, I plan to go back and look at all the files Turo's found for me." She started to walk away.

Silvio hesitated and then caught up with her. "I think we should do that together, Sister. Two people can go through the files faster than one, don't you think?"

Sister Daniela drove the truck into Siena and parked it at the terminal. Walking inside, she glanced around and then headed to the ticket booth.

"I'd like to speak with a manager," she said. "Where are the managers?"

"Along the far wall at the top of the escalator."

Sister Daniela turned and started to walk away.

The woman behind the counter yelled. "You'll need an appointment, Sister. They won't see you without an appointment."

Sister Daniela heard her but kept walking. At the top of the escalator, she noted the doors on the far wall. She walked toward one door that stood ajar but, at the last second, veered toward the closed one. The second door sported a sign reading *No Entry*, but she reached for the knob anyway. It opened. A man, sitting behind the desk, looked up just as she closed the door behind her.

The manager was middle-aged. What hair he had left was graying. He stood when he saw that the young woman was wearing a habit. "Excuse me, Sister, but you've come in the wrong door. You need to talk with my receptionist in the next office."

"But this is very important," she said. "I'm working with the chief investigator concerning the problem on the tracks the other night."

"I didn't know they'd contacted the team in Roma. After all, there were no bombs."

"No, but the person I work for doesn't believe it's nothing. Why would anyone try to block that train?" She watched his eyes look down at her habit. "I'm just a gopher," the nun confessed. "In fact, I'm a temp. The chief investigator needed someone who could do the job fast. I used to do investigation work before giving myself to God—so here I am."

"Your boss must know about the wine."

"Wine? What do you mean?"

"A shipment of wine was removed from the train when it stopped."

"I take it that's in your report."

"Well—uh—this is the first I've heard about an official investigation."

"I can come back," she said, hearing a chair scrape the floor in the receptionist's room next door. "By the way, why was there wine on the train?"

"Because the shipment was supposed to leave the Siena-Ampugnano Airport that night. You should have known about it. No investigator's office would hold onto you if you didn't understand the crime."

"I know. I'm so glad you told me," she started to turn back to the door. "Isn't that odd? Do you often transport wine by train and then by plane?" She put her hand on the knob, ready to open the door.

"Yes, it's a regular shipment."

"By whom? Which winery are we talking about?"

"Several of them do that. I don't know which one was being transported that night."

The door to the next office began to open. Then the phone rang, and the receptionist stepped back to answer it.

"You don't know. I can't get this straight in my mind. Wineries send wine by train here, and then a truck or something takes the wine to the airport. A plane then takes the wine to a destination."

"Yes."

"It can't be the Classico region here because that wouldn't need a train. Where do these shipments come from?"

"This particular shipment—the one that disappeared—came from the Rufina region."

Sister Daniela heard the phone in the next office click, and the chair scraped the floor again. "Thank you for your help. You've actually saved my temp job. I'll come back tomorrow and pick up that report. I'll tell my boss that you're cooperating in spite of the obvious lack of communication between our departments."

Just as the door to the next office opened to reveal the receptionist, the nun slipped out the one to the terminal and closed it behind her. She stepped onto the escalator before crossing herself and asking for forgiveness for her lies.

Sister Angela and Silvio returned to the station. Detective Sergeant Turo had left boxes on a desk near the front counter, and the nun eagerly opened the first one.

"This is my desk," said Silvio. "Please have a seat. I'll go out and get us drinks. I'm starving, aren't you?"

But the nun didn't answer. She was already reading reports about the cases that occurred near Castel Valori around the time of Pia's appearance at the convent.

When Silvio returned with the food, he found sheets scattered over the surface of *his* desk and the two desks on each side. "Have you found something?"

"I'm trying to separate them. There are a number of parking tickets and moving violations among them. I'm trying to weed out offenses that probably wouldn't impact how the child ended up at the convent."

"You mentioned that there were domestic disputes in town."

"Yes. I have these over here. And then there was the accident I read about. I have all the reports for that on this side. I suggest we eat first. Then we can go to the addresses with the domestic disputes."

Silvio handed her a sandwich and napkin. "I thought you'd like a roast beef with olives."

"Come to think of it, I'm starving," she said, tearing open the paper wrap. "Did you get any chips with this?"

"Yes." he said, offering her a bag. "I also have some pickles if you want one of those. And I have some soda for you."

The nun inhaled the smell of the sandwich as Silvio handed her a pickle.

Silvio took a large bite out but then put his sandwich down on a napkin. "The car accident sounds interesting."

"The hit and run?" she asked, dropping a straw into her soda can. "That does sound interesting, but from what I gather, there are few details. Someone called in a crash. We can visit the woman who called. By the time the police got to the scene, the car was against a tree and the driver, still inside, was dead. The woman was apparently alone. No one saw the vehicle that hit her, and there's a question about how it managed to hit the car on the rear fender on the passenger side."

"I take it we don't have the woman's car to examine."

There was a pause as both sleuths took bites of their sandwiches. The nun then wiped her hands. "We do have pretty good snapshots here," she said handing him the photos.

"It looks like the other vehicle first hit her from behind, and she lost control and hit the tree."

The nun put down her bag of chips and grabbed the pictures back from Silvio. She examined them through Silvio's descriptions. "The suspect's car would have to be going pretty fast to move the vehicles into a tree."

"Both cars would've been going fast, although the road's dirt. It would've been easier for her car to slide down the embankment."

"That makes this not a hit and run accident, but a homicide. From what direction was she coming? There's a note that she was heading away from Castel Valori."

"And there would've had to be two sounds if she was facing the wrong way," said Silvio.

"I don't see that in any of the reports. We'll have to revisit the witness who called it in. But if the suspect hit the victim's car from behind and then from the side, the fatal blow to the driver, wouldn't that have harmed his car too? I'm surprised he got away."

"Check the evidence from the tire tracks," said Silvio. "What kind of vehicle was it?"

The nun wiped her hands again and then leafed through the reports. "It was a pickup. This should've been investigated further."

"Who was the victim?"

"No purse or wallet on her. The killer must have stopped the pickup and retrieved her ID." Sister Angela tapped her finger. "And no other evidence in the car."

"If she had a child, there'd be something. What about hair or bodily fluids?"

The nun looked at him. "You're beginning to

sound like a detective."

"I'm in a police station most of the day. I pick up that sort of stuff."

"According to the examiner, there was hair in the car, but the only matches were hers." She continued to tap her finger on top of the desk.

Silvio   waited,   watching   her   spellbound expression.

"I don't think they ever thought to see if anything might have been from a toddler."

"Why would they? They knew nothing about a child until two years later."

"Why was the victim driving on that dirt road when she could have been driving on the asphalt road that passed right by the convent? Why would you get off the main road, Silvio?"

"I might if I knew someone on that minor road," he said. "Has everyone been interviewed?"

"Or you might because you thought you were being followed. When she looked in the mirror she saw someone on her tail. Maybe if she turned off, he would pass by. He didn't. She knew then he was following her."

"So she doesn't stop and try to turn around. Perhaps this road went a ways and then turned back to the main road. She kept going on the dirt one…"

"And he rammed her. I have a chill just thinking about it. She must have been so frightened." The nun stopped to take a bite of her sandwich. "So he gets out of the car and grabs her purse, the car registration, and removes the license plates. Let's just say there was a baby in the backseat. Was he after the baby?"

"He has the victim's ID. Does he want Pia too? He must have taken the child and everything having to do with her."

"But would he do that and then leave her at the convent? Why not leave the child in the car and let the police handle it. The two year old wouldn't be able to identify him."

"You know, Sister. We have hairs from the car. We could see if the hair from the car matches the kidnapped child's hair. That would be proof that she was in that car."

Chapter Twenty

Sister Daniela stepped off the train and headed toward the terminal doors. For the second time in as many days, she traveled to Triesa. After dinner the night before, she discovered Carlota La Barca had left a message on her cell phone asking her to return to Triesa. Carlota needed to talk with her.

Making her way to the café where she'd met Carlota the first time, the nun bought two espressos and two rolls. Then she strode down the road to the house she'd searched from attic to basement.

Carlota was there to let her in. "We're alone," she said. "My parents are again at the shop. This is a good time."

"Why did you want to speak with me?" Sister Daniela asked, placing the coffees and rolls on the kitchen table. "Do you know where Pia is?"

"No. But I have a confession to make."

"I don't usually hear confessions, but if it has to do with the case…"

"It does. When you asked me if I knew about the body, I told you I didn't?"

"You were aware there was a body in the amphora?"

"I didn't know there was a dead body inside. I just knew the victim."

Sister Daniela tipped over her coffee and ran to collect paper towels to clean up the spill. When the table was clean she sat down again to listen, her heart pounding.

"His name's Alrigo Nocera."

The nun wrote furiously on her pad. "How do you know him?"

"He came to the winery a few times. I was alone. Martino always seemed to be away doing business. Alrigo showed up and wanted to know if there were jobs for him at the winery. I told him he'd have to come back when my husband was there."

"Did he ever talk with La Barca?"

"Not at first. As far as I know, he only came by when I was alone. After the second visit, I felt sorry for him. I invited him in for coffee."

"What did you find out about Nocera?"

"He told me his wife and child had been killed a few years earlier and that he lost his job at another winery because he found it too difficult to go back to work right away. I nearly cried for him right there. What a husband he must have been."

"And he visited you again?"

"Yes. I wanted to comfort him."

"Did you have sex with him?" Sister Daniela almost blushed. She wasn't used to being so forward, but the stakes in the case were high.

Tears began to appear at the corners of Carlota's eyes. "I tried to comfort him. He was so vulnerable."

"How many times did you two meet?"

"About five times. I have to confess that my desire was to have children by my husband, but Martino always resisted and took protection. He said he wanted to get the damned business going. When Alrigo came along, I thought I might go around my husband, get pregnant by my lover, and pass the baby off as Martino's."

"Did you?"

"Get pregnant? No."

"Did your husband ever suspect?"

"I don't know. He probably did. I tried hard to keep the house looking clean and neat so he wouldn't question me about having a guest."

"Did your husband ever meet Nocera?"

"Yes. The night before I left. Martino found Alrigo by the fence."

"Outside the orphanage?

"Yes. Alrigo told Martino he'd asked me about a job. I think my husband knew something because we had a big row that night."

"Did he say he suspected you were having an affair? Nocera must have told him more."

"I don't know. I packed my bags the next morning and hid them in the closet. When Martino told me they were short of help the next day and asked me to check the amphorae, I did."

"And you saw nothing extraordinary about the aging wines."

"No. That part's true. I don't believe Alrigo was dead before I checked them. The chemicals in all ten amphorae were at normal levels. I signed the charts. The next train to Triesa was scheduled for five that afternoon. I left him."

"You're aware that your statement makes your husband appear guilty. He hadn't only met Nocera, but maybe figured out you were having an affair?"

Tears ran down Carlota's face, and Sister Daniela handed her a tissue. "What do you know about Pia's disappearance?"

"At first I didn't know a child was kidnapped."

"According to the timeline, that must have happened before you left—the night of the row. Nocera was out in the field, waiting for the children to go to bed. He took Pia out of the orphanage. By the next afternoon, he was dead, and Pia was missing. When you were with Nocera, did he ever mention Pia's name?"

"No."

"Did he ever ask or say anything about the orphanage?"

"If he did, I didn't hear it. We didn't talk. I concentrated only on reaching my objective."

"Aside from the story about his wife, did he ever say anything about where he came from?"

Carlota dabbed her eyes and then rose to throw out the paper cups. She stood in front of the sink and stared out the window. Then she turned around and said, "Rufina. The first day when he asked me to get him a job at the winery, he said he had experience. He'd worked at a winery in the Rufina region."

"Did he give you the name of the winery?"

"No. I suppose my husband would've asked him if he knew he wanted a job."

"When did you learn about Pia?" asked Sister Daniela.

"I read about it in the papers after I arrived here."

"What did the story say?"

"Just that a child had disappeared from an

orphanage in Filari."

"You worked at the orphanage and knew the orphanage was next door to your husband's winery yet you called no one to inquire about it?."

"Yes, I worked at the orphanage and knew most of the children, but I wouldn't call about what I thought was a runaway," said Carlota.

"Now that you know about the case, can you tie Nocera or your husband to the kidnapping?"

"I once knew both men, Sister. I don't think either man would be involved in a child's kidnapping."

As soon as Sister Daniela was seated on the train, she took out her cell phone and called her friend. The more mature nun was back at the Castel Valori police station about to go out and visit those involved in the reported domestic disputes.

"I know who took the child," Sister Daniela blurted out.

"We can go out now and pick up Pia. Where is she?"

"No, I know who the old nun is—or was. His name was Alrigo Nocera. He was from Rufina."

"Where did you get the information?"

"I'm in Triesa. Carlota La Barca confessed to having an affair with our victim."

"Did La Barca know about it?"

"Carlota isn't sure, but La Barca did meet him. He questioned Nocera when he was by the fence near the orphanage. Nocera told La Barca that he'd asked Carlota for a job. Carlota claims her husband returned to the house very angry, and the couple had a fight. She ran away the next day after testing the wine in the amphora. She told me Nocera was alive the night of the quarrel and that the checks on the aging wine were normal the next day."

"Do me a favor and contact Ricco. Maybe he can get something more out of La Barca."

"Wait. Nocera told Carlota his wife and child had been killed. You don't suppose…"

"I suppose nothing. If he was Pia's father, he could've asked for his child. Why kidnap her?"

Turo walked out of his office and handed Sister Angela a sheet of paper. "Here's the mechanic's report on the vehicle."

She read the information. "The VIN had been sanded. After the person in the second vehicle took the time to clean out the victim's car and take the plates, I'm not surprised. My colleague did find out that our kidnapper, and victim, is from Rufina. He told the winemaker's wife that he worked at a winery there. Now that's a clue we might be able to run with."

"What about the domestic situations?" asked Turo.

"I'm just on my way out the door, Detective Sergeant. Is Silvio around?"

"I think he's with his motorbike."

The nun opened the door to find Silvio just outside, revving the motor. He handed the nun her helmet. "Hop on," he said. "Do you have the addresses?"

"Yes. Most are in town. One's on a farm a bit farther out."

"Let's start in town. Hang on."

The two took off on a narrow drive just off the piazza that led them down the hill. Silvio made a sharp left turn at the bottom and goaded his bike up about half a block before slowing to a stop.

"This is Signor and Signora Sultana," said the nun, dismounting and taking the few steps up to ring the bell.

Silvio followed as soon as the woman appeared.

"Please come in," she said. "I have hot tea, if you'd like.

"We have questions about a report you made against your husband four years ago."

"It doesn't matter," she said, pouring a cup of tea for the nun. "He's dead, bless his soul."

"Please tell me what happened."

"My husband hit me. He did it a lot. A neighbor heard my screams and called the police."

"You stayed with him?" asked Silvio.

The old woman shrugged her shoulders. "You've a lot to learn, my son."

Waiting for the tea to cool, the nun rose from her chair and walked over to the mantel. "Who are these children?" she asked, pointing to a row of photographs.

"Those are mine."

"You have young children?"

"No. They're old pictures."

"Do you have grandchildren?"

"I have two great grandchildren, Sister."

"How old?"

"They're just starting school."

"When did you see them last?"

"I haven't seen them at all. My grandchildren live in England. They send pictures, though. I framed them and put them up over there in the hallway."

The nun walked over to the photographs. "Are all of your grandchildren grown?"

"No. Some are still in school. Why?"

The nun sat down again and sipped her tea. "Because four years ago a child was left at the Sacro Cuore della Francesca. Sometimes there are problems in a marriage that might force the parents to give up a child."

"You think I'd do that? I had seven children, Sister. I'd never do that to one of my children. My husband would've killed me if I had."

The second house was above the grocery near the terminal. Again Sister Angela dismounted while Silvio lagged behind.

"I know this family," he said. "Are you sure it's them?"

"Perhaps it's better if you didn't come in. It might be embarrassing to both you and the family."

A woman opened the door and led the nun up the steep stairs. "Hello, Sister. Are you asking for alms? I can give you what I have, though I'm afraid it isn't much."

"No, no." said Sister Angela, beginning to huff and puff as they neared the landing. "I'm here because of a police report from four years ago."

The woman stopped in her tracks. "Sorry? I didn't know the church would be involved with the police."

"I'm not here representing the church, Signora Ussi. I came to this house trying to find out why a two year old was left off at the local convent four years ago. The police came to your home then because of a domestic dispute. I was wondering if the child belonged to this family."

The woman held her chest like she was going to swoon. "Four years ago, the police came here because my son and I were arguing. He wanted to work in town instead of continuing with his schooling."

"I'm sorry to bring it up. He didn't have any children?"

"Now he does, but not then. He works for my husband in the shop downstairs in order to have an income for his wife and child. Excuse me, but I don't think it's right that four years later the police want to visit the situation again."

"No. It doesn't sound right. The child involved was recently kidnapped, and we're trying desperately to find out where she came from. I'm so sorry to interrupt you, Signora Ussi. I'll report to the police that your family isn't involved."

When the nun stepped outside in front of the grocery, Silvio revved his engine and sped out from between two buildings on the opposite side of the street. "Now for the farmhouse?" he asked.

Silvio kept driving well past the last houses of the village. The hilly countryside spread before them— yellowing grassy fields with lines of cypress and beautiful estates.

"There was a domestic dispute out here?"

"You don't have to be poor to have problems, Silvio."

"How would you know that?"

Sister Angela let the warm breezes glance off her face. "Only God knows."

Suddenly the motorbike slowed to a stop.

"What's the problem?"

"I'm not sure if we're in the right place," he said.

"There's a postbox up there. Let's check the number." As he slowed the motorbike, she checked the number on the box with her list. "This is it, Silvio. You're better at this than even you know."

Silvio pulled the bike up to the gate and pressed a button.

"Who are you?" a scratchy voice through the tiny speaker squeaked at them.

After waiting for the gate to open, Silvio let the nun off at the front door. Sister Angela knocked and waited until a woman came to open it.

"Signora Colletta?" the nun asked.

The woman stepped aside to let her enter. Signor Colletta's in his study. I'll let him know you're here."

"Just let her in, Dona," he spat. "Of course I

know she's here. If you'd done your job and answered the intercom, then I would've *needed* to be told. He approached the door. "Please come in, Sister. You'll have to forgive the help. They're all hopeless. I don't know why I pay them."

The nun entered and sat down on the soft loveseat. "Signor Colletta, I'm here concerning an incident that resulted in a police report four years ago."

He gave her a withering stare, but Sister Angela didn't shrink away. "So the police are checking up on me now? For God's sake, you're seriously reexamining a case that happened four years ago? Why's the Church involved, Sister? Did something happen to my ex-wife?" He lit a cigarette and paced the room like a wild cat.

"So Signora Colletta and you are divorced."

"We settled just a few months after the complaint. The witch married me for my money and figured out a way to take much of it with her."

"Were there children?"

"No, thank God. She was well past her prime when I married her. She came from a supposedly affluent family. She's a Brit. Her father made his money in industry, but I think she made her fortune through all her marriages. She'd been married four times before. The whole relationship was a joke. I must have been out of my mind. It lasted less than a year." He stopped to snuff out his cigarette in the ashtray on the coffee table in front of the nun. "I suppose you disapprove."

"It sounds terrible, Signor Colletta. I'm sorry you had to go through that," she said, rising from her comfortable throne.

"So tell me why you're here. Is she dead?"

"I've no idea. I've never met her. I'm investigating the kidnapping of a young child for the police. If there were no young children involved in the separation with your wife, it doesn't concern me. I can see myself out. Thank you for your help."

Chapter Twenty-One

Viviana braced herself against the top of the marble headstone to look closer at the picture of Mara. She'd been so alive just weeks earlier.

Viviana didn't hurry when she first heard Mara had taken ill but immediately visited her when she was told her mother was in the hospital. Mara was already unconscious. Had her mother realized she was there or was she already preparing to leave this world? Was Nonna's death so hard on Mara?

Aunt Clarissa and Aunt Lucilla hadn't even bothered to show up at the funeral in Roma. They said they were too busy selling Nonna's house. Isabella, Viviana's elder sister, couldn't leave her new family in Malta, but she too was devastated.

The young woman stood up, wiped her eyes, and walked toward the small hotel just blocks from the cemetery. She felt very tired and needed to lie down. In the morning, she would catch the train to Corsa Pietra and her husband. At least Mara had seen her younger daughter married.

It was all very romantic. Giulio and Viviana were wed in a grassy field where more grape stalks were to be planted. Mara and her sisters were present as well as more De Capuas than Viviana had ever met. Included were a few members of the community, but overall the group was small. Ermanno was the best man, and Isabella, her sister, was her matron of honor. There was plenty of wine shared among the guests, and the outdoor table just outside the farmhouse offered several dishes.

Viviana was lovely. Before the ceremony, Mara took Viviana into Corsa Pietra, but there were few gowns so they visited towns and villages all over the area in search of something that was appropriate for such an illustrious occasion. Most of the local stores had old-style dresses with antique lace, buttoned-up bodices, and long veils. Viviana wanted to look more fashionable.

In Firenza, they finally found a striking gown that emphasized Viviana's slim lines, though soon those lines would disappear. It had wide silk gauze straps and a low-cut front. The waist was high. The skirt, brocade of white and gold, wrapped her long thighs and glowed when the sun hit it.

On her head, she wore a tiara, and on her feet, gold shoes with four-inch heels, something that would catch the groom's eyes.

Her bouquet wasn't timid. Vivid purple bougainvillea poured out of her hands in long strands, while Isabella, in a purple gown, carried white mums.

Giulio looked happy. Surprisingly, Ermanno seemed to be enjoying himself too. They both ushered their mother to a seat in the front row. But Giulio was still unable to take his eyes off his beautiful bride.

The priest from the church in town married

them and then blessed the couple. The two were driven into the city offices in Corsa Pietra to make everything official while the guests raided the food and wine.

As soon as the bride and groom were seated at a long table under an equally long awning that flapped in the late autumn breezes, Ermanno stood to give the toast. "Welcome everyone. We're sorry to pull you away from your businesses at such a busy time of year. My brother has always had trouble timing everything. Thankfully, he and his lovely bride have agreed to put off their honeymoon until winter and help with the fermentation. I just want to make sure Viviana understands that she isn't expected to get up and serve wine to you all. This is the couple's big day, and we all want her to relax and enjoy it."

Viviana was relieved when it was over. The newlyweds retired to Giulio's boyhood bedroom. She was so exhausted she fell asleep in his arms right away. The two were awakened at six the next morning by a persistent buzz.

"Hand me my phone, Giulio. I suppose it's your brother, telling us to get to work." She put the phone to her ear. "Hello?" Seconds later, she dropped the phone onto the mussed sheets and rose to grab her clothes.

"What's wrong? Surely that wasn't Ermanno."

"No, it was Mamma. Nonna died during the night. Since she couldn't come to the wedding, I should've gone to the nursing home and shared our day with her. I have to go to Clarissa's."

Giulio remained silent. "Am I expected to go too?" he finally asked. "Ermanno wants me at the winery."

Unsuccessfully trying to button her slacks over her growing belly, she let out an exasperated sigh. "You don't have to come with me. I know you're expected to work. I hope Ermanno doesn't require my help too." Tears made their way down the side of her nose.

Giulio rose and put his hands on her shoulders. "I'm so sorry, Viv. I know you're hurting. It's just that we're trying to make this place viable. The competition's tough, and we're just a little winery. No one will notice if we fail—except our suppliers, who'll probably go down with us. I promise I'll try to make it to the service when your family decides on a date and time." He kissed her on the nose.

Viviana turned back to find some looser clothes in his overcrowded closet.

"Maybe Mara can take you shopping for maternity clothes. At least you'd be more comfortable."

"Do you think they'd go with my five-inch heels? I don't believe you'd let me serve customers without my heels."

"We'll get someone else to serve customers. Business will be light until spring. Then you won't be able to wear heels anyway."

Giulio showed up at Nonna's funeral in the old church in Corso Pietra. When his exhausted wife had trouble standing at the burial site, he stood behind her and let her lean against him. Mara stood next to her daughter, sobbing. Viviana was surprised her mother cried so hard. After all, Viviana had come to Corso Pietra in the first place because Mara wanted to work rather than come care for her mother.

Afterward, the small group of mourners gathered in the parish hall to eat and talk. Clarissa dabbed her eyes as she flitted from one group to another. Mara sat down and hardly uttered a word to anyone. Viviana tried to speak with all present but soon sat down beside her mother.

"Are you all right?" asked Viviana. "It isn't like you to be off on your own. Your uncle even came. Have you spoken to him?"

"I'm sorry. I'm very tired."

"Have you seen a doctor? I noticed you have a little cough. How long have you had that?"

"It's nothing, Viv. I'll be fine when I get back to Roma. The work there's piling up."

"I confess I don't want you to go. Why can't you stay here with me?"

Mara finally smiled. "I'm flattered but until you have the baby, I'll have nothing to do. When's the appointment to find out if it's a boy or a girl? You do want to know, don't you?"

"In a few weeks, Mamma. Yes, I want to know."

"What about Giulio? What does he want?"

Viviana bit her lip to keep it from trembling. "I suppose he wants a boy, but he doesn't say much about it."

Viviana never got the opportunity to tell her mother about the sex of the baby. Two weeks after Mara returned to Roma, a friend found her unconscious in her apartment.

The hot summer sun poured in through the open window. Viviana could feel the sweat trickling down her back and quickly got up to turn on the air. It was late. She showered and headed for the kitchen. As she passed the front room, she noticed her mother-in-law in a chair, knitting.

"I'm sorry I'm up so late. Have you had coffee?"

"No," said the older woman. "I haven't eaten either."

"I'll get you a cup right away," said Viviana, rubbing her back as she waddled into the kitchen.

When breakfast was on the table, she helped the old lady to her chair.

"Have *you* eaten?"

"I have a roll, but I'm not really hungry," said Viviana. "Please don't wait for me."

"Why are you dressed up? Are you going somewhere? You aren't allowed to mingle with the customers when you look so big."

Viviana smiled. "No. I want to speak with Ermanno. It was my understanding that Giulio would be back for his child's birth. It's in two weeks, and I haven't heard a word from my husband."

"He has work to do, Viviana. You shouldn't expect him to be here. Husbands are no use with women in labor. As long as you have a doctor, you'll be fine. Let the men get their work done."

"I suppose you're right," she said.

"My room's a mess. The bed hasn't been changed. I'm sure that's on your agenda today."

"Yes, of course, Mamma," she said, putting the cup to her lips but still unable to take a sip of espresso. "Give me a few minutes, and I'll get to work directly."

Standing, she slipped out the door and toddled toward the winery. The truck was in the drive as she rounded the corner. Stopping to catch her breath at the back of the truck, she watched the strong men, their arms glistening in the heat, slowly carry inside the boxes. Suddenly she felt a searing pain in her side. She sat down on the truck ramp next to a box to wait for the pain to subside. It was then she noticed the writing on it. "Fine wine from the Amalfi Coast," she read aloud.

Rubbing her belly, she made her way into the shade of the large building. In back of Ermanno's desk, the young woman, recently hired to temporarily replace Viviana, gathered the receipts and began to file them. Viviana shuffled up to greet her.

"Oh, hello," the woman said. "I'm Donata. By the looks of it, you must be Viviana. I was just neatening Ermanno's desk before he returns."

"What about the customers?"

"There's a lull between tour buses. You look hot. I'm so glad there are fans all around here."

"Ermanno doesn't usually like people cleaning up his desk."

"Really? I've been doing it for weeks. He hasn't complained."

"And the paperwork for the delivery outside?"

Donata smiled. "All taken care of. The receipts are in his drawer."

"Do you know where Ermanno is? I need to know the whereabouts of my husband."

"Giulio's up north in Verona. It's a winemakers' convention, I think. Then he goes to Milano to a lovely restaurant on Via Gesu."

"So he has no plans to come home anytime soon?"

"I don't think he'll tell his brother to come home. When Ermanno needs to send more supplies, he usually asks me to take them to him. Why?"

Viviana could feel the heat on her face.

Donata brushed her auburn hair off her wet cheek and stepped out from behind the desk. "It looks like I'm done here. I guess I should go back to the tasting room where I have air conditioning."

For the first time, Viviana realized Donata wasn't the young innocent girl she was told Giulio had hired. Donata was several centimeters taller than she was. As the young woman slipped away, Viviana watched her shapely legs strut through the doors into the sun. On her shoes, she wore heels—five inch heels. Viviana felt another pang and grabbed her side.

That evening after fixing her mother-in-law dinner, Viviana suddenly screamed. Serena helped Viviana into the car and drove her to the hospital in town. Serena sat with her sister-in-law as she writhed in pain. Twelve hours later, Viviana gave birth. Serena had already left to go to work. No one from the family was there.

Chapter Twenty-Two

Sister Angela sat down in front of another box of evidence provided by Detective Sergeant Turo. "Let me see," she said aloud. "Concerning the accident, we haven't any identification for the driver and nothing on the vehicle. What about the DNA, Sergeant?"

"We have that but no matches."

"Missing person's reports. Surely there's been something in four years."

"We saw many. We followed up on those missing persons reports within weeks of the accident. Nothing."

"And beyond the five weeks?"

"There were too many reports to continue to investigate them all. Most of the missing persons are found or eventually show up. Of course, we still examine local missing person's reports, but none seem to be related to this accident."

"Where's the body now?"

"Interred in the church cemetery. Of course there's no name because we don't have one."

Sister Angela rested her chin on her palm. "Perhaps this woman went missing, but those who knew her wanted to keep her disappearance a secret. If the family didn't know about it when it happened, surely they would've inquired about her when she didn't turn up—even months later."

Turo stopped clicking his keyboard and, sighing, sat back. "If you want to go through all the missing person's records over the past four years, you're welcome. I'm afraid you need to get the information from Roma. Perhaps they have it all online. We didn't hold onto ours because we don't have room to keep everything."

Sister Angela smiled. "That's an idea, Sergeant Turo. If we decide to, I can do that. But I've been informed that our victim in Filari came from Rufina. It might be easier to concentrate on those missing from Rufina zone."

Sister Daniela stood in front of her classroom once more, but it was difficult to put the thoughts of the investigation and the La Barcas out of her mind. She glanced through the windows that overlooked the vineyard next door and shivered. Had Nocera been casing the classroom days or even weeks before the kidnapping? How did Nocera get into the orphanage?

She stared out at her students who looked back at her expectantly. "I'm sorry," she said. "I see by my notes that you're all in the middle of reading projects. Why don't we continue with those? Allegra, would you please come up and organize the groups? I have to step out for a few moments." Sister Daniela began to walk toward the door, but hesitated. "Evelina, would you come with me?"

The two walked to the lower stair treads and sat down.

"I'm still troubled about the situation that allowed the kidnapper to enter the building. Let's go over your steps that evening again."

Evelina took a deep breath and let it out slowly. "Let me see. At about ten o'clock, I walked over to the front door and made sure it was latched."

"Was it secured or did you have to lock it yourself?"

"I don't remember. I was used to doing both so I wouldn't have thought twice about it."

"Then where did you go?"

"I always followed that by heading for the kitchen and the back door that leads to the outside landing. Sister Carmela's usually locked that already, but I still check it."

"Has it ever been unlocked?

"Yes. But it's usually when Sister Carmela's visiting the nuns in Siena or when she's sick."

"Then you retraced your steps?"

"Yes. I walked past the staircase and followed the passage to the nurse's room."

"You mentioned you did this every evening."

"Yes. I'm the only one who does it because it's so spooky with all the equipment in there."

Sister Daniela looked surprised but regained her composure. "So you walked down the passage and went into the nurse's room…"

"I went in and checked the door. It was locked, as usual. Then I turned off the lights downstairs and followed the others to bed."

The nun stood and brushed off her black skirt. "Follow me," she said. "Let's do this together."

The two climbed the stairs to the main floor. This part of the house was more quiet than usual.

Was it always so peaceful when the children were downstairs with her? The only sound came from the kitchen where Sister Edita was preparing lunch.

"So, it's five to ten, and you're watching television with the children in this room. Where did you sit?"

"No, I was in the dining room. That's where a few of the others were still studying. I was reading a book."

Evelina sat down in one of the chairs at the dining room table, and Sister Daniela slid into a chair next to her.

"Ding. Ding. Ding. You look up. It's ten o'clock. What do you do?"

"I tell those around me to put away their books because it's time to go to bed."

"And you wait for them to leave the room?"

"No. Many of the younger ones are slow to make it to the stairs. I'm probably the second or third to get up. I walk through the television room and flip off the TV. The children groan but start to rise. I keep walking until I get to the front door."

Sister Daniela continued to follow her.

"I put my hand on the knob and rotate it." She shows the nun. The door opens. Evelina closes it and flips the lever below the knob. Then she tries it again. The door doesn't move. "This is how it was. It wouldn't move. I remember that now."

The nun flipped the lever back, opened the door, stepped out, and closed it. "Lock it again," she said to Evelina, still standing on the inside. Sister Daniela unsuccessfully tried to open the door. Then she examined the keyhole. No sign of tampering. She knocked, and Evelina let her back inside. "Who has a key?"

"Sister Carmela has one in her room."

"Who else?"

"No one. Everyone else uses the basement door. You have one for the basement, don't you?"

Sister Daniela fingered the key in her pocket. "Who else has one of these?"

"I'm sure Sister Natalia has one. I'm uncertain about the others, though I suspect some of them do. Sister Carmela has a few on her wall for some of us who have to go out at night and need to get back in."

"I hadn't even thought that any of you might want to go out."

"We don't have a nurse. Last fall, some of us got the flu. A nun came from Siena to take one of us, Grazia, I think, to the doctor."

"What happened to the key?"

"I don't know. You'd have to ask Sister Carmela."

"Perhaps the sisters at Mercy House have some keys too."

"I have no idea."

"And as far as you know, the La Barcas don't possess one. Sometimes neighbors keep them in case you get locked out."

Evelina stared at the nun. "Someone's always here to let us in, Sister. Why on earth would we give one to the neighbors?"

"Okay, you've checked this door. You turn around. Stop. You are about to cross through the television room again. What do you see?"

"The television's off. Cammeo and Elenora are on the couch. Liliana's pulling Pia out of the chair."

"Pia's still up? Ten's a bit late for her, don't you think?"

"Pia's resisting. Liliana has probably awakened her and is helping her up to bed."

"Perhaps," said Sister Daniela. "She could be throwing a tantrum."

Evelina scrunched up her eyes and tried to concentrate on the scene. "I'm not sure. We could ask Liliana, I suppose."

"So you walk through this scene and then through the dining room. Stop. Who's left in here?"

"I see no one. Someone's turned off the lights."

"Do they normally do that?"

"No, but often enough. Someone probably thought they were helping me. It depends on who was in here last."

"But you can see enough to know there's no one still lingering."

"Actually I trip on one of the chairs because it's dark. I confess that I swore. No one called me out on it so I figured the room was empty. Touching the wall, I make my way to the kitchen." She pushed open the door.

"Stop. Can you see?"

Busy fixing lunch, Sister Edita and Elenora look up but don't say anything.

"Yes. There's a nightlight on in the kitchen. Sister Carmela doesn't want all the lights out in case she needs to tend to someone during the night."

"Is there anyone in the kitchen?"

Evelina hesitates. The two cooks stop to listen, but when Sister Daniela stares at them, they turn away and resume their work.

"Yes Grazia's getting a drink of water."

"She takes a glass with her?"

"No. We aren't allowed to take a container of liquid upstairs at night. The nuns worry that there'll be accidents—bedwetting."

"So how does Grazia get her water?"

"She crawls up onto the counter and turns on the tap. Then she leans over to sip the flowing water."

"Like a fountain?"

"Yes."

"She gets down and passes you as she leaves the kitchen?"

"Yes. She gets down but she doesn't pass me."

"She stays in the kitchen?"

"No. There's a door just left of the one to the outside landing."

"This little door?" the nun asked, opening it.

"Yes. There are back stairs to the second-floor rooms. It lets us off right next door to Grazia's room."

"So anyone can come downstairs to get water and such anytime during night."

"I suppose, but they're taking a risk."

"What do you mean?"

"If Sister Carmela catches anyone using *her* stairs, she makes them do double their chores."

"Did she catch Grazia that night?"

"I don't think so, but she once caught Terza, and Terza had to clean the bathroom by herself for a week. I've never seen her use those stairs again."

"All right, Grazia climbed down from her perch and scrambled up the stairs. Then what do you see?"

"Nothing."

"Did you turn this way to see if Sister Carmela's light's on?"

"I'm not sure, but I still wouldn't be able to tell. She always has a nightlight on in her room and her bathroom too. She's afraid of the dark, I suppose." Evelina turned toward the door. "I check the door to the outside landing. It's locked. No surprise."

"Nothing unusual then. The hairs on your neck don't stand up. You don't look toward the window to see if anyone's watching you?"

Evelina stared at Sister Daniela again. "No, but I probably will from now on."

The two women retraced their steps to the dining room.

"Stop. Is the dining room light still off?"

Evelina hesitated. "No. I don't think it is. I flip it off at the far switch. As I'm walking through, I check under the table."

"Why?"

"I don't know. I just wanted to make sure no one's there before I turn off the light." Evelina continued to the television room.

"Stop. Who's here?"

"No one. The light's on, but the children are gone."

"Did you think to look in the office right off the television room? Is the door closed? Are the lights off in there?"

"I didn't notice anyone. I don't remember if the door was open or closed. It's usually open, I suppose."

The nun walked into the office and checked the windows. They were all latched—except for one. Sister Daniela tried to latch it but couldn't. "What do you know about this window?"

"I don't know anything. We usually don't come in here."

Sister Daniela headed through the front door and down the steps. The window was behind the branches of a thick bush and just above her head. Nocera would've had to have some kind of ladder to gain access through that window.

She retreated inside and found Evelina. "Okay, you pass through the television room and turn off the light."

"No. I leave it on. I walk past the stairs and head down the passage to the nurse's office."

"Stop. Did you check the door again? Could one of the children still remaining in the television room have opened it before going upstairs?"

"No, I don't check the door. I don't think one of the children would do that."

"Is the bathroom door open or shut?"

A crease formed between Evelina her eyes. She stared in the direction of the bathroom. "I don't remember."

"Is the light on?"

"Again, there's a nightlight. I'd see that whether or not the door's open or shut."

"Is there a light in the passage to the nurse's office?"

"No. During the day there are windows but not at night."

"Grazia mentioned that the moonlight made it lighter outside."

"Perhaps. I'm not sure if it was light or dark. I walk this every night and don't expect extra light." Evelina got to the office door, automatically reaching into her pocket to pull out a key.

"Stop. What's that?" Sister Daniela put out her hand for the key and turned it over in her palm. "It's my understanding that the key to the landing's missing, but we *do* have one to the door to this room."

"It's a regular key."

"Who else has one of these?"

"As far as I know, this is the only one, but I don't *really* know. This one belonged to the last nurse. Sister Carmela took it directly from the nurse as she was leaving and handed it to me."

The nun pushed it into the lock and opened the office door. The room was sunny with windows on both sides. From one, she could see La Barca's vineyard. The other view offered the landing. After the two women entered, Sister Daniela closed the door behind them.

"Why do you need to do that?"

"I was wondering if when you locked the door someone inside could still get out. We'll test that on the way out." The nun faced the exterior door and turned the knob. The door opened.

"The outside door opens without a key when one goes out but automatically locks afterward."

"So when you check this door, you must assume it's locked."

"Yes, but I still bolt it by turning the latch above it."

"It's unlatched now. Does someone do that in the morning?"

"I don't know. Sometimes it's open. I've never seen anyone come down the passage to use this office."

"When you locked it that night, was it open?"

Evelina hesitated. "I'm not sure."

Sister Daniela turned around to see a desk and a few tables. Equipment sat on top of them, including a microscope and scale. It was difficult for the nun to identify the other machines. They didn't seem to be plugged in. The cords wrapped the contraptions in various loops and knots.

"How long has it been since you had a nurse?"

"More than five years, maybe seven or eight."

"And why did the last one leave?" Sister Daniela squeezed between pieces of discarded furniture, stacked neatly in columns. She bent down to see what was under an examination table.

"Sister Carmela claimed that we didn't need a nurse when Filari opened a clinic."

The nun pulled on a pile of cushions under the table and tugged at a colorful object between them. "Ah, a little elephant," she said, examining her find. "Perhaps the nurse used stuffed animals to comfort her patients." She stood up. "I suppose no one opens this window." She attempted to push up the pane of a nearby window.

"No. I've never seen that one open."

"Go to the passage outside this door and lock the door like you usually do when you leave."

Evelina stepped out and locked the door from the passage side.

The door opened easily when Sister Daniela turned the knob from the inside. "That answers that. If someone could enter from the landing, he could easily get inside the main house."

Evelina traipsed back down the passage.

"Stop. You're passing the bathroom. What do you see?"

Evelina came to a halt. "The door's closed. Someone must be inside. I didn't see or hear anyone go inside, though."

"Grazia claimed to have heard you lock up. It could be Grazia."

"I don't know. I don't wait. I don't recheck the front door. I just mount the stairs and go to bed."

"The light to the television room and the dining room are off?"

"Television room—no. Dining room—yes. I usually turn out TV-room light before I go upstairs."

"After that do you turn on lights for the stairs?"

"No. I go up in the dark."

"Is Grazia in bed when you get to the top?"

"I don't know. She doesn't sleep in my room."

"But you don't see her at the window outside your room either."

"No. I think I'd notice that."

"How could you make it up the stairs in the dark?"

"I'm used to them. It doesn't have to be light for me to make my way up." Evelina hesitated. "Wait a minute. It isn't dark at the top of the stairs."

"Because there's still a light on?"

"No. There's moonlight bouncing off the wooden floor. There's an empty chair by the window."

"Do you look out the window?"

"No. There's something else. I don't fall asleep

right away. After about an hour, I begin to doze, but I'm awakened by a noise."

"Perhaps you hear the intruder."

"No. I hear the scrape of the chair on the wooden floor. I start to get up, but I can't move my feet. I hear another noise."

"Do you think it's Grazia opening the window?"

"No, the sound's farther away."

"What do you mean? You hear something elsewhere in the house?"

"Yes. I hear something downstairs or outside. I'm not sure."

"Why don't you awaken someone else?"

"I think I might be dreaming. I sit up and wait for another sound but don't hear anything more. I turn over and finally go to sleep.

Chapter Twenty-Three

Sister Angela tossed and turned. Rolling onto her side, she stared at the alarm clock. The alarm was set for five-thirty, when everyone would awaken to go to prayers. At what hour did Chief Detective Pagano arrive at the station?

The fan in her window helped, but the air was still sticky. Rising, she slid a wooden chair in front of the fan to sit and think. What did she know about the Rufina region in northern Tuscany? Had she ever been there? It was just an hour or two east of Florence, wasn't it? Nocera told Carlota he'd worked in a vineyard in Rufina. If Nocera wasn't related to Pia, why did he remove her from the orphanage? It must have meant he'd been hired. By whom? Perhaps the family? Sister Angela shook her head.

In her mind, she went over what she and Silvio found out about the vehicle on a small dirt road not so far from the convent. Did the car come from Rufina? The little gray sedan had a dent toward the back. The driver could see the other automobile in her rearview mirror. How long had it been following her? The driver must have left the main highway to see if the pickup would exit too. She veered off at the last second and then watched in horror as the other vehicle remained behind her. Surely she thought that if she kept going straight ahead, she'd find another entrance onto the highway. But instead, the little road narrowed. Unable to turn around, she drove on, accelerating to raise dust so the vehicle would stay back. But the pickup had more power. She was an easy target. There in the field, bordered by single, stubby tree, gangly bushes, and dirt drives that led beyond the eyesight of possible witnesses, the car behind her slammed her. Once Twice. She tried to stay on the road, but the final blow spun the car around. Her head hit the steering wheel with such impact that she was nearly thrown from the seat. The culprit or culprits had no need to leave evidence. They only took the time to remove it from the car. Did they remove anything else? Did the police get DNA from the back seat? There was no evidence of a child in the car.

She sighed. Tears for the victim mixed with a sleepless night filled her eyes. Someone had suggested they exhume the young woman's body. But what information could they glean from that? No, it would be better to follow up on Nocera and see if he and the accident were connected.

She must have fallen asleep. Sister Angela's head snapped up when the alarm went off. Her neck cracking, she rubbed it as she stood. Why on earth hadn't she returned to bed when she started to nod? She donned a robe. Seizing her towels and toiletry bag, she made her way down the hallway to shower.

Downstairs, the kitchen was empty, but the door was open. She could hear the chant emanating from the chapel across the garden. Noticing there was no coffee or tea ready to be served, she scurried to the chapel entrance. The prayer service had already started. Slipping into a back pew, she immediately joined in.

"I'm glad you could make it, Sister," said the prioress. "Sister Concetta left the service early to heat the rolls and brew the espresso. I hope you'll join us."

"Yes, please," Sister Angela said. She felt for the red phone in her pocket. Perhaps she had a bit of time to eat before she made her phone call.

"Did you sleep well?" asked Sister Oriana, sitting down next to her at the long table.

"Yes. It's a perfect room for me," she said, slightly distracted. "Do you remember an automobile accident less than a kilometer across the field four years ago?"

The other faces at the table looked blank.

"I remember one on Via Veneto," said Sister Tiberia. "Was it four years ago? I'm not sure." She took a bite of her roll.

"It was about the time that you got the child."

"Really?" said Mother Patrizia. "Perhaps it's because of the child that we forgot there was some sort of accident. I really don't recall one. Was anyone hurt?"

"Yes. The woman driving was killed."

"Via Veneto's a bad road," said Sister Tiberia. "It has lots of bumps and potholes. Perhaps she lost control and ran into a fence or bush beside the road."

"There seems to have been another vehicle involved. Of course, the police never found the second one."

"But how can you tell if there was no sign of another vehicle?"

"The car had been hit. There was damage to her vehicle."

"I'm surprised I didn't see that in the papers," said Mother Patrizia. "Perhaps Father Montez remembers the victim."

"The police held the body for identification. Without an ID, she couldn't be buried by the Church."

"And you're investigating this accident why?" asked the prioress.

"Because Pia was delivered to your doorstep a day or so later."

The nun excused herself as soon as the conversation lulled. She retired to her cell to call the chief detective.

"Hello, Sister Angela. Have you found anything new?"

"Yes, Ricco. I'm not sure where it's taking us, but I'm working on it. Have you let La Barca go?"

"Yes. We could've kept him. The murder happened at his winery, after all. But his *avvocato* convinced us that La Barca wouldn't leave the area. Considering the value of his assets, he has too much at stake."

"I agree. I don't think La Barca murdered Nocera. I actually doubt he was trying to cover up the crime either."

"Then we don't have much."

"Actually, I think the evidence lies in Rufina. I haven't set up my itinerary, but I'd like to make my way there today. I want to know more about Rufina. If Nocera worked there, one of those wineries probably employed him. I'd like a list of the wineries. Can you get me that?"

"Got it. What else?"

"I'd like to talk to the senior detective in the Rufina region. Can you set that up for me?"

"That would be in Corsa Pietra. I'm afraid we have no detectives there. I can introduce you one of the agents, however. Let me call them so they can protect you."

"I don't need protection but would welcome information."

"By the way, Mother Faustine from Mercy House forwarded an email from Sister Daniela's mother superior, reminding us that your young friend must return to Montriano. If she wants her teaching position back, she'll have to be at the school by this weekend. We'll miss her help."

"Ah," Sister Angela responded. "I assume there'll be a note waiting for me in my email too. I really must speed up the investigation."

Sister Tiberia had a eighteen-year-old nephew, Dino, with a car. She suggested Dino drive Sister Angela and her for a winetasting tour of Rufina, less than two hours away by automobile. The nuns were on the road about fifteen minutes later.

Pagano sent the short list of wineries to Sister Angela. There were only two large ones dominating the sales of wines in the region.

"Are there no others?" asked Sister Tiberia.

"Yes," said Sister Angela. "There are smaller ones, but if Nocera worked in the region, he probably worked for one or both of the big ones. We'll taste wines there first. I'm worried about Dino, however. If he tastes too, we may not make it home tonight."

Sister Tiberia smiled. "He doesn't like wine. He won't taste any. I did promise he could help you investigate, though."

"Good. We may need a bodyguard."

Dino flexed the muscle of his free arm.

Sister Angelo directed Dino up the long well-groomed drive of the first winery. "This one's on Pagano's list. We'll start here. Dino and the two nuns passed the outdoor tables and went inside. A few people stood at the long counter.

"I'll try your Chianti," they said to the man behind the counter.

"Where are you ladies from?" he asked.

"I'm from Castel Valori and my companion is from Montriano," Sister Tiberia said, expectantly holding up a wineglass she'd picked up from the end of counter.

"Did you know that the Rufina area's slightly more mountainous and less gently hilly than the

Classico zone?"

"Yes, and the nights are cooler," said Sister Angela. "That causes the grapes to ripen more slowly."

Sister Angela held up her empty glass, but the gentleman behind the counter ignored them both. "I think you'll find that in the last thirty years, Chianti Rufina's become richer. We consider the wines here as being serious contenders for the best Chianti in the world."

"Prove it," said Sister Tiberia, no longer smiling.

"We usually have guests take the tour before tasting."

Sister Angela smiled. "Do you mind if we talk with your superior? I'm working with the State Police in Siena. While we're waiting, we wouldn't mind a taste of your fine wine."

The bartender retreated to a door at the end of the bar.

Sister Tiberia leaned over the counter to see if he was returning with a bottle. "I'm not sure that's the response I'd go for."

In less than a minute, another man entered through the door carrying a bottle. "How do you do?" he said to the nuns, uncorking the new bottle. "My assistant said you needed to speak with me. How can I help you?"

"I have a picture of a man by the name of Alrigo Nocera. He spoke of having worked in some of the wineries here."

"What's the matter with him?" asked the manager, staring at the picture.

"He's dead."

"It doesn't really look like him, but I know the name. I believe he worked with my family in one capacity or another over the years." He poured each nun a taste of wine. "This is the *riserva,* our best."

The nun took a sip. It was indeed good. She hoped he'd offer another, but saw him recork the bottle before either woman could ask. "Very nice," she said. "I don't understand. You know his name as having worked here but don't know how he was employed or for how long."

"You must understand. We have hundreds of contractors who work here, especially during the harvest. I wouldn't keep records on them. I only do that for those I hired directly.

"Is there an agency you use to get contractors when you need them?"

"No. We don't have any large towns with businesses that handle that. They come to us looking for work. I guess they aren't really contractors. Let's call them temporary workers."

"If he was from around here, do you know if he had a family?"

The manager's eyebrows rose into perfect Roman arches. "I'm afraid I'm too busy here to know everyone in Rufina."

"I can imagine," Sister Tiberia said. "I'd be surprised if you knew many of the people who live here. I suppose you don't attend church."

"Thank you, Signor…"

"Signor Pagnozzi."

Sister Angela stared at the label of the corked bottle in his hand.

"I'd appreciate it if you didn't bother my

bartender. Please contact me directly if you need more information." He handed her a card and disappeared through the door with his bottle.

"Nice man," said Sister Tiberia. "Who was he?"

"He's one of the owners," she said, showing her the card. "Let's find Dino. I hope they didn't talk him into going on the tour."

The nuns got a similar response from the second winery. While they were more generous with the flights of wine, they didn't reveal any more information about the victim.

"I remember him," said the manager. "He didn't work very hard. I let him go after the picking season was over."

"Do you have employment records?" asked Sister Angela.

"No. I don't keep them on temporaries. If he'd proven to be an asset to the company, I would've hired him."

"Would these temporary seasonal jobs pay well enough for him to live in this area?"

"Unless he was working full time, no. I imagine most temporaries have family to fall back on."

"Let's say you were a temporary. If the two largest concerns refused to hire you, where would you go?"

"If I felt I could only do labor in the fields, I guess the only other place would be some of the zone's startups or small family wineries. We do have some of those. They don't pay as much as we do, but they still try to compete for workers. Why don't you visit some of them, Sister?"

From there, the nuns checked on a few of the lesser-known wineries that the first manager recommended. No one seemed to recognize Nocera at all.

"I think we should return home," said Sister Tiberia. "We don't seem to be getting anywhere. These smaller wineries don't serve anything anyway."

"I'll need a cup of espresso if you expect me to drive all the way back," said Dino.

"There's a small café just as we go into one of the villages," said Sister Angela. "Maybe there'll be something to snack on too."

Dino pulled up to the curb, and the three walked into a café to order coffee and sandwiches. Sister Angela hesitated and grabbed a newspaper on the shelf on the way in. After they ordered, the nun opened the paper and began to read.

"Look at this," she said, folding back the first few pages. "A small winery in the area is actually growing. It seems to be having an impact on the two large conglomerates we just visited."

"Why didn't we call upon them?" asked Sister Tiberia, glancing at her watch. "I guess it would be too late now."

"It wasn't on the list the last winemaker gave us. Perhaps that's because they're worried this upstart company might grow and become a competitor."

The waitress brought their food and coffees.

"Have you heard of this winery?" Sister Angela asked the waitress.

"Yes. Their wine's quite good."

"May I keep this newspaper?"

"Of course. If you go there to taste their wine, let them know that Stella sent you."

Chapter Twenty-Four

Sister Angela missed morning prayers and breakfast at the convent. She didn't show up at the police station until after ten.

"You look drained, Sister," said Turo. "Perhaps you tasted too much wine yesterday."

"That must be it," she said. "We tasted wine but accomplished little else."

"Then we have to go back and look at our evidence again."

"I wish we knew who brought Pia to the convent," said Sister Angela. "That would tell us much more."

"Did you contact the people who used the child care facility at the avalanche site?"

"Yes. I emailed each one and called those who didn't respond to the email," said the nun, sitting in at one of the desks, rocking the chair from side to side. "No one remembers an extra child or anything odd happening during the catastrophe. But I'm not sure that's so unusual. Most people would be worried about their own situation."

"What about the bank robbery?"

"The heist told us nothing."

"Then you don't believe it was someone who had too few resources and left the child."

The nun stopped fidgeting. "Nor do I think it involved any of the families who were having marital or monetary difficulties four years ago."

"What about the car accident?"

"What about it? The car's gone. We have the driver's DNA but no other DNA that might indicate that a child was there. We can compare Pia's DNA with the victim's, but that'll take time. It's been too long since the accident. We must find witnesses to get anything new."

"Silvio was looking for you earlier today. He's been continuing to investigate the accident. I sent him out on an errand. He should be back in a couple of hours."

The nun wasn't listening. "I know it has something to do with the area around Corsa Pietra. I just don't know who to approach. Obviously the high-and-mighty Chianti winemakers don't want to bring unwanted attention to the area. It might hurt them in the middle of the tourist season."

"I'm not sure that would stop you," said Turo. "I need some coffee. Did you have breakfast? If not, can I order you something?"

"Please. I didn't have breakfast because I didn't feel hungry. But now that I'm back into the middle of clues, I could use a roll of some sort—something light to hold me over until lunch."

The detective sergeant glanced at his watch. "Why don't I just get us some lunch? That way we can work through the conventional lunchtime."

After their meal, Turo decided to continue their

conversation. "What makes you say you know it has to do with that zone?"

"Nocera was from Rufina," said Sister Angela, sweeping the crumbs from the table into the palm of her other hand. "He kidnapped the child and then became a victim himself. There's got to be a connection."

"So we have to look at Nocera more closely."

The nun's face lit up. "Do you have anything on him?"

"No, but I did write the police in Corsa Pietra. Albeit a short one, our Alrigo Nocera does have a record."

"What do you mean *short?*"

"Most of his menial crimes were settled outside of court, but he was arrested for disorderly conduct, theft, and public drunkenness."

"The arrests themselves would tell us where he was working and if he had an *avvocato*, correct?"

"We're banking on that, yes. The police are forwarding his file. We should have it this afternoon." He looked at his watch. "In the meantime, Silvio should be back from his assignment. He mentioned needing to speak with you about what he discovered when he went over the evidence again. It would be nice if you could indulge him."

"Of course I must. Silvio's got a good head on his shoulders. He'll make an excellent detective someday. We're partners."

Sister Daniela stood on the landing outside the second-floor bedrooms. The chair that Evelina and Grazia both mentioned was no longer in front of the window. Where did it go? She gazed at the vineyard next door. *Who watched over the wine while La Barca was in jail? Would Carlota return in time to help pick the grapes?*

The young nun's eyes dropped to the column of vines that ended at the fence. *What did Grazia tell Sister Angela she'd seen?* She squinted, trying to imagine the victim in a nun's habit looking back up at her. Grazia told everyone that the full moon made it easy to see the old nun. That was true. The position of a full moon would've lit the whole field. *What else did Sister Angela say Grazia told her?*

Turning, Sister Daniela hurried down the stairs to the main floor. She could hear the banter of children in the dining room. She looked at her watch. She had fifteen minutes before she had to be back in the classroom.

The chatter stopped the second she set foot in the dining room. She eyed the group and found Grazia on the far side of the table, awkwardly gathering her dishes to deliver to the kitchen counter.

Sister Daniela crossed the room and offered her assistance. "Let me help you, Grazia. It looks like you have too many dishes to take all at once."

"Thank you, Sister Daniela. I spilled on my blouse. I must go up to my room and put on a clean one before class starts."

Sister Daniela dropped off the dishes and followed the young girl up the stairs. Grazia found her clean shirt and began to change. "You mentioned to Sister Angela that the old nun had a sparkly ring, didn't you?"

"Yes. It was beautiful."

"Grazia," the nun said. "I ran into someone the other day. He told me he belonged to you. Did I understand him correctly?" She removed the pink stuffed animal from her pocket.

Grazia's eyes lit up. "That's Sampson. He's my friend."

The nun let her give the elephant a hug. "Do you want to know where I found him?"

Grazia looked up at the nun, her eyes hinting that she knew. "Yes, I don't know where I could have left him."

"What about at your *fortezza?*"

"It isn't a fortress. It's a castle."

"It looked very comfortable." When Grazia turned to leave, Sister Daniela gently clutched her arm. "Did the old nun come to the door while you were in your castle?"

"The nun held up her hands in prayer. I thought she was cold outside."

"When? When you were at the window that night?"

"No. She was in the field the night before." Tears filled her eyes. "I saw her in the field. She wanted to come in."

"But you didn't go down to let her in that night did you."

"No. I worried about her all the next day. The following night I saw her again. I pointed to the back of the orphanage."

"Why? Evelina had locked all the doors. Did you go down again?"

"No. I didn't go to bed when she told us to. I hid in the bathroom. When I heard Evelina climb the stairs, I went back to the castle and unlatched the door to the landing."

"How did you get into your castle room?"

Grazia turned over the pink elephant and worked her tiny fingers into the seam under its ribbon collar. After wrestling with it for a few seconds, she pulled out a key.

"But how did the door get locked again after the old nun left with Pia?"

"You can lock the passage door by pushing the button before closing it. The interior door automatically locks." She finally gazed up at Sister Daniela's face. "I didn't know she would take Pia. I thought she was a real nun."

"Where's the old nun's ring?"

"What do you mean?"

Sister Daniela took the elephant from the little girl and stuck her fingers through the seam. She could feel it but not get it out. She handed it back to Grazia. "We need the ring as evidence. Please remove it and give it to me," she said.

Grazia reached inside and produced the diamond-encrusted men's ring. "Am I kicked out of the orphanage?"

Sister Daniela winked at her. "I'll tell Sister Carmela and Sister Natalia that you're my special assistant. I don't think they'll be too angry. Please hurry. Class is starting."

On the way down the two flights of stairs, the young nun slipped her phone out of her pocket and dialed Sister Angela.

Silvio made an appearance in the early afternoon, offering to show the nun something at the accident site. Donning a helmet, Sister Angela grudgingly climbed on board the back of the motorbike, and Silvio revved the engine.

"I don't know why we don't just walk," she shouted near his ear, but he didn't seem to be able to hear her.

The motorbike slowed as Silvio guided it onto the dirt road and then sped up until the dust trail from the front wheel blew back over his passenger's helmet. By the time the two arrived at the site, Sister Angela could taste the grit between her teeth and spat, attempting to dislodge some of it.

Silvio retrieved a file from a saddlebag below Sister Angela's seat. "This is what I found out about the car accident that took place here four years ago. The automobile was coming from the same turn-off we used when we left the highway. The female driver was followed by another car."

"You can't prove that."

"Wait a minute. The report of the accident said that the car couldn't have been hit from behind because there were no dings across the back fender. More likely, she drove off the road on her own and slid into a tree over here."

"What tree?" the nun asked, shading her eyes and looking all around her.

"There was a tree there. It's in the photo.

Someone must have chopped it down."

"They called it a hit and run in the report *I* saw."

"But that wasn't the final report. This one is. No one followed up on this because the case was closed."

"If she was driving in the same direction we just were, the tree would've caved in the passenger side," said Sister Angela. "This report doesn't agree with the one the medical examiner gave us."

"I believe it was more complicated than that. There's a small possibility the car got turned around before it hit the tree."

"There was no one else involved?"

"If I drive too fast on this dry dirt, my bike starts to fishtail. If I slam on the breaks in a fishtail, I turn my bike all the way around."

"I wonder how many time you had to prove that to yourself. I believe you, but that doesn't drive you into a tree."

"So now we have one car pointing this way and the car that tailed her facing her directly. She was staring into her assailant's evil eyes. Do you think she recognized him?"

"Cut the drama and tell me your theory."

"I think she tried to go down the embankment enough to go around him. He let her drive by, and then, as she managed to steer up and onto the roadway, he backed up accelerating until he hit her on the back corner of the passenger side, forcing the car down the embankment and into the tree."

"Let's assume she was killed," said Sister Angela. "He—if it was a he—gets out of the car or truck and walks down the embankment, sees her dead, takes anything that might ID the car, and the child in her car seat, and takes off. When he gets back to the main road, he, for some god-forsaken reason, excuse my French, turns right toward town. Suddenly he sees a convent, and bless the Lord, he can now get rid of the child too."

"No," said Silvio. "That would be silly. He'd never do that. I think he didn't get out of his vehicle at all. This whole thing must have caused some noise. He wouldn't know if anyone lived close by. What if they came snooping around? I believe he took off to consider his options."

"You think he called the mastermind?"

"If he had one—or he realized he needed to make sure she was dead. He's facing this direction. He keeps driving but doesn't find an entrance onto the highway. He turns around and approaches the site again. No one's around. The dirt road must have muffled most of the sound. He gets out of his vehicle and climbs down to the car, opens the door, and her body falls out. He cleans anything that might tie her to him and leaves satisfied. He's accomplished his mission."

"What about Pia?"

"I haven't solved that part yet. He either took her, the car seat, and all the paraphernalia that parents lug around for their youngsters, and then left—*or* someone else came along and did that before he came back."

"In order to open up the case again, you're going to need new evidence. How are you going to do that when we no longer have a car, a body, or a child?"

Silvio opened his file on the seat of the bike. "Look at this photo. The police were looking for a dent on the back fender of the car. If she were heading toward town he'd hit the fender on the rear toward the driver's side. It's like playing pool. If you hit her car here, she loses control and drives toward the tree. But she'd be on the opposite side. If she did a one eighty and tried to go round him he would've hit her where you actually see the dent in the photo. Look farther along the fender. This wasn't her first accident. I'm sure the police saw it and figured the dent was from an earlier scrape. After all, she was a terrible driver who couldn't steer herself away from the only tree around."

The nun held the picture close to her eyes and then turned to face the direction in which the car would be pointing. Then she looked up to see the landscape around where the tree in the picture once grew. "You're right. In the snapshot, there's a telephone pole. It's in the middle of the field in the direction out of town. Do you have a picture of her?"

"Yes, it's the same one that was in the evidence we leafed through. She's hanging outside the door, which was probably opened by the assailant."

"Oh, and look at this. The back door behind her isn't latched. Do you think he went into the back seat area to find evidence that might ID the car or did he open the door to retrieve the child?"

"My gut tells me he didn't take the time to recover the car seat and other baby stuff," said Silvio. "Why would he if he were going to drop her off up the road?"

"Then where did those items go? They never ended up at the convent."

The two glanced around.

"There's a fence here," said Sister Angela. "That means there's a farm nearby. I think there are people living around here. As for your gut, the nuns are good at relieving that. Let's stop off at the convent and have some espresso and a treat."

Chapter Twenty-Five

Weary, the pair returned to the convent to find most of the nuns working in the garden. After a cool drink and a roll, Silvio drove back to the police station.

"You look tired," said Sister Tiberia. "Why don't you sit here in the shade? I'll go in and brew you an espresso."

"Thank you. Maybe that'll do the trick. I really don't have time to sleep. I must solve this case before Sister Daniela and I return to Montriano."

Sister Angela emptied the cup with one last sip. "Those were delicious ricotta cookies," she said. "I'll have to get the recipe before I leave here." She sauntered into the kitchen to wash her cup when she heard the front door open and then shut. Sister Oriana chattered away as she accompanied someone to the kitchen.

"Sister Angela, look at these beautiful tomatoes and carrots. Signor Petrini has shared some of his harvest with us."

"How do you do, Signor Petrini?" she said, wiping her hands on the napkin still tucked behind the rosary beads hanging from her side. Sister Angela put out her hand, but the gentleman didn't respond.

"Signor Petrini's our special friend," said Sister Oriana. "He was in an accident when he was a boy and still gets confused."

"But I can see he's a good farmer," Sister Angela said, examining one of the tomatoes. "Is this from his farm?"

"Yes. He lives not too far from here. He's done very well considering his hardships."

"Do you still need a nap, Sister?" asked Sister Tiberia.

"No. Silvio and I planned to go back out after I've rested a bit. He should be here soon to pick me up."

Not fifteen minutes later, they could hear Silvio rev the motor of his bike as he tried to climb the short drive.

Sister Oriana and Sister Angela emerged onto the front porch to meet the young man with hopes of becoming a detective like his uncle. Sister Angela handed one of the tomatoes to Silvio and introduced him to her colleague.

An old man limped out of the front door, nodding his head. "*Vroom, vroom*," he said, hobbling down the steps to the drive.

Silvio looked lost.

"*Vroom, vroom*," Petrini repeated, as he passed them on the drive. "*Screech, bang!*" he said, clapping his hands to make the explosion sound even louder. Then he toddled to the road below and, after checking for traffic both ways, crossed it.

"Where did you say he lived?" asked Sister Angela.

The nuns consulted each other. "I don't know exactly," said Sister Oriana. "Somewhere out there." She made a sweeping gesture in the direction he'd just taken. "Perhaps one of the other sisters knows."

Silvio handed the nun her helmet before donning his own. "We can find out at the station, though I'm not sure how the man can help us."

Sister Angela climbed on and encircled his waist, knowing the trip down the drive would be a bumpy one.

At the station, Detective Sergeant Turo barked instructions into his phone.

"I'm not the only one who didn't get much sleep," said the nun.

Turo let out a long sigh. "I was talking with Agent Alba with the Corsa Pietra police. They haven't sent us the information on your victim, Nocera. Perhaps they're having trouble with the winemakers too."

"Sounds like police practices in the region are lax. Have they given us anything?"

"They said they're overrun with tourists. Many of the vineyards are beginning to harvest this weekend. Lots of strangers in town means increased petty crime and heaps of reports. They've neither time nor the inclination to interrupt the town's biggest business. I did ask about this vineyard you found in the paper. He warned me that they were the most popular. They're growth in the last five years has been phenomenal."

"Really? And the other wineries?"

"I guess neither the big vineyards nor the other startups have benefitted as much from the bigger draw."

"Their wine must be good. Silvio and I should take another trip there and investigate."

"Silvio's too busy to romp around the Rufina zone," he said. "You'll have to find someone else to take you."

"What about my theory concerning the car accident?" asked Silvio.

"What about it? It's a sound theory, but where does that get us?" asked his uncle. "We have no new evidence. Find me the identity of the driver or an eyewitness. Then we've an investigation."

Sister Angela logged into Turo's laptop and checked her email. Sister Daniela asked her mentor to call her when she got a chance. Sister Angela stepped outside to dial her friend.

"What do you have?" she asked.

"The ring. I told you about getting Grazia to admit she unlatched the door for the old nun, um— Nocera. What I didn't have time to tell you is how we both missed something about what she described. You told me she mentioned being mesmerized by the glint of the nun's ring. When I looked down at my own, I conclude it looks too tarnished to reflect moonlight. I gazed around at the other nuns at the orphanage and saw that they didn't possess anything that might sparkle either."

"What ring? Nocera didn't have a ring on his finger when we found the body. I suppose if I'd thought about it I would've concluded that the murderer saw it and took it, thinking it might be worth something."

"No. According to Grazia, the old nun gave her the bling when Grazia left the door open and guided her to it. Nocera placed the ring on a table in the nurse's office for her. Grazia showed me the key to the former nurse's office by digging it out of a stuffed animal. After questioning the existence of the ring in my mind, I decided to poke deeper into the little elephant and discovered the ring."

"What does it tell us?"

"Signor Nocera was no slouch. The ring has diamonds and sapphires on it. I took it into town, and it appraises well. Our victim wasn't a picker."

Sister Angela thought about what the winemakers in the Rufina zone had insinuated. Perhaps they hired him for a bigger operation and discovered he was a thief. Why didn't they say anything?

"I believe I'll have to go back to Rufina. Nocera had a record, but the offenses were minor. The Police in Corsa Pietra don't seem to want to give us more. Sounds like a bigger operation than we thought. Thanks for the great detective work. You might have delivered the biggest clue we have yet."

Dispirited, the nun returned inside to take a short nap.

"I'm glad you're here," said Mother Patrizia. "I promised Signor Petrini that we'd deliver some eggplants to him since we didn't have time to pick them for him this morning."

"Those are beautiful, Reverend Mother. You have some great gardeners here too."

"He brought us some equally beautiful tomatoes and carrots. We'll have a tasty salad this evening. Would you mind delivering them for us?"

"Not at all. I could use the walk to keep me awake. Do you know where he lives?"

"He's off the next road down."

"Via Veneto?"

"Yes.

"The turnoff's quite far, isn't it?"

"If you go all the way down the main road before you turn off, yes. But just a few hundred meters from here is a pedestrian path. It's beside the house with the birdhouses hanging from the eaves. Follow the path down the hill until you get to Via Veneto. Then turn up the road toward town."

"I didn't see any houses along that road."

"If you follow it up about a hundred meters, you'll eventually see a narrow dirt drive leading down through some rangy bushes. You won't see the house from the road, but it's there."

"Will he recognize me?"

"Of course. He's neither stupid nor dangerous. You're wearing a habit. He'll recognize that. He has trouble communicating, but that doesn't mean he fails to understand."

Sister Angela took her package and spun around, coming face to face with Silvio. "I have an errand to run. Do you want to come with me?" She started for the door but quickly stopped. "I don't think we need the bike. I'd like to walk this time."

The two sauntered down the driveway and crossed to the other side. Then they trudged down the road toward Via Veneto.

"I hope you don't plan to walk to the accident site. It's a distance to the entrance and an equally long trip back up the dirt road."

The nun smiled. A few hundred meters along, they came upon a row of houses. The nun took a left beside a house with long vines and birdhouses hanging from the eaves.

"Where are we going?" asked Silvio.

"This is a shortcut," she said.

When they got to the dirt road, she turned left again.

"I think the accident site's in the other direction."

"No, no. I have to give these eggplants to Signor Petrini. He lives just up the road here."

After walking about ten more minutes, Sister Angela noticed a narrow dirt drive.

"Is there a house back here?" asked Silvio.

They continued through the arch formed by the tall bushes and immediately saw the house. It looked more like a hovel. The outside plaster was chipped, the shutters worn and unpainted. A barn nearby leaned into the house, its door left open to reveal a rusty tractor, gardening tools, and miscellaneous equipment.

The two passed the open barn, walked up to the door, and knocked. Suddenly a man carrying a rake hobbled around the corner and stopped to stare at them.

"Signor Petrini, I'm Sister Angela. We met at the convent this morning, remember? You brought us fresh carrots and perfect tomatoes. The prioress wanted you to have a couple of eggplants." She held out the bag.

Petrini stumbled forward and took them, all the time staring at Silvio.

"This is Silvio, the young man with the motorbike," she said, hesitating.

"Vroom, vroom."

"I saw your tractor in the barn," said Silvio. "How old is that? Surely someone might want to pay you for it." Silvio walked over to the barn door and admired it.

Sister Angela and Petrini followed.

Silvio saw the objects first. He turned to the nun and pointed at the back corner.

"What are those?" she asked the farmer.

"Baby," he said.

Silvio stepped over the pile in front and lifted a car seat out of the smaller pile. Under it was a faded bag. Silvio picked it up by the straps and held it high so Sister Angela could see it.

"I didn't know you had a child, Signor," she said, feeling her heart beat hard against her chest wall.

"No, those for the convent."

The nun smiled. "But they don't have a baby, do they?"

"Gone," he whispered.

"You gave the baby to the nuns," she said, holding out a hand to help Silvio and the evidence navigate the way out of the piles.

"Baby cried."

"Where was her mother?"

"Sleeping."

The nun looked at him. His eyes filled with tears.

"How did you know there'd been an accident?"

"*Bang Bang.* I run."

"How many cars were involved?"

"He held up a single finger. *Bang!* Tree."

"So you took the baby and left it with the nuns."

"Play games. Grow food. She love me."

"No one else has asked you about that day? Did any detectives or other strangers come here to inquire about the accident?"

"No. Mamma not move. Sleeping."

"Thank you, Signor Petrini. You've been most helpful," she said taking the diaper bag from Silvio and beginning to walk back up the drive.

The farmer didn't leave the spot. He watched the two leave with the baby's items. When they got to the arch in the bushes, Silvio turned to make sure the farmer was okay. Petrini set aside the rake, gave a slight wave of his free hand, and then turned toward his front door.

Silvio spun around and ran to catch up with the nun. "What do you think we should do?"

"I believe you should take the evidence to your uncle."

"What does this prove?" asked Silvio.

"It tells us who delivered Pia to the nuns."

"But Uncle Estes is going to say that it's irrelevant because it doesn't solve the case."

The nun stopped in her tracks at the end of the drive. "It verifies that Pia was in the car where her mother drove off the road and was killed. We've determined that there was another vehicle involved and that second vehicle hit her car. Now we have to identify the mother to see if she came from the same place as the murder victim. If Pia's alive, she's probably there."

Silvio tripped, and the nun waited for him to catch up. "I don't see the connection between Pia and the murder victim. Why did this Nocera guy need to take the child home?"

"Why would he take the child at all? If we find where he came from and identify his connections—his friends, business partners, who he owes money to—then we might get a clue of where Pia has been taken. You don't solve cases by jumping to the final clue. Mysteries take you on an intricate path of discoveries that together, hopefully, leads to the reason for and cause of a crime."

Sister Angela and Silvio finally arrived at the convent both thirsty and tired. Silvio strapped the items from Petrini's barn onto the back of his bike.

The nun took his canteen and filled it with cool water. "Tell Detective Sergeant Turo what I told you. Sister Tiberia and I will head to Rufina first thing in the morning. Your uncle must call the police there so they'll be available to assist us."

Chapter Twenty-Six

The two nuns were silent as the big 1985 silver Buick Riviera bumped over the ruts of the E78 carriageway.

"I can't believe this car has survived drives like these," said Sister Angela.

"I don't take out my baby often. That helps. The mileage in the nearly twenty-five years I've had it is still less than two hundred kilometers."

"Why didn't I see this car at the convent before?"

"My mechanic hates me to take her out. He thinks she belongs in a museum and keeps her at his garage for safekeeping."

"How did you get it? Did someone donate it?"

"It's mine. Dino wanted a new car, the one we rode in last time, so he gave me his old one. The Buick was already used when *he* bought it."

The car rattled as they hit another bump.

"This road's a travesty," said Sister Angela. "I read they planned to bring this carriageway up to European standards long ago, but they didn't finish it. We have four lanes of crumbling surface and have to drive like snails."

"We're almost there," said Sister Tiberia. "My baby will make it there and back. I think I'll still be driving her when Dino's car is disassembled for parts. This Buick's a gem."

The steep valley walls were revealed as the car crested the hill. Sister Tiberia pulled over so Sister Angela could better consult her map for directions.

"Are you sure you don't want to drive into Corsa Pietra first?" asked Sister Tiberia. "If someone at this vineyard's behind the murder and kidnapping, he might be dangerous."

"I don't want to destroy the reputation of this up-and-coming vineyard if everyone there's innocent." Sister Angela paused. "At least I want to make sure we get a taste of their Chianti first."

Sister Tiberia parked the Buick along the edge of the driveway and stepped out of the car.

"It looks busy," said Sister Angela.

"There's a table in the corner of the patio. Let's see if we can get that one."

A young woman with sweeping auburn hair wriggled between the tables and chairs, crammed close together on the patio. Men reached out to paw at her long bare legs.

"How can I help you?"

Sister Angela quickly glanced at the badge pinned just below her low-cut blouse. "We'd like to taste your wine, Donata." said the nun. "Do we need to order something first?"

"No," Donata said, swiping at the hand resting on her backside.

The guilty customer guffawed.

"But we have some tasty sandwiches that would

go well with the Chianti. There's also a prosciutto and melon salad."

"I'll take one of those with a taste of your Chianti," said Sister Angela.

Sister Tiberia nodded eagerly.

"Make that two," said Sister Angela. "By the way, my friend and I have been here before. It's been a few years since we made the trip." She tucked her napkin through the loop that held her rosary beads so it wouldn't blow away. "I'd say it's four or five years since we've been here. Isn't that right Sister?"

Sister Tiberia smiled and nodded again.

"Donata," Sister Angela continued, taking hold of the waitress's hand. "My friend and I promised to meet up with a young woman who used to work here. This young woman had long sandy hair and was roughly your age at the time."

Donata's face paled. She started to step back, but Sister Angela still held onto her hand, admiring the large diamond on her finger. The gentleman at the next table continued to take liberties with Donata's backside, and she sighed. "I've been here about four years. There was a waitress before that, but I'm not sure I really met her."

"You have a lovely ring. Your husband must love you very much."

Donata glanced toward the winery office and warehouse but quickly turned and pushed through the chairs and tables blocking her route to the tasting room.

Sister Tiberia giggled. "Bravo," she said. "I wish you'd let her go sooner, however, because I'd have a glass of wine by now with which to toast your performance. Did you see those heels? They must be at least four or five inches. Even my legs would look good in those."

"As much as I'd like to partake of my wine and salad, I'm afraid I'll have to further explore the premises. I wonder if there's a ladies room around here." She handed her red cell phone to Sister Tiberia. "If I don't return in ten minutes, call the police in Corsa Pietra."

Sister Tiberia stared at the contraption in front of her. "I've never used one of these before."

"Dial 1-1-2 and tell them to come immediately to the Amarena Balda Vineyard outside of Corsa Pietra," said Sister Angela. She hesitated. "Tell them I choking."

Leaving her tote, Sister Angela navigated her way past the tables. No hands dared to reach out for *her* backside. When she got to the asphalt drive she turned toward the next set of doors. A large panel truck was parked in front of the entrance. Sister Angela peered inside the dark cavernous winery. It was quiet.

She continued to the rear of the truck. The door was down, forming a ramp. Sister Angela peeked through the opening. No one was in the truck, but a few boxes were stacked in the far corner.

Turning, she found a closed door and inched it open to glimpse inside. Suddenly the doorknob was wrenched from her grip. Someone was emerging from what appeared to be storage warehouse. The man stopped short and stared at the intruder.

"I'm sorry," said the nun. "I must be in the wrong place. I was searching for a restroom."

"You're definitely not in the right place," said Ermanno, gently pushing the nun out of the doorway and closing it behind him."

"Ah. I was having lunch at your tasting room, and I thought your wife pointed me in this direction."

"No. The restrooms are in back of the tasting room."

"I'm sorry to disturb you," she said walking with him toward his office. "After lunch, my friend and I would like a tour. What time do you have tours?"

"I'm afraid we don't have any. It's harvest time, and we're very busy." He slowed in front of the entrance to the cavernous winery. "And Donata isn't my wife. She's my brother's fiancée."

Sister Angela had to think fast. She hadn't yet learned what she needed. She repeated to Ermanno her story about knowing the former waitress before he could turn and leave her there. Ermanno stared at her. His jaw muscles twitched, and a crease formed on his brow.

"Donata mentioned she replaced her about four years ago. I'm looking for the former employee you see. I'm a friend of the family and was asked by them to tell her they were thinking of her."

Ermanno took her arm and led her to his desk, situated on an island surrounded by steel drums and oak barrels.

"Oh, this must be the winery. Surely someone can tell me how the grapes turn into your delicious Chianti."

Ermanno gestured to another worker. "Sister, this is Guillermo, my assistant. Would you please escort this woman…?"

"Sister Angela," the nun said.

"Would you please give Sister Angela a tour of the premises? She's interested in how we make wine."

"I have a team working on the press as you asked. I really should…"

"The team can handle that. Sister Angela's come a long way for a tour, and I'm asking you to make her wish come true." Ermanno turned to face the nun. "You said you had a friend with you? I can go fetch her."

"Oh," she said, trying to come up with an answer. "We planned to meet here after lunch. She has to work through the noon hour and…"

"Are you saying she isn't here yet?" he asked, interrupting her. He held her by the shoulder nearly shaking the response out of her.

"Yes. She won't be here for another hour."

"I'm afraid it'll be too late for the tour in another hour," he said, removing his hand.

"That's all right. I'll take the tour by myself and tell her about it later." She spun around to follow Guillermo's retreating figure.

They began at the large press just outside the back door. Guillermo abandoned her for a few minutes to instruct his team. Sister Angela took the time to look at her watch. Sister Tiberia would be calling the police in three minutes.

"Sister," said Guillermo. "I assume you've seen bunches of grapes before…"

"Ah, what a beautiful scene. It makes me want to remain out here all day. Tell me, is that the farmhouse? The red of the tile roof is stunning against the blue sky. And look, beyond is Corsa

Pietra. Family members can look across the valley whenever they want."

"Yes, that's the family who owns Amarena Balda."

"Does Donata live there with her fiancée? I'm afraid I got her chatting about it when I saw her ring. How long have you worked here?"

"I've been here nearly ten years. Let's go inside. I can talk to you about fermentation."

"Just one moment. If you've been here ten years then you know about the woman whom Donata replaced."

The worker urged her toward the door. "Viviana? She hasn't been here for a while."

"Yes. I'm a friend of the family, you know. They told me Viviana loved working here. I heard she left, but you know how family is. Was she fired?"

Guillermo squeezed her arm and forced her through the door.

"What did I say?" she asked. "Did I say something?"

Ermanno approached. "What's wrong?"

"She's asking about Viviana," said Guillermo. "I'm not sure I should be the one to tell her anything about a previous employee."

"What do you want to know, Sister?" Ermanno demanded. "Please follow me. I can't leave my work right now, but we can still talk." He turned to leave.

Sister Angela sped up to stay with him.

"Tell me about Viviana's family," he said. "What do they want to know? Did the woman run away from them too?"

The nun nearly tripped. What had the assistant

said? Why had Ermanno assumed she was missing? *He must know something about her demise.* "It's true I haven't seen Viviana for several years. Her family never spoke of the situation. I assume that means she was fired and ran away ashamed." Breathless, she continued. "I suppose your brother's *avvocato* possesses the signed divorce papers."

Ermanno stopped. "What do you mean?"

"No one would let Donata marry him unless Viviana was dead, or she and your brother were divorced."

He walked away, the long strides of his gait making the nun trot alongside. Sister Angela wasn't watching where they were going. She had to concentrate. The nun slowed her pace. Letting her eyes scan his retreating figure, she searched for a weapon kept near his waist. She couldn't make one out. The nun listened for sirens. Silence. Didn't Sister Tiberia make the phone call?

"Forgive me, but maybe this is a bad time to ask for a tour. I see we're passing the entrance. I can leave now if it would be better for you."

"It's a bad time to make your exit, Sister. My tour starts over here. If you wait for me inside this room, I can uncork some of the *riserva* so we can sip wine while I show you how fermentation works. He opened the door at the end of the winery and flipped on the light."

"What room is this?" she asked as the lights went out again. The door shut behind her. *My guess is a jail cell.*

She made her way back to the door and flipped the light switch on the wall next to it. The bulb didn't go on. She'd just have to sit and let her eyes adjust to the dark. She remembered catching a glimpse of stacked boxes on the opposite wall and inched her way forward until she found a box away from the taller stacks. Sitting down, she fingered her beads. *A little prayer wouldn't hurt. Why can't I hear sirens?*

Sister Tiberia fumbled with the phone for five long minutes after the time she was supposed to call the police. Finally she managed to press 1-1-2 and explained where the two nuns could be found. The police in Roma put her on hold. She listened to the clicks until someone else picked up.

"Is this Corsa Pietra?" she asked.

"Yes."

"This is Sister Tiberia. My friend Sister Angela and I are at Amarena Balda Vineyard, but my friend's turning blue. I think she's choking. Please come as quickly as you can."

"Sister Angela from Castel Valori?"

"Yes, but she's actually from Montriano."

"Detective Sergeant Turo in Castel Valori told us to expect her. She never turned up here."

"We stopped at Amarena Balda to investigate, but she's had an accident. Please, please hurry."

"We dispatched an *ambulanza* to Amarena Balda. Are there any other instructions?"

"Please send a cruiser too. Look, this is just my opinion, but it might be wise if you don't use your sirens. I think someone here at the winery might have committed a homicide."

"What?"

Sister Tiberia held the phone away from her ear and instructed Donata to put the plates and glasses of wine on the table. "Sister Angela should be back in a minute. She left something in the Buick." She waited until Donata was a few tables away before she placed the phone to her ear again. "We're working on a homicide. We need help. I think Sister Angela's in trouble."

The police cruiser slowly made its way up the drive. Sister Tiberia, wine glass in hand, wriggled past the busy tables and stepped out to greet it. Two more police cars soon followed. She ran up to the first and asked the uniformed man to open the window. Behind him, one of the policemen stepped out of his car.

"Sister Angela went up the drive to the winery," she told him.

"Stay here," he said, waving to the others to follow him.

Donata stopped and stared at the group, a procession inching up the drive.

The large warehouse had two doors. As the agents approached the first one, they noticed a nun emerging from the second.

"There she is," he said.

She cocked her head, warning them that there was someone behind her.

"Take cover," he yelled as the rest of the agents scattered.

The person holding the nun's arm tried to pull her back into the storage chamber, but she refused, twisting out of his grip. That's when the shooting began. At first, Sister Angela's brain didn't comprehend what was happening. When it did, she jumped back, spun around and scuttled around the corner of the building.

It didn't take long for the shooting to stop. Ermanno was the only armed man, and the police soon talked him into giving up his weapon.

"Sister Angela, this is Agent Alba. It's safe to come out now," said the policeman in charge.

When she didn't appear, he went looking for her. He rounded the corner. She wasn't there either. It was then he saw the farmhouse.

Had she been shot? Following Sister Angela's possible trail while scanning for bloodstains on the walkway, he made it to the dining area just outside the kitchen. All was quiet. Where was the nun?

Sister Angela heard the creak of the kitchen door as the police entered the farmhouse. "There's a gun pointed at my head," she called out.

The old woman slammed the butt against the equally hard back of Sister Angela's head. She hit the floor face down with nothing to break her fall.

Alba called out from the kitchen. "Put it down. My partner's got his gun pointed directly at you."

Mamma de Capua spun around to investigate his claim and tripped over the nun's conveniently-placed foot. Her gun hit the floor and went off, tearing through the painting of a Tuscan hill village on the wall.

The agent offered Sister Angela his hand and helped her up. "Agent Alba," he said. Then he picked up the weapon.

A second policeman appeared in the kitchen doorway and stepped up to handcuff the old woman.

"Thank you," said Sister Angela. "I suspect, however, that we aren't through. I believe Signora de Capua carried a gun to keep strangers out because she's hiding someone."

"Let me do it," Alba said. "You have a large bump on the side of your cheek."

"And on the back of my head." The nun touched it and winced. "I'll look around this area. Your men can take the top floor."

The group dispersed. Several minutes later, they reconvened at the bottom of the stairs.

"I didn't find a basement door," said the nun. "There's a tool shed or something I can see through the window. Come with me. It'll probably be locked."

A padlock hung from the shed's door latch. Alba pulled a small lever-like instrument off of his belt and slid it into the padlock. He hit the end of it with the butt of his gun, and the padlock fell apart.

The nun opened the door wide and pushed aside a gas can and a few hand tools. In the corner lay a makeshift bed. She squeezed through stacks of pots and extra roof tiles. Her black curls stringy, the child pressed herself against the corner under a work table.

"Pia? My name's Sister Angela."

Sister Tiberia's face emerged from behind her friend, and the child's face suddenly lit up.

Chapter Twenty-Seven

Sister Tiberia slowed as she turned the Buick up the embankment in front of the convent. On the backseat, Pia, who slept in Sister Angela's arms most of the way from Corsa Pietra, roused.

The front door opened, and the nuns tumbled out of the convent onto the porch.

Pia smiled.

"Do you want to greet them?" asked Sister Angela.

Pia nodded and slid toward the door. She ran to them for a group hug.

Emerging from the car, Sister Tiberia tried to warn them the child needed a bath, but no one seemed to care.

"We must take the train to Siena at eight tonight," Sister Angela told the prioress.

"Detective Sergeant Turo told us about the rescue and also that you must leave. We've planned a little dinner party for five o'clock so friends in Castel Valori can say good-bye. The detective sergeant and Silvio will be coming. They can drive you to the terminal."

Mother Patrizia returned, placing an ice pack on Sister Angela's cheek.

Sister Tiberia took Pia's hand and led her inside to the bathroom. "We'll be ready in about a half-hour," she announced.

The detective sergeant and Silvio arrived as did Signor Petrini and Father Montez. The group stood around in the kitchen, waiting for Pia to appear. Sister Oriana had to rush to a shop in town and buy the child a dress because she was unable to clean the one Pia wore.

Sister Tiberia walked a well-scrubbed Pia down the long hallway. Pia could hear the voices and scampered toward them.

The prioress gave Pia some orange soda, something she bought for Sister Angela's visit, and introduced her to the detectives and priest.

When they got to Signor Petrini, the old man said, *"Beep, beep,"* and Pia giggled.

Sister Concetta served up soup, and everyone sat down to supper.

"How did you know to investigate Amarena Balda?" asked Turo when they were seated.

"I didn't. I just thought it was odd that this startup was growing so fast. It turns out they were bringing wines in from the Amalfi Coast and supplementing their own grapes with the Campanian wine. Their grapes would never have produced enough wine to export as much as they did. That crime wasn't murder, but money often leads man to commit more serious crimes. Remember, I knew a woman had been killed in an automobile accident and that Pia was discovered in the same car. I just pretended that I was a friend of the family and started asking personal questions. Donata, the waitress and fiancée of Viviana's widower, responded like she knew what I was talking about. I doubt she was aware that Giulio couldn't remarry because he needed either a dead body or divorce papers signed by his wife." The nun tore off a piece of bread. "Nocera was Ermanno's assistant at Amarena Balda. Remember the old nun's ring? He probably received it from the family for his dirty deeds. Nocera ended up our murder victim in Filari."

"How did you find out her name?"

"Viviana married Giulio de Capua. Giulio's brother, Ermanno, didn't like her and hid from her what was going on with the winery. Ermanno also made sure Giulio spent all his time on the road and away from his young wife."

"So this Giulio was weak," said Silvio. "He listened to his brother too much."

"Actually it's more complicated than that. After their child was born, Giulio did come home, but he still didn't stand up for his young wife. Viviana must have realized that Giulio was attracted to her replacement—our waitress. As a new mother, Viviana was in charge of caring for the De Capua matriarch along with her young baby. Mamma de Capua was very demanding. Knowing her husband was cheating and unable to please any of them, Viviana decided to take the baby and move out."

"Why didn't we hear from Viviana's relatives?" asked Turo.

"Good question. We're still trying to track them down. I did hear the car she drove wasn't currently registered in Corsa Pietra. Evidently, it was one they used around the winery. The Castel Valori police wouldn't have been able to identify the vehicle four years ago. She was just another missing person if any of the family tried to find out where she went."

Silvio finished his soup. "Someone must have told Nocera to kill her. I think Giulio was too soft to do it."

"Maybe, but Giulio didn't mourn Viviana's loss very long. He was already having the affair with Donata. He sounds more like a rogue than a softy."

"Then Ermanno must have planned the murder. He sent Nocera to get rid of her."

"Actually, both men seemed to conspire to do the deed, but the real manager of the De Capua clan was Mamma. Everything they did, including spiking their wines with grapes grown outside the Rufina zone, was orchestrated by Mamma. Their punishment for that crime alone is the loss of the coveted title and label as a Rufina Chianti—a relief to the two bigger local vineyards, I'm sure."

"Very nice, Sister," said Turo. "I guess I didn't realize just how good a detective you are. You're welcome back anytime."

Sister Angela smiled. "And your nephew makes an awesome detective himself. His gut feelings actually guided my investigation."

Sister Concetta presented a cake, celebrating Pia's return. Cake and espresso were followed by more hugs, kisses, and promises that Pia would visit. And then Turo drove Sister Angela and Pia to the terminal to catch the eight o'clock train home.

At quarter to ten, the train arrived in Siena. Sister Liona's car idled beside the curb. Pia recognized the nun right away, but couldn't stay awake long. Just out of Siena on their way to Filari, Pia again fell asleep in Sister Angela's arms.

The lights were still on at the convent, and faces were plastered at each window when the car pulled up. Pia was released first to run inside and be with her family.

"Thank you, Sister," said Sister Carmela. "Oh look at your face. That'll be a nasty bruise. Sister Natalia refused to go home to Mission House until after you both arrived. We saw the La Barcas back at their winery this week. I suppose they were innocent. Then who kidnapped Pia? Who dressed up as Sister Octavia and why?"

"You'll all hear the story tomorrow morning," said Sister Angela. "Sister Liona told me the chief detective and Sacco are coming over for breakfast. Sister Daniela and I will now go to her sister's place to pack. We have to hightail it to Montriano or lose our jobs."

"Yes, we heard that Sister Daniela was leaving us. We have a new woman coming in next week. She's not a nun, but she possesses good teaching skills. We asked Sister Daniela not to leave, but she said Susanna was better. We think she really misses Montriano."

"I need Sister Daniela. She's the best detective I

have. She figured out how Nocera got into the orphanage that night."

"She hasn't told us the story," said Sister Natalia. "She kept insisting it was an accident. Perhaps you'll let us know tomorrow morning too. We need the information to keep it from happening again."

Sister Daniela came up to give Sister Angela a hug. "It's so good to see you. I'm glad you'll be able to say good-bye to Michel and Susanna before we go. I'm afraid Michel and Maximo were very busy with the harvest so we won't see much of them."

"It was such a shock to hear you're coming with me. Mother Margherita must be thrilled. She's missed you very much."

"I can imagine. She loves being the administrator, but when I left, she was relegated to the classroom again, training my replacement," Sister Daniela said quietly. "I guess I've missed her too."

"You'll be cured of that all too soon. Tell me about Susanna. Is she really well enough?"

"Yes. There are no signs of her cancer. We celebrated with another bottle of *riserva*. Sorry, we didn't save you any."

"I have to tell you. Pagano and Sacco were both very impressed with your investigative talents. They were actually afraid you might get hurt if they let you do your own work. But you didn't. You used your instincts wisely and saved the La Barcas from any more embarrassment or worse."

"I was just investigating. I had no idea they were innocent. I'm not so sure Elmo thought I was a proficient detective. I'm afraid he had to save me more than once. Remind me to ask the detectives about the orphanage receiving the old nun's ring. I think they should sell it and keep the money for the orphanage."

"I believe the police will need it to lay out their case that Nocera was the kidnapper. You should talk to them, though. Perhaps they can give it back to the orphanage when they're done. And what about Grazia? Why haven't you told the nuns what she did?"

"She's a child. I thought you and I could broach that subject tomorrow. Hopefully she won't be punished too hard."

"You believe everyone, Sister Daniela. You aren't allowed to be both a teacher and trusting."

"I'm trying hard to be like you. If I have a soft touch then I must have learned it from my instructor."

Sister Angela put her arm around her friend. "You proved yourself, and I look forward to working with you again in Montriano."

Sister Daniela giggled. "If Father Sergio agrees to let us alone together."

Sister Angela laughed. "Poor Mother Margherita had to lie to him in order to let me come. I hope he didn't bother her too much about it. Montriano's probably riddled with crime because its best detectives aren't around to keep order."

The two nuns watched Sister Carmela round up the children and push them toward the stairs. "It's bedtime. Evelina?" she called. "Where are you? Someone has to lock up after our detectives have all left."

Evelina kissed Sister Daniela on the cheek.

"Allegra and I are teaching the class until the new teacher comes. Hopefully you have time to drop by and see us."

"I already know you two can do it. I'm leaving the children in good hands. Sister Angela and I will be back in the morning. Our train doesn't leave until tomorrow evening, but we'll be too busy talking to the police to help you out. They're all yours."

Pia was several steps up the stairs when she turned around and stumbled back down. She approached Sister Angela and Sister Daniela, hugging them both around the legs. Then she took Allegra's hand and began to climb the stairs with her.

Chapter Twenty-Eight

Sister Angela accompanied her friend into the classroom where for the last year Sister Daniela taught. Allegra was at the helm, going over a lesson for the younger students. She quickly sat down with the others when Sister Daniela entered.

"I didn't want to interrupt the lesson, Allegra. If you want to finish first, please do. I can join the older children in the back of the room for this lesson."

"No, I was finished. Perhaps all of us should come together now to wish you good-bye. Is Sister Liona going to pick you up when it's time to go?"

"Our train doesn't leave until this evening, and my sister and brother-in-law are taking us to the terminal."

"What about Pia? When's she joining us?" asked Evelina, moving up to take a seat closer to the front.

"Pia's with Chief Detective Pagano," said Sister Daniela.

"It's called a debriefing," said Sister Angela. "We have evidence against those who took Pia, but she knows things about her kidnapper that we don't. What she tells the police now will help us put away the perpetrators."

"We're happy to have her back," said Cammeo. "I can't wait to see if she got to ride on the broomstick."

"As soon as she's finished with the chief detective, she'll join us in the classroom," said Sister Daniela.

The children started to cheer.

"But before that, we're going to have to get some work done."

"Do you know who's going to be our new teacher?" asked Liliana.

"I don't know her, but I hear she has a good background."

"But is she nice?"

"I also heard she's very nice. I think you'll all love her. She's supposed to be here in a week. I would've liked to have met her too, but my mother superior said I must return to Montriano right away."

Grazia walked into the classroom, a small pink elephant under her arm.

Sister Daniela approached her before she sat down and led her back out. "Please proceed," she told Allegra.

The nun and the child sat on the lower treads of the staircase.

"You were with Sister Natalia, weren't you?"

"I was with her and Mother Faustine."

"But they let you come back, didn't they."

"Yes. They told me what I did was bad. I let the old woman into the orphanage, and that led to the kidnapping. I'm not sure Pia will ever forgive me."

"You thought the kidnapper was a nun," said Sister Daniela. "They must have realized you didn't know she was dangerous."

"They understood that. They said they could fix the problem by closing off the nurse's office so that someone like me can't get in and out so easily. But they also told me that I've done things that make it difficult for them to teach me."

"That's also true, Grazia. Perhaps you should try a little harder to follow the guidelines the nuns have set down."

"Like?"

"Like going directly to bed without spending your sleep time staring out the window. You could also talk to your teacher or Sister Carmela or even Evelina if you see something strange going on. Think about it, Grazia. A nun standing in the middle of a vineyard is very odd."

"Do you think they'll choose to send me away?"

"Definitely not. I think they believe in your ability to learn from your mistake. You're a bright and wonderful child and can use your talents of observation to their benefit."

"Huh?"

"In other words, they must love you very much."

Pia was sent to join the class. The nuns convened with the two detectives in the office just off the TV room. Sister Edita delivered sandwiches and soda so they could eat and talk at the same time.

"What did Pia tell you?" asked Sister Angela, ignoring the food to satisfy her hunger for more information.

Pagano swallowed a bite of his sandwich and took a sip of soda before telling them all about their interview. "Pia thought the old nun was someone coming to take her home."

"Home?" asked Sister Daniela.

"Evidently, home's the convent in Castel Valori. She doesn't seem to remember her mother, but she does recall how happy she was with the nuns at the convent."

"When did she realize she was in trouble?" asked Sister Carmela, her eyes drooping from lack of sleep.

"She says the nun took her to some building and let her go back to sleep. I described La Barca's winery, and she thought that's what it looked like, though it was dark, and she didn't really see much before she nodded off."

"Did she see La Barca or Carlota?" asked Sister Daniela.

"No. She said the next day, a man woke her up. I showed her pictures, and she identified Nocera, who had discarded his habit by then. Nocera walked her to the road. A car stopped them. Nocera knew the driver so they both got in. Nocera argued with the driver. The car stopped and the two men got out. Pia was told to stay in the car. After a long while, the driver returned alone to the car and drove Pia to Rufina. He didn't say a word to her, but she saw him again at Amarena Balda."

"Did she still think she was going to the convent?"

"She said she prayed and prayed that they were going there. When they arrived at Amarena Balda, she was taken to the farmhouse and given a beautiful room with a canopied bed and dolls and stuffed animals. The woman who lived there said she was to call her Nonna."

"I assume she realized she was with her blood family," said Mother Faustine.

"She probably didn't understand what a real family was," said Sister Angela.

"You're right," said Pagano. "She didn't understand, and Pia told us that Nonna got increasingly annoyed with her. The old woman needed someone to wait on her, but Pia complained about having to do that. About a week before you arrived at the winery, Sister Angela, Pia was relegated to the shed."

"What about Viviana?" asked Sister Daniela. "What've you found out about Pia's mother?"

"Viviana Mioni was her name. She has family, but they moved out of the country before the accident. She worked for the De Capua's for about a year before Giulio de Capua married her."

"Giulio must be Ermanno's brother," said Sister Angela. "Ermanno admitted that he himself was Viviana's brother-in-law."

"Yes. Giulio is Ermanno's younger brother. Pia's his daughter by that marriage. He's now engaged to another young lady."

"Yes, Donata. Giulio seems to be quite adept at choosing good-looking women," said Sister Angela. "I know you haven't had the opportunity to interview any of them yet, but I assume you're getting your information from Corsa Pietra."

"Yes, Elmo was present at the interviews. Ermanno de Capua runs Amarena Balda. He's never been married. From what Elmo could gather, he never approved of Viviana, though he forced his younger brother to marry her because she was pregnant. As you're already aware, there was wrongdoing occurring at the winery for the several years."

"Yes. The management was spiking its Chianti with Campanian wine. The boxes being delivered to the winery were labeled 'Wine from the Amalfi Coast.' Of course, the De Capuas probably wouldn't have been jailed for the crime, but they would've lost their Chianti label and most of their business."

"Perhaps Viviana found out about the deceit and threatened to report them," said Sister Daniela.

"It's also a coincidence that the bomb scare that stopped a train you were on, Sister, had to do with a shipment of wine from Amarena Balda. If I'd figured that out sooner, we might have been able to find the child. But this had nothing to do with the kidnapping. There were investigators that were checking the cargo coming into the Siena terminal. Someone from Amarena Balda found out and stopped the train to get their shipment off. "

"Maybe that's why no one in the Rufina region ever checked the size of Amarena Balda with the winery's yield. The brothers were always two steps ahead," said Sister Angela. "That might have exposed the operation before the crime got out of hand. So who are they going to go after for the murder?"

"I believe they'll go after both brothers for the murder and the mother for kidnapping," said Pagano. "They'll probably try to use Donata's testimony to implicate the family. Elmo got the impression she knew what was going on. That means Ermanno must have trusted her and probably revealed things about

Viviana and Nocera."

"Do you think Donata can be turned?" asked Sister Daniela.

"She's a tough cookie, but I believe she'll be easy to convince that life in prison isn't worth her loyalty to the brothers," said Sister Angela. "As for Nonna, the old woman most likely won't live out the sentence for the kidnapping charge."

"Did either brother confess to killing Nocera and Viviana?" asked Sister Natalia.

Pagano smiled. "He didn't confess, but Ermanno revealed that his younger brother did it."

Sister Angela nearly rocked her chair too far. "Giulio did it? So much for romance. That means Viviana came face to face with her husband. She didn't get out of the car and run into his arms. She tried to go around him—probably knowing he'd take Pia if she gave up."

"What about La Barca and his wife," asked Sister Daniela.

"I don't think we can prove that La Barca or his wife tried to cover up Nocera's crime. Signora La Barca admitted she had a short affair with Nocera, but that's not a crime either. She's back, you know."

"Carlota came home?"

"Yes. She mentioned how wonderful you are, Sister Daniela. She said you reminded her that forgiving her husband and trying to save her marriage would probably be the right thing to do. I hear the two are now trying to have a family."

"What about the Amarena Balda?" asked Sister Angela. "I assume it'll be sold."

"I heard that Serena de Capua, who's lived in Corsa Pietra since her brother's marriage to Viviana, is interested in saving the winery. She wants it to be a family-run business again, though she'll have to work hard to retain the CODG's Rufina Chianti label."

"All by herself?"

"No. She has a boyfriend, Guillermo. He was working undercover for the Corsa Pietra Police Department. He also called the department for back-up before your friend from the convent was able to get through."

"I wish them happiness. Guillermo was quite attractive. I'm glad he's on the right side."

Sister Daniela's face gleamed as the group broke up. "We make a good team," she whispered to Sister Angela.

"I'm so relieved you're coming back to Montriano with me. Together we'll be able to get more cases."

The two women returned to the classroom. At about three, Sister Natalia came down to fetch them.

"Please, Sister Daniela, Sister Angela. You must come upstairs. We have visitors."

The two nuns stopped at the top of the stairs. A young man and woman were being led through the TV room.

"Let's go into the office here," said Sister Natalia. "These are the nuns I was talking about, Signora Quinto. They tracked down your niece."

Sister Angela felt the chill. "You're Viviana's sister?"

"Yes. My husband and I now live in Malta. I found it nearly impossible to uncover the details about my sister's disappearance. Naturally I knew she'd disappeared, but the police told me very little. We suspected she was dead."

"Did you know about the child?"

"Yes, she was pregnant at their wedding. I have a picture from the hospital in Corsa Pietra. Viviana sent me the photo. She called her Mara after our mother. I just found out that her name had been changed to Pia."

"The nuns at a convent found her on their doorstep. She was just a toddler who couldn't tell them her name so they called her Pia, the feminine form of pious."

"We'd like to adopt her," said Isabella. "It's our right, isn't it? We're the next of kin."

"There's a procedure," said Sister Natalia, hesitantly. "We can go through it, if you like."

Sister Angela smiled at them. "There's nothing more wonderful for Pia than to be with a loving family. Do you have children?"

"Yes. We have two children, a boy and a girl. The boy's seven and the little girl's three," She took her husband's hand and squeezed it. "We believe she'd be a perfect addition for our family."

"I do too," said Sister Daniela. "But we must take this one step at a time. I think you should get to know her first. Will you be around for a few weeks?"

"We have to get home to be with the other children," said Isabella, her shoulders drooping.

Sister Daniela looked across at Sister Natalia, who nodded. Then Sister Daniela rose and went to the stairs to fetch Pia.

As they waited, Sister Angela talked to the couple in a low voice. The children and nuns here at the orphanage and the ones at the convent in Castel Valori are Pia's family. It'll take time for her to see you as her family—more than one week, I'm afraid. If you really want to adopt her, you're going to have to make the trip several times."

But Signora Quinto wasn't looking at the nun. Tears filled her eyes as soon as she saw Sister Daniela leading the child through the TV room.

Sister Daniela bent down and said, "Pia, this is your aunt and uncle. They want to get to know you."

Pia clung to her young teacher's knees.

Furiously wiping her eyes, Isabella crouched. "Pia, you look just like your mother."

Pia searched her teacher's face. Sister Daniela smiled and nodded.

"I have her picture," said Isabella.

Signor Quinto blew his nose into a handkerchief. The noise made Pia giggle.

Isabella approached Pia. I have a photo of you and your mother. She handed it to the child when she was close enough.

Pia stared down at it. "Me?" she asked. "I look like a doll."

"Like a very pretty doll," said Isabella.

"Would you like to talk to Signor and Signora Quinto for a while?" asked Sister Daniela.

Pia looked frightened and lifted her arms to the nun.

"They just want to talk. Why don't you read for them? I have your book here. I'll stay with you too. No one's leaving here, okay?"

Dinner was served in the conference room early so the nuns could catch their train. Michel and Susanna were invited to dine with them. It was still quiet in the dining room, many of the children studying too hard to make any noise.

"I liked Isabella," said Sister Angela. "She was patient with Pia. I do hope that works out."

"She agreed to come here this week for about an hour each day," said Sister Natalia. "We'll put up pictures of the family and her cousins on the wall of her room so she doesn't forget them. They plan to return at Christmastime with their children. I give it six months. Pia will come round by then, and we can finish the adoption process. I'm so excited. You don't know how rare it is to have someone want one of the children." She dabbed at her eyes.

"I don't mean to make you cry harder," said Sister Angela. "But Sister Daniela and I have to leave to catch the train. Sister Daniela said she had to use the restroom, but I suspect she's with the children."

Sister Natalia and Sister Carmela rose to give the nun a hug.

"You're our heroes," said Sister Carmela. "Please don't hesitate to come back and visit."

Sister Angela said. "I'd ask you to adopt us, but Mother Margherita might balk at the paperwork involved."

Take a quick look at the first book in the
Sister Angela Mystery series:

L'Oro Verde

~ One ~

Struggling up the side of the hill, Bernardo
glanced over his shoulder to see who shadowed him.
He could almost hear the raspy pant below but still
could not make out his pursuer. Gulping for air, he
paused to listen again. The wheezing stopped, but it
started again as soon as he began to climb. He
checked his watch—nearly two in the morning.
Bernardo knew he was being stalked. He needed a
place to hide and away to escape. But his mind raced,
and he could not think clearly. Who was after him?
How much time did he have? Would the stalker kill
him? The former altar boy was not afraid to die. He
had a strong faith and believed he would be with God
after death. He did not feel bad for or think of
himself. He thought of those who loved him and
regretted the pain they would endure if he did not
return. The light from the three-quarter moon
shimmered as the sultry heat of summer condensed
over the grassy fields and curvy rows of grapevines.
But Bernardo did not look up until he got to the top
of the hill. Before him, his hometown of Montriano
unfolded over the crest. The ancient walls that once

protected it on all sides had crumbled and were replaced by flowering thickets for shade with benches so visitors could look out over rows of grapevines, splashes of olive trees, and undulating mist shrouding the farmhouses and fields.

Slowing to catch his breath, he stopped to stare at the deserted streets, slithering like snakes down the hill and disappearing into the blackness of the village. He should consider his flight, which way he planned to go. The road to the right would take him to his parents' house where his father could protect him. The center one meandered down to his church, San Benedetto. The stocky spire of the parish church barely peeked over the nearby rooftops and was not as high as the town's two towers. He imagined himself standing in the steeple and ringing the bell, summoning help to keep the stalker at bay. The street to the left led to the medieval towers, Polini and Grossa.

Bernardo spun around until he could see the Milky Way in the starry sky above the towers. He knew the spot well since he often went there on summer evenings to study the heavens.

One night months ago as he carefully identified the constellations, moonbeams spilled across his hand and forearm. It reminded him of a high school art lesson on Leonardo da Vinci's use of moonlight in a famous painting. Bernardo owned a copy of it—*Leda and the Swan*. He kept it under his bed and pulled it out often to marvel at its beauty. He would run his fingers down Leda's thigh, imagining what it would be like to feel a real woman, warm and soft. The boy never figured out what the moon and the stars had to do with the light in the painting. He never understood the lesson.

At school conferences, his teachers told his parents he was slow, assuring them, however, that his handicap was surely temporary. Most of them said he would catch up with the other students soon enough. But Bernardo was already well past twenty, and he never caught up. Would he need to go back to school to catch up? He no longer wanted to learn Da Vinci's secret of the moonlight. He could make out the constellations and a galaxy as well from the steps of Polini Tower. He saw it all for himself and that was enough.

A dog barking in a distant field brought Bernardo back to the chase. He must find a place to hide soon or be captured. Gazing past the Montriano skyline, he raised his hands to the heavens, brown on black. He scrutinized the darkness and wondered if he wanted to keep running. There were few lights, but the plastered brick facades of the ancient structures within the walled village held the glow of dusk. Which of the three roads should he take?

He decided to go right to see if his parents were still up. Edging deeper into the shadows of the walls and buildings, he scampered down the twisty road. But when he got to his parents' house, the gate was locked. Pulling away from the building, he looked up. The windows were shuttered. When he lived with them, his father, Giuseppe, explained that parents need their sleep and that he should not wake them unless it was important. Was this important? A dog barked two yards over and lights went on in that house, but his parents' house remained dark.

Bernardo glanced up the road and was relieved that it was still deserted. Spinning around, he followed this street until it curled to the left, leading back into the center of town and the small piazza in front of San Benedetto Church. Pausing at the main road, he waited, listened and peered intently in all directions before quickly moving on.

The thirteenth century Romanesque-style church had been written up in a brochure for tourists. Bernardo taped the picture that appeared there to the mirror in his bedroom so he could look at it every morning before he went to school. The outside of the church was unadorned; the front had a single door. It was arched but somewhat narrow, not grand like that of San Francesco Church farther down the hill. The interior, however, was beautiful. Chevron-patterned terracotta tiles decorated the floors, and dark beams crisscrossed overhead. High stained-glass windows tinted the rays of afternoon sun. Frescos graced the walls, but not so many as in San Francesco. Bernardo memorized the Biblical stories told in each one, but though famous artists painted them, he could not remember their names. Perched above the high altar, a beautiful Madonna, painted in the fifteenth century, looked down over all the parishioners. Bernardo knew she was there to protect them. He prayed to her often, asking her to care for his parents. Then he asked her to perform a miracle and heal the brain injuries that made him forget things and misunderstand them. The front door would be locked but Bernardo knew where he could get in. Veering right at the steps, he circled the building and turned left into a dark alleyway across from the rectory.

Scaling a wall and dropping into the bushes behind a bench in the priest's contemplative garden, he followed the stone walk to the sacristy and let himself in.

The sacristy was always open. Rumor had it that Father Augustus broke the lock when he came in from the wine festival one night. Bernardo smiled to himself. Father Augustus now lived in a retirement cottage in Petraggio. Last he heard, the old priest was still drinking his favorite whiskey, a habit he had picked up in seminary. No one ever bothered to fix the lock because the wall and a locked gate protected it.

In the sacristy, Bernardo sat down and fingered the phone. He could call for help, but he did not want to wake anyone. Maybe he could rest here for a while and dial someone in the morning. Sitting back, he thought about one service in particular where he saw the old priest drunk. On Via San Lorenzo, old Valentino Rinaldi was dying. At eleven the night before, his daughter, Elena, called Father Augustus at the residence asking him to come to perform last rites.

Unfortunately for the priest, it was a slow death. Rinaldi's lungs sputtered and wheezed as the man made a last effort to hold onto his spirit. Elena was afraid and did not want the priest to leave. She asked that he delay last rites until the end and offered Father Augustus red table wine. Chianti was not one of the priest's favorites, and it would take more wine than whiskey to gain the effect. Father Augustus was tired though and would need strength to administer the final sacrament. He probably promised himself that he would sip small doses so it did not disturb his blessing. Old Valentino finally made his exit at four, and in the last minutes, Father Augustus offered the final sacrament—with a flourish, it was said. But it was then Sunday morning, and the priest needed to preside at the ten o'clock mass. Bernardo assisted. The priest made it through the sermon with few slurs, or so it seemed to Bernardo who rarely listened to the whole sermon anyway. But in the middle of the blessing of the Eucharist, the sanctuary and nave of San Benedetto fell silent.

Father Augustus had bowed down to place a piece of bread into his mouth and never came back up. Bernardo, his heart beating wildly and his hands still clasped tightly together, pretended to take his hushed prayers closer to the altar. The priest's cheek was slumped against the paten, his pursed lips dotted with crumbs, his eyes closed. Bernardo's heart sank. Aware somewhere deep down that the show must go on, Bernardo grasped the chalice of Christ's blood, raised it high in the air, and then drank the sweet wine. When he brought the cup down with a thud against the altar, Father Augustus started. Bernardo pointed to the next prayer, and the mass continued without further interruption.

Bernardo was so deep in thought he almost did not hear the noise. There it was again—the swoosh and crackle of bushes in the garden. Not even thinking of the phone, Bernardo moved toward the nave door. The white albs that hung along the wall glowed in the moonlight, and he fingered them tenderly. For a split second, he wondered if his was still there and had the urge to pull it over his head one more time. Perhaps the Lord would recognize him and spare him as the senior altar boy who faithfully assisted at all those masses. Until just a few years ago, he carried the processional cross up the long center aisle and sometimes swung the censer. Clouds of incense pulsed from the openings, making him want to sneeze, but he did not, recognizing how important it was to keep the censer steady. He often held the paten for Father Augustus during communion because even then the old priest's hand shook uncontrollably.

But Bernardo had to get out of there now. What was wrong with him? Why could he not keep his mind on his task? Turning around, his hand found the knob on the nave entrance. He twisted it to the right and then quickly to the left. It had a funny catch that no one bothered to fix. The only people who used it knew you had to manipulate the knob to open the door.

Bernardo slipped into the dark church where he paused to let his eyes adjust, but he did not really need to. He knew the layout by heart. A foot to his right, his eyes settled on the offertory candles, all of which had flickered out. The smell of hot wax and incense was overpowered by the musty stones and decomposed humanity that inhabited the pews over centuries. Bernardo loved that smell—the scent of his ancestors held aloft in the damp air that mingled with the smoky prayer emanating from the candles. He lingered to inhale the memory, but hearing the squeak of the sacristy's outer door, he did not wait there long.

"He's coming," he whispered to the figure on the crucifix.

Turning his back to the altar, he gazed down the long aisle, racking his slow and unreliable brain for a place to hide. Then it came to him. He remembered a small crawl space behind the vault of Giovanni Cardinal Bartoli who oversaw the diocese in the 1400s. A sleeping body, carved in granite, lay sprawled over the stone lid. When he was nine, Bernardo once watched in horror as his cousin, Tonino, and his friend, Piero, tried to pry open the lid to see if the body was still there. The cover would not budge because the top was far too heavy, but years later, Bernardo still dreamt about a shriveled corpse with yellowing teeth jumping out at him.

A marble statue of St. Francis of Assisi stood over the tomb, his arms outstretched, his fingers that once supported a bird, broken off long ago. Bernardo knew the story of the saint's life and felt protected by him. When praying, he would often run his fingers over the smooth folds of the robe, feeling uncomfortable because he had heard a preserved piece of the saint's vestment was actually rough and worn.

He knew he would be safe, having hidden here before. Tonino once tried to find him in the church and could not. He could see Tonino, though, observing him through a tiny hole and trying not to laugh when his cousin scratched his head. With his cheek against the floor, Bernardo could make out the sanctuary and altar as if he were a mouse peering through its front door.

It did not take long for Bernardo to hear noises in the sacristy. The pursuer must have discovered the unlocked entrance. But the footsteps did not seem to come directly into the nave, making Bernardo breathe easier as the sound faded. Perhaps it was someone who worked in the parish, someone who had left the lights on downstairs or an altar lady arriving to press the albs. But his relief did not last. The stomp of footsteps began again. For the first time, Bernardo noticed the gait was somewhat uneven.

Thump-ka-thump. The steps got louder until he heard the familiar right-left rattle of the knob.

Thump-ka-thump. He watched a figure cross the floor in front of the sanctuary, pausing to cross himself at the altar.

Bernardo wanted to cross himself too but could not extricate his right hand from the narrow space beside him. His breaths were short as he waited—waited for his pursuer to turn and try to find him.

The figure finally spun to face the pews, and Bernardo realized it had no face. The cowled visage topped a long coarse robe. Was he crippled? Why did he waddle and why did he hold his side?

More labored steps, and the shadow passed out of Bernardo's line of sight. Thump-ka-thump, *thump-ka-thump*. The steps got louder. And suddenly, they stopped. Drawn toward the victim like a magnet, feet suddenly appeared directly in front of the young man's peephole.

Bernardo thought his heart had stopped. Screwing up his eyes, he examined the pair of shoes not a foot away. The rough fabric of the robe draped gracefully over the highly-polished shoe tops, and when the toes turned toward him, Bernardo watched the folds sweep eerily to readjust themselves.

Relieved, the boy slithered backward out of his hiding place. "Father, please forgive me. I have no place to go," he whispered as he struggled to his feet.

Unable to distinguish the face in the hood's shadow, Bernardo leaned forward for only a second before the blow came. A heavy object split his skull in the middle, giving him less than an instant to identify his assailant. But Bernardo was slow and would probably never have really recognized the face anyway.

Fine lines of tiny bones and a web of arteries popping out of the wrists, a pair of hands maneuvered the bludgeon to the side, and within seconds, yielded a blow to the ear. Bernardo must have never felt the second hit.

If the boy had recognized his brutal attacker, his eyes did not reveal it. They rolled upward, creating the face of a martyr, beseeching the heavens to let him enter. The slight smile on his lips suggested his mind was filled with other images. The second strike sent him into the marble rendering of St. Francis, where Bernardo finally crumpled, prostrate at the feet of the patron saint against dying alone.

The figure brushed the hood back and slid out of the robe. There was work to do. Bernardo's violent end had left a pool of blood on the floor and spatters on the walls. A long red stripe adorned the white folds in St Francis' vestment. The body of Bernardo was hurriedly crammed back into its hiding place, the blood methodically mopped up with the hooded robe.

Had Bernardo been watching through his peephole, he would have observed the figure, dragging a long object and robe, pause again to face the altar, and an arm pass first up, down, and then from shoulder to shoulder. As the shadow paused in front of the candles, a stream of smoke would curl upward. Bernardo would have heard the coins drop noisily through the slot and seen the figure kneel for a moment to pray. But he could witness none of this— at least in the way that one on this earth knows or senses things. Nor could he listen to the person follow the indirect passage through the sacristy or hear the outside door finally close as the shadow merged with the darkness that shrouded the tiny hill village of Montriano.

About the Author

Coralie is a native of California and graduate of the University of California at Berkeley. Having visited Italy four times, Coralie has traveled extensively for her books. She and her husband and her golden retriever now live in Massachusetts.

CPSIA information can be obtained
at www.ICGtesting.com
Printed in the USA
LVHW012205130622
721151LV00008B/786

9 781505 533293